PRAISE FOR THE SHERRI TRAVIS MYSTERIES

"The Sherri Travis Mysteries started out well and have gotten better . . . The writing keeps getting tighter, and Smallman knows how to crank up the reader's tension . . . One can't help wanting more and anticipating the next book in this entertaining and fast-paced series." —*National Post*

"A series that gives the reader a casual style and storytelling with staying power." —*Hamilton Spectator*

"Florida has never seemed so appealing and appalling as it does in the Sherri Travis novels." —*Toronto Star*

"In Sherri Travis, [Smallman] has created a sassy, plucky heroine who isn't afraid to get her hands dirty and ask the questions that need to be asked." —*Cozy Mystery Book Review*

ALSO BY PHYLLIS SMALLMAN

Sherri Travis Mysteries

Margarita Nights

Sex in a Sidecar

A Brewski for the Old Man

Champagne for Buzzards

Highball Exit

Singer Brown Mysteries

Long Gone Man

MARTINI REGRETS

PHYLLIS
SMALLMAN

TouchWood Editions
touchwoodeditions.com

LIBRARY AND ARCHIVES CANADA CATALOGUING IN PUBLICATION
Smallman, Phyllis, author
Martini regrets / Phyllis Smallman.

(A Sherri Travis mystery)
ISBN 978-1-77151-090-5

I. Title. II. Series: Smallman, Phyllis. Sherri Travis mystery.

PS8637.M36M375 2014 C813'.6 C2014-902764-8

Editor: Frances Thorsen
Proofreader: Vivian Sinclair
Cover images: Martini glass—sidewaysdesign, istockphoto.com
Tropical background—Amoled, istockphoto.com
Author photo: Jen MacLellan

Canada Council for the Arts Conseil des Arts du Canada

We gratefully acknowledge the financial support for our publishing activities from the Government of Canada through the Canada Book Fund and the Canada Council for the Arts, and from the Province of British Columbia through the British Columbia Arts Council and the Book Publishing Tax Credit.

The interior pages of this book have been printed on 100% post-consumer recycled paper, processed chlorine free, and printed with vegetable-based inks.

1 2 3 4 5 18 17 16 15 14

PRINTED IN CANADA

This is for the other big men in my life,
Larry, Darryl and Tom Smallman.
Thank you for your love and support.

CHAPTER 1

The Florida Everglades are a place of serene beauty and sudden death. Spread across one and a half million acres, they're a wilderness where snakes and alligators rule—out there, mistakes can be fatal. It wasn't a place where I, Sherri Travis, ever meant to end up alone late at night.

And it isn't just nature you have to fear in the Glades. The people living in this inhospitable place can be just as dangerous. Down here we call them swamp rats, men who know every gator hole and every way there is to turn a dollar, both legal and illegal. They use the Glades to strip down stolen cars or use their airboats to pick up drugs dropped from the sky. And there are guys who find the swamp the perfect place to make unwanted people disappear. There's not much evidence of a crime left after a body passes through an alligator or a python. The wetlands of Florida are a depository for all kinds of unwanted things, living and dead, a spot to hide a multitude of sins.

When I was eighteen I made my first solo crossing of the Glades, and my father, Tully Jenkins, laid out the rules for traveling Alligator Alley. Tully's first rule was, "Never travel through the river of grass after dark. Leave it to the crazies and criminals." This decree was followed by "Always keep your doors locked, and always have a full tank of gas." And then there was the most important rule: "Don't stop for anything."

And even a dozen years later, I didn't take that crossing for granted. I thought I had it all under control until that night when things went so horribly wrong.

I'd been down in Miami for a long-overdue weekend with a girlfriend, a situation that had created considerable tension between my fiancé, Clay Adams, and me. He didn't understand the need to catch up with friends. He wanted me to buckle down and plan a wedding, the sooner the better, while he worked eighteen hours a day selling real estate. You see, for him, life wasn't about enjoyment and good times but about winning. I'm not exactly sure what he was trying to win, but it had a lot to do with using money to keep score. The man had a plan and a driving need for us to improve ourselves. He was all about business, while I was all about partying. Right away you can see the problem.

Sunday afternoon, I called Clay to put off my return to Jacaranda because Kelly's friends had suggested a sunset booze cruise. He wasn't happy.

I promised Clay I'd be home before midnight, but then, when I was already late leaving Miami, Kelly suggested a martini at a hot new club. What's another hour? Besides, how many holidays did I take in a year? This was the first time I'd gone off on my own since Clay and I moved in together. I deserved it. At least, that's what I told myself.

When I left Miami, not quite sober, it was already nearly twelve. I was well behind schedule. I checked the gas. Half a tank if I looked at it optimistically, just over a quarter if I broke the mold I came from and was honest. Okay, even with a quarter of a tank, it should be no problem making it to Naples, the first spot for gas on the west side of the Glades. After all, it wasn't like the old days when Dad's crapped-out piece of junk got ten miles to the gallon. A quarter of a tank was enough. I'd be fine.

As the lights of civilization faded to the darkness of the wilderness, kamikaze bugs threw themselves against the windshield. I turned on the wipers and sprayed a weak stream of water at their bodies, turning them into a gelatinous smear of mush. "Shit." The windshield washer was nearly empty of fluid from the trip over, insects being one more of the nasty things that live in the big swamp. I should have refilled it. I sighed out loud at this further evidence of my failure as a responsible adult.

I turned off the wipers, which were just making the huge smear worse, and cursed my failure to prepare, but no way was I turning back. I was already late and needed to make up time.

I drove a little faster just to compound my stupidity.

Not entirely comfortable with my decision, I glanced down at the gauge. Definitely well below the line. Tully's warning buzzed around in my head like a demented bee, calling me a fool.

A weathered billboard loomed out of the night and proclaimed, LAST GAS BEFORE NAPLES. It probably wasn't true. Billboards in Florida aren't known for truth in advertising. What really caught my eye was the little white add-on at the bottom: OPEN 24 HRS. I slowed, trying to decide. I was at the turnoff before I really made up my mind.

It was the name of the road that caught me and pulled me in. It was called Last Chance Road. Silly and laughable—last chances don't come with signs—but I braked and pulled onto the narrow strip of pavement leading away from the highway, hoping for one final opportunity to get it right.

Only inches above the water, the long dark road was a narrow chute through six-foot-tall grasses. Devoid of buildings and leading nowhere but to the gas bar, it had an ominous and lonely quality. It made me feel trapped.

Red eyes shone in my headlights. A gator. I slowed, barely at a crawl as I went by him. If I hit the twelve-foot-long monster . . . not something I wanted to think about. When I was a kid, alligator sightings were much rarer. Now, after thirty years as a protected species, they're everywhere, including the roads.

I drove on towards the faint light glowing above the grasses to my right, wary and cautious. A litany of scary possibilities could be waiting at the end of Last Chance Road. If the station was closed, I'd have wasted precious resources. There was no place to pull over or turn around. Going back wasn't an option until I got to the end. Last Chance came with no choices.

I was half expecting the sign to be lying, but when I swung into the small clearing, created from a mound of shells scooped out of the swamp, I saw two pumps and a small store. The lights were on; it seemed a normal, everyday gas station. While the bright neon was reassuring, there was no vehicle anywhere on the parking apron. Was the building empty? Were the pumps working?

The sound of gas actually running into the tank brought a heartfelt sigh of relief. I hadn't made a mistake. I congratulated myself on getting something right for a change.

While the tank filled, I pulled my top loose from my body, shaking it to let the hot night air circulate over my skin, and then leaned back against the pickup to study the soft spring night.

CHAPTER 2

March is the dry time of year in Florida. Wildlife moves into areas where there is water, becoming concentrated and dense. Gator holes are surrounded by wading birds and all manner of mammals taking advantage of the water. It would be worse this year. We hadn't had any real rain since October.

Five months, and the Glades were drying up in an alarming way. But everything would be reborn when the rains came. Nothing stays barren for long in Florida; it teems with life and fecundity and new beginnings. With the monsoons beginning in May, rivers would pour south from the upper parts of Florida to flood the southern tip of the state and lay down a foot of water over the Everglades. In another month or so, it would go from sand-dry, with grass crackling and breaking under your every step, to swamp-wet and impossible to pass through without watercraft.

Standing there I thought of all those things and more. Where would Clay and I be when the rains came? I became aware of how badly I'd screwed up, or maybe it was just the regret and depression that follow too much alcohol. Whatever it was, it actually had me considering an alteration in my life; the party girl was starting to seriously consider leaving the festivities. Over the weekend, even at the height of the good times with noise and laughter all around me, I found myself feeling lonely, and realized I was missing Clay. It was an uncomfortable surprise. Still, it hadn't stopped me from going for that last martini, had it? That old saw "I can resist anything but temptation" should be tattooed on my forehead.

The buzz of insects making nice with each other all around me underscored my conviction to put things right in my own life. I needed to get home and make nice. Big-time.

I was hanging up the nozzle when a harsh yowl, almost like the sound of a human in pain, rose from the wilderness. It had been a long time since I'd heard that sound. Tully had taught me to identify that wail while we were sitting around a campfire and I'd never forgotten it. That call had terrified me back then, but now the panther's cry brought a smile to my lips.

Perhaps the panther was calling for a mate. March is mating season for the panthers, their time for making nice, and in three months there would be a couple more blind little kits out there in their natural habitat to defy the doomsayers. The experts keep telling us that panthers have disappeared from the wild, that there are less than a hundred left. I've lived all my life in Florida, trekked the backcountry with my father, and only seen two panthers. One was at nightfall on a narrow trail in the Myakka Wilderness Preserve; the other was dead on the road near Everglades City. But panthers travel mainly at night, bedding down on hammocks and sleeping during the day. I want to believe that's the reason we don't see them.

"Keep on screaming, baby," I whispered to the far-off animal. "Don't die on us." I leaned against the truck and waited, but there was no answering call in the night. Maybe I was hearing a lonely howl of frustration in a world only one panther occupied. Ain't that a bitch? Being the last one of your kind gives loneliness a whole new meaning.

I cleaned the windshield and waited some more, but the panther stayed silent, so I grabbed my purse and headed in to pay for the gas.

The front windows of the building were plastered with posters and flashing neon, advertising brands of beer and high-caffeine drinks guaranteed to keep you awake for a week. I couldn't see inside but I wasn't worried by that. It was just the normal, everyday kind of spot we all need and use safely without thinking. Nothing told me there was anything unusual happening in there—no hair raising on the back of my neck to warn me.

As I stepped inside and the door sighed shut behind me, the two people in the store looked up with panic-struck expressions. The dread was so strong on their faces, I looked back over my shoulder to see what had caused it. Nothing. When my eyes turned back to them, they'd relaxed. I wasn't the person they were waiting for, so they ignored me and returned to their conversation—or, more accurately, their argument. I watched and tried to decide what was happening. The guy arguing with the clerk behind the glass enclosure was in his late teens. Lightning bolts were shaved in his close-cut hair. His feet were bare and his jeans were wet to the knees.

I'd expected to be the only customer in the store because there were no cars out front. Where had he come from? He must have pulled around to the back of the station, because no one walked to this lonely place, but why would he hide his car around back?

"Help me," he said in a voice full of fear and panic.

My senses went on high alert. Something bad was happening here. Alarm filled me. I glanced around. My instinct was to get out of there, but I told myself that was ridiculous, told myself I had too much imagination. Whatever was happening, it wasn't my problem and in two minutes I'd be gone. I'd just grab an iced coffee and get a Popsicle out of the chest freezer and then I'd be on the road again. The weekend was catching up to me, leaving me snoozy for the long drive ahead, although the shock of their conversation had woken me up a bit. Still, it would be a roll-down-the-windows-and-crank-up-the-music trip home.

I gave them a pass and headed for the back of the store, hurrying past display units that jutted out into the aisles so that you almost had to turn sideways to walk down them. The whole place was like that, a tiny warren of narrow aisles. Wire shelves holding two-day-old white bread crowded up against shelves of jars of peanut butter and headache pills. Glass-fronted fridges containing six-packs of beer and soda lined the far wall. It was an uncomfortable and claustrophobic place.

Back at the counter, where merchandise crowded the narrow entry and left room for only one person at the glass partition, the boy turned sideways, making room for me at the clerk's window but blocking my way out. Even though he made room for me, he didn't stop arguing. "C'mon, Angie, you gotta."

The girl, pretty and Hispanic, had a small ring through her bottom lip and a silver stud in her nose. Her hair was long and straight and black. Focused on the boy, she acted as if I didn't exist. She hissed something at him in Spanish and huddled as far away from the window as she could get.

I cracked the Popsicle in half on the edge of the counter and waited. What made their problems more important than my needs, their lives more immediate than mine? Annoyance hummed through my veins. It was the middle of the night, in the middle of nowhere, and I still couldn't get served. It seemed the anthem of my life. I read a big sign warning that the clerk's cage was locked and all cash went immediately into a locked box the cashier couldn't access.

"No one will find out you helped me," he said. "Please, you got to help me, Angie." He reached out his hands in desperation and panic, planting his palms and forearms on the glass as if he could touch her.

The girl, secure between the cigarettes and lotto tickets behind the glass, replied, "He already called . . . knows you're headed here."

"Excuse me." My voice was too loud in the small room with all of us crunched up together. I didn't care. I wanted their attention. More than that, I wanted out of there. Whatever was going on here, I wanted no part of it. It was definitely something bad they were talking about, a problem that was going to end violently. "Can I just pay for my gas?"

The boy swung to face me. His large black eyes were full of tears. He swallowed and stepped aside. It was almost a courteous act.

I held up the orange Popsicle. "Just the gas and these . . . my dinner." They didn't smile. In fact, they looked like they'd never smile again. But then, my words were a pretty pathetic attempt to lighten the mood.

The girl ignored me and launched herself to the edge of the counter. "I'm not getting involved in this."

If the girl was afraid, I was terrified. I didn't know who was coming, but I didn't want to be there when they arrived. I put my credit card away and dug through my wallet for cash while the boy pleaded, "Let me take your car."

"I can't get mixed up in this." Her voice was harsh in its intensity.

The boy laid his cheek against the glass and whispered, "I saw. They'll kill me."

I glanced frantically around, hunting the danger. For the briefest second I considered leaving without paying for my gas, but that was stupid and would only lead to more trouble. I fumbled the cash onto the counter.

"They're on their way." The girl leaned back again, distancing herself from whatever risk he represented, and bumped up against the shelves of cigarettes.

He slapped the glass with his palms and pressed his chest against the surface as if to break in. "You told them," he screamed.

"Get out of here while you still can. They're coming for you." She pointed to the door and yelled at the guy, "Get out of here, now!"

"But how?" he wailed. "Please, Angie." He banged his fist on the glass, making it tremble, and shouted, "You have to help me."

She wrapped her arms across her chest, cradling herself. "Hide in the grass until it's safe."

He shook his head frantically. "Not good enough. I've got to go farther."

I slipped three twenties into the trough under the glass.

Wound tight as a spring and in deep despair, the boy with lightning in his hair watched me out of the corner of his eye while pretending not to, freaking me out even more.

I slid past him without waiting for my change. As I went out the door I dug my keys out of my shoulder bag and headed to the truck at a jog, glad to be out of there before anything happened.

Putting them out of my mind, I calculated how long it would take me to hit Fort Myers and how angry Clay was going to be with me when I finally got home. I opened the door of my pickup and threw my purse inside. That's when the guy with lightning in his hair hit me from behind and knocked me to the concrete.

CHAPTER 3

I slammed hard onto the pavement. The air rushed out of me, and the concrete scraped the skin from my arm. I heard the bottle of iced coffee shatter and felt cold liquid splash up my arm.

The boy put his foot on my wrist and bent over to grab the keys out of my hand. He stood over me for a second, menacing and intense.

"What?" I said. I meant, *What's happening? Why are you taking my keys, and what's going to happen to me?* I wanted to know a whole lot more besides, but all I said was that one dumb word.

"Sorry," he said.

What kind of a dumb-ass thief apologizes?

I was still on my back, wondering what the shit had happened, when he jumped into the truck and slammed the door. That got me on my feet. I grabbed the mirror and banged my hand against the door as the truck jerked forward. I lost my balance and fell to the asphalt, scuttling backwards out of the path of the rear wheels as he peeled away.

Then I was running after him, as if I might actually catch him or he, seeing my desperation, might change his mind. I watched the brake lights flash on as he slowed to take the ninety-degree turn at the exit. It wasn't enough. The truck fishtailed dangerously before he got control and disappeared behind the wall of grass. Seconds later the sky brightened over the reeds as the headlights came on. I followed the progress of my truck by the glow of the lights as it headed back to the highway without me.

I waited in shocked disbelief for this impossible thing to correct itself. Maybe time would rewind. Perhaps I'd get a do-over, or a mulligan. Maybe he'd change his mind. The only thing I knew for sure was that some giant mistake had been made.

But he didn't stop. I watched my life vanish as the glow moved away from me. My ID, my credit cards and my cell phone, even the hot new outfit I'd spent too much money on down in Miami, had disappeared. All the flotsam and jetsam that kept Sherri Travis functioning had been taken away. The only things left were the clothes on my back: capris, a white top that left one shoulder bare and pink flip-flops. Everything else was gone.

My only choice was to go into the building and call the cops. If I was lucky, Angie would let me call Clay to say I was going to be very late. In my mind I was already making excuses and marshaling arguments for why this so wasn't my fault.

I was halfway back to the booth when the lights over the pumps went off, leaving just a soft blush of light behind the glass on the pumps.

"No," I protested. The inside of the store went dark. Only the spotlights on the corners of the building remained lit.

I bolted for the door, slamming into the glass with arms outstretched before I grabbed the handle and tried to drag it open. The door didn't yield. Pushing and pulling and kicking, insane with fear, I screamed, "Let me in!" I pounded the glass with my palms.

No one answered.

I pressed my face against the glass, cupping my hands around my eyes. There was no sign of the girl in the dim interior. The boy had called her Angie. "Angie," I yelled, pulling on the door. "Angie, let me in. I've been robbed. You have to help me."

She didn't call out. Nor did she come and open the door to offer me refuge. And then it hit me. She wasn't going to come to my aid. She didn't help the boy, and now she wasn't coming to save me.

I swung away from the door and searched the small paved square for somewhere to hide. I didn't know what I was hiding from; I only knew I needed to disappear. There was nothing here but this barren piece of pavement, surrounded by hundreds of acres of grass hiding venomous snakes and alligators. At five foot seven, I was shorter than the grass, and if I stepped into it to hide, I might disappear forever.

I turned back, pounding harder on the glass and begging, "Please." My voice broke and tears streamed down my cheeks and onto my neck. "I won't hurt you." But how do you reassure a stranger of that? And why would she be afraid of me in the first place?

"I've been robbed," I sobbed.

No one answered.

There were no welcoming footsteps, no click of a lock opening the door to me, no words of comfort. Again I cupped my hands around my eyes and peered inside, half expecting to see her staring back at me. But in the radiance of the neon window signs and the dim pot lights in the ceiling, nothing moved. There was no one.

I rattled the door. "You can't leave me out here." I was still pounding the door when a light-colored sedan shot out from behind the concrete structure and sped towards the exit.

I ran after the car, waving my arms and yelling, "Wait."

But the sedan didn't slow. Rocking at a crazy angle and threatening to flip at the sharp bend onto the road, it turned out onto Last Chance Road.

I ran after it, waving my arms in the air and shrieking for Angie to wait for me. Not even a flicker of brake lights. Angie definitely wasn't stopping for me, wasn't even looking back. I stood in the middle of the road and watched her go, shocked and frightened.

With the dry, dusty scent of grass in my nose and the sound of my sobs joining the refrain of nature, I stood in the middle of Last Chance Road, hugging my arms across my chest, waiting to be rescued. A sense of absolute loss was followed by a tiny flicker of hope, a crazy expectation. Maybe Angie would regret leaving me behind and come back. How quickly my despair could be overcome by an ingrained optimism. That small sliver of hope kept me in the center of the pavement, waiting for her to return.

It didn't happen. Even hope was gone.

The darkness closed in on me. The night sounds grew louder and more menacing than they'd been when I was standing under a shelter of lights.

The cry of the panther splintered the night. Terror freed me from dazed inaction. I ran back to the store.

CHAPTER 4

I needed to get inside. There would be a phone in there. The windows were heavily barred, and a steel grate had been pulled across the inside of the door. But maybe I didn't need to be inside to bring help. I searched for something to smash the glass. Surely a break-in would set off an alarm and alert the police. That's what I wanted most right now, sirens and flashing lights and someone with a gun to protect me.

I couldn't find a rock big enough to even scratch the glass, let alone shatter it. The area was stripped down and barren, probably to prevent just what I was contemplating. I stared down at my rubber flip-flops. Not even a stiletto heel for a weapon.

Maybe there was another way in. I searched the sides of the building for a pay phone or other entrances. Even a police battering ram would have trouble breaking down the heavy steel grill over the back entrance, and no matter how scared the girl had been, she had still taken the time to lock up the building. The washrooms on either side of the back door were locked. Each of them had a small window, set high above my head—too high and too small to give me access. The building was a fort.

"Calm down," I told myself. Taking long deep breaths and struggling for control, I searched my surroundings again for a hiding place. I had the crazy idea that if I could clamber up onto the roof I could hide there and be safe at least from nature. I just needed something to stand on, but the barren parking lot was empty. There wasn't even a garbage can to use as a ladder or a dumpster to hide in. Hoping I'd missed something, I circled the concrete-block building one more time, slowly. Security lights flashed on to highlight my passing. There was nothing. The defenses of the tiny hut were absolute. This place of convenience was locked down and secured like the most dangerous prison. Everything that could be stolen or used to break in had been stripped away, leaving no place to hide from man or nature.

Wild thoughts, impractical and dangerous, chased each other through my brain. I had no way to start a fire to signal for help, no hope of yelling loud enough for anyone to hear. Walking out to the highway to flag down a car seemed to be my only way out, but the memory of red eyes glowing in the lights of my pickup killed that idea. The prospect of a walk along the concrete ribbon through the tall grasses, a gauntlet of wild and dangerous slithering and sliding things on both sides, frightened the hell out of me. Chances were, I wouldn't even make it to the highway to be raped and murdered.

Even if I could make it out to Alligator Alley, how would I know if I was being rescued or thrown into a new hell? Women are raped and killed with impunity in the heart of the city. I didn't want to think about what the wrong man would do to a woman out in the wilds. Whether it was true or not, I felt that the only people out here late at night were going to be the wrong ones to turn to, the ones Tully had warned me about, deviants and crazies. Upstanding citizens were home safe in their beds. Hitchhiking in the Glades at night was a perfect way to make myself disappear forever.

The only other option was staying where I was and waiting. Sooner or later, someone was coming to this station looking for lightning-bolt man. The only thing was, he'd said they were going to kill him. That didn't sound like someone I could count on to rescue me. I tried to think of another way out.

A flock of birds, dark against the night sky, flew up over the sawgrass. Something had startled them into flight. Someone was coming. I stepped back under the overhang and huddled under a light above the door. Defeated, I slid down to my heels, my back against the cool glass. Squatting there on my haunches, I waited for what would happen next. I'd made a mistake and now I was going to pay for it.

Clay says I suffer from poor planning, never looking ahead, never sticking to the agenda or carrying through with the plan. The truth of his words had never seemed clearer than they did now. I should have left when I said I was going to. And then there was that last martini. That was what I regretted most of all.

I'd compounded my error by passing on the offer of a bed for the night, so sure I had everything under control. It would have been so much easier to explain to Clay why I was a day late than why I ended up alone at night in the middle of a swamp.

Now that I'd accepted that all my frantic activity was useless, I became aware of the pain. I lifted my arm and checked out the wound. I was missing skin, stripped away by my impact with the pavement. A thin trickle of blood ran down to my wrist, a feast for all kinds of bacteria and insects. I dabbed the clotting blood away with bottom of my blouse but tiny pinpricks of red welled and filled the patch as I watched.

A line of light appeared over the grasses to the left of the station, moving towards me. I got slowly to my feet. Lights, bright lights, headlights of at least one car, were coming down the empty road to the station. For a moment the lights seemed to separate. Two cars coming for gas? They were heading here for another reason.

What had the girl said? *They're coming for you.* Maybe it was the police. For one brief moment hope sprang to life again. But Angie was afraid of the people coming. Would Angie be afraid of the police? And if Angie was afraid of the people who were coming, I was petrified.

They're going to kill me. It wasn't the police who were coming.

I wasn't involved. I'd witnessed nothing and was no threat to anyone. I was just an innocent victim of a crime, so they had no reason to harm me. But somehow I didn't think innocence was going to protect me.

CHAPTER 5

One thing I was sure of: the approaching lights weren't coming down Last Chance Road to rescue Sherri Travis. And I was also pretty certain they weren't coming for gas.

Maybe when the men in the cars saw that the lights were off in the store and there were no cars on the apron, they'd leave, wouldn't even get out of their cars and look around. Sure . . . that was a likely scenario . . . in someone else's nightmare. If they were coming way out here, they'd search back and front, and no matter where I was, they'd find me.

Still, no problem: I'd tell them everyone but me had gone, explain that my pickup had been stolen. What would happen then was either a lift to the next exit or something I didn't want to imagine. In any case, I wanted it to be my decision whether they found me, and I needed to see them before I committed to showing myself. If they were normal people only interested in pumping gas, I could just pop out and bum a ride. But how do you tell regular people from psychopaths?

I scanned the shadows around me. I'd been around the building more than once and knew it offered no concealment. Where could I secrete myself except in the grasses? It was a terrifying prospect. It wasn't just alligators I feared. In the summer a python had been killed with a whole alligator inside of it. The python had just squeezed its body down along that bumpy surface, swallowing and spreading itself, until it had ingested the entire gator. I wouldn't even be a challenge.

I ran around to the back of the building, out of sight of the lights that would soon sweep the gas bar. Flattened against the wall, my heart racing, I searched for cover. I spied a small opening, a little break in the line of shrubs across the back of the parking lot. I headed for it with no clear idea of how it would help me. What I found was an opening to a twelve-foot-wide drainage ditch. Drainage canals run along Alligator Alley from Naples to Homestead. They were created when material was scooped out from the ditches to raise the pavement above the water in the swamp, keeping the road from flooding. Now these canals are a roadway for migrating gators and other forms of wildlife.

There was a canoe. I'd found my way out. There was only one problem. While the bow was pulled three feet up onto the sand, the paddle floated in the water just beyond my reach. If I wanted it, I had to step into the black water to retrieve it. I hovered there, with only the toes of my pink flip-flops in the stream, thinking of what swam beneath the surface and trying to find some forgotten courage.

The full moon shone on the water like a spotlight, outlining the trees and shrubs along the channel. Something moving under the dark surface was causing a shiver of motion on the top. Ripples. Small waves of movement, from some unseen thing, disturbed the glassy plane. The canoe swayed in its wake.

I wasn't going in the water. But maybe I didn't have to; maybe I could get in the canoe and reach over the side to grab the paddle. I grasped the fiberglass sides, pushing the small craft off the sandy bank. The tiny waves from the movement of the canoe pushed the paddle farther away from me.

The lights from the cars swept around the corner, entering the parking area and shining over the building to light up the night sky.

There was no time to worry about possible threats when a real one had just arrived. I had to get that paddle. I lunged into water up to my knees and grabbed the smooth planed wood. I threw it into the bottom of the canoe and then I followed. Too frightened to be careful, there was no three-point entry, no bracing myself on the gunwales to distribute my weight and stepping in gently. It was more like a belly flop into the unknown. The canoe tipped wildly, threatening to roll. I braced myself, praying to stay upright, and watched one of my pink flip-flops bobbing on the small waves.

The canoe settled. I had to get out of here, but which way should I go? There were only two choices, right or left. Left went deeper into the Glades. Right went back towards civilization. Right was the direction for me.

I dug in with the paddle, following the silver path of the moon. I took six strokes and then looked back over my shoulder. Drainage ditches are as straight as a surveyor's pole and you can see down them for a long way. Anyone coming for lightning-bolt guy could look down the ditch and mistake me for him.

Heavy brush grew along the sides of the water, offering concealment. As I moved closer to them, dripping fronds swept down to touch me, marking me with their dampness. I used the paddle to push the canoe deep into the overhanging tangle of vegetation, hoping the red canoe couldn't be seen through the underbrush.

Surrounded and hidden, I still didn't feel safe. My billowy

white top caught the moonlight and stood out like a beacon. I slid down below the gunwales. The ribs along the bottom cut into my shoulders and hips, and water soaked into my clothes. I stayed perfectly still and tried not to imagine the spiders and snakes and other vicious things in the branches above me, more things to kill me than I could actually name. But there was more than imagination to fight against. I heard rustling in the overhang. I stared up into the tangle. Was it some small creature repositioning itself or something moving towards me? God, don't let it be a snake. My heart pounded against my rib cage, a wild animal attempting to break free, and my breath came in short, sharp pants.

A park warden had once told me there are over fifty species of snakes in Florida but only six of those are venomous. Making me able to name six ways I didn't want to die was the wrong way to try to cure me of my fear of snakes. I whimpered involuntarily. I quickly cut off the sound by slapping a hand over my mouth. I lay there stiff with fear, positive that living creatures were crawling over me. The steamy night closed in around me. Mosquitoes gorged themselves on my blood. I waited. Eventually, my heart began to beat more evenly and my eyes adjusted to the darkness. Second guesses had time to mature. Was I making a mistake by hiding? Did I really have anything to fear from these unknown people? Maybe I'd misheard. These might be the good guys. Could even be cops. I thought I heard footsteps and rose halfway to a sitting position. The canoe rocked and ground against the brush.

The crunch of feet on shells was quite clear now. And then a light passed by me on the water.

A man's voice said, "We know you're here, Tito. Angie told us where to find you. We only want to talk."

Half raised from the bed of the craft, I tried to decide whether to speak, but then another voice, this one less reasonable and conciliatory than the first, yelled, "You son of a bitch, we're going to get you, and then we're going to kill you for this, you little dickhead."

I eased down. The canoe wobbled, rubbing against a branch and squealing in protest. I didn't breathe again until the rocking stilled.

The light swept by. Would the metal along the topside of the canoe catch the light?

"He's gone in the canoe." One of them was talking on a cell. "Angie was right. I can see where he came in the canoe and then pushed it back out. He may be coming your way, going back to the nursery." The man went silent, listening, and then said, "All right. We'll stay put until you get here."

His footsteps crunched on the shelled area by the canal as he walked away.

CHAPTER 6

Fighting panic, I tried to remember word for word what I'd heard. They knew Tito hadn't gone with Angie, but they didn't know about my pickup. They were looking for Tito on the water. No, they were looking for me. *He's coming your way.* Someone was on the water looking for him. If I left the safety of the underbrush I could run into him. Which way was this person coming from? I had to guess. Nursery. Did that mean children or plants? I hadn't noticed a sign for either at the few turn-offs I'd passed.

And then there was the biggest question of all. Was it better to hide here in this tangle until morning, or should I try to make for some safe place farther on? A thousand mosquitoes fed on me; I slapped my arm where the skin had been scraped away. Sitting still and being attacked by bugs was impossible. Besides, doing nothing has never been my way. I was going.

I knelt, hips against the seat, and fought my way out, using branches to push myself backward through the tangle. In the swamp, it seemed every plant came with prickles. They grabbed me, tearing at bare skin and clothing. Finally, almost free, I shoved the paddle deep into the muck and pushed. As I yanked the paddle free it struck the side of the canoe with a sharp crack. No one could mistake the bang for a natural sound. The men would know exactly what it was.

Terror gave me strength nature hadn't. I pulled hard on the paddle, trying to distance myself from the sound. Clumsy and slow and out of practice, I gained feet and then yards with each stroke.

Traveling through the blackness, worrying about snakes and gators and strange men, fighting down panic until I could hardly breathe, I prayed I had escaped. But I knew I hadn't. Somewhere out on this canal, possibly coming towards me, was a boat heading to the station. I listened for the sound of an engine between strokes. There was only one thing I could do. I had to find a place to hide until it passed.

A hundred yards from where I'd begun, the landscape changed. On my left, the narrow waterway opened up into a small, marshy pond. Large clumps of reeds grew where the two waters met. Was this my chance to get away from anyone traveling the canal? I could hide here and then go on after they passed. I listened for an engine but there was nothing.

This marsh marked the start of the true Everglades, unaltered by man, and the farther I went into them, the thicker and taller the grasses would be. And now, in the grip of the dry season, the water would only be six inches to a foot deep in places, too shallow to paddle. I'd have to walk and drag the canoe. Without even the small protection of the canoe . . . I couldn't finish that thought.

And there was another problem. Even if I tried to walk through the needlegrass and prickleweed along the edge of the channel, hoping to bypass anyone heading for the gas station, I could easily get disoriented. In the river of grass, the reeds close behind you as quickly as you pass. With no markers, I'd be lost in the million and a half acres of the Everglades.

I had to make a decision. Stay on the canal and risk meeting the men on their way to the station, or risk the Everglades and all they contained? A night bird called, beckoning me into the wilderness.

The safety the grasses offered was too frightening. I took a deep breath and paddled twenty feet past the opening to the little bay and was once again contained in the narrow tunnel of the canal.

Slowly my eyes adjusted and my night vision improved. The darkness that had surrounded me like a heavy blanket was no longer so dense. Overhead a new moon shone and there were more stars in the sky than I remembered there ever being. I began to pick out details of the landscape. Bushes growing out of the black water became separate entities and not just one huge mass. Lighter areas, shadows really, separated from the midtones of night and from the black unknown at water level. Fear sharpened my senses. I smelled the rank mud of the bank and felt tender air against my skin. Insects bedeviled me but I shut them out, intent on the larger threat. My eyes searched from side to side, covering the water and the vegetation along the edges, hunting for danger, but it was the egrets that warned me. A white cloud of them rose from the dark outline of a tree down the channel. They circled into the lighter sky ahead of me, squawking and complaining, before settling down again. I listened, holding the paddle above the water. Drops slipped off the end and fell to the water, loud in the night that was suddenly silent.

A faint cough . . . a human sound. Quickly, without thought, I rammed the nose of the canoe deep in the canes. Thorns and barbs grabbed at me. I reached up to protect my face and knocked the paddle out of my hand. It clunked against the side and disappeared into the water. There was no time to search for it. First I needed to disappear in the overhang. I needed to hide.

I tugged on the overhanging greenery and pulled myself in deeper. Making sure none of the canoe jutted out into the channel, I stretched out along the bottom as I had before. More water soaked my back and matted my hair. A small bug crawled across my face. I pursed my lips and tried to blow it away. Overhead a branch bent towards me; a leaf fell on my chest. It was hard not to bolt upright, to rush away from the unknown. I bit down hard on my lip to remain silent. Tears slipped down my cheeks and tickled onto my neck. "Stay still; don't move," I warned myself.

I heard the chug of an electric motor. The canoe, rocking in the wake from the boat, rubbed up against a mangrove root and groaned. I prayed they wouldn't recognize the sound for what it was, that they'd think it was only one branch rubbing on another in their wake. I didn't risk looking up to see them go by.

Minutes passed and there was no sound of the motor. Aware of my body, of its discomfort, hard ridges digging into me and scratches and bites enough to drive me mad, I had to force myself to stay down. My hands were clenched at my side like I was laid out in a coffin, the blisters on my palms burning. Perspiration dried and cooled me. Goose bumps rose along my arms. I lay in the bottom of the canoe long after the sound died away, straining my hearing to super strength to hear if they returned. Were there any more men coming down the canal? I listened for the sound of the motor. Only the night sounds of the marsh.

I couldn't stay where I was. If they came back and searched the underbrush with flashlights . . . it was too frightening to contemplate.

I sat up. Water dribbled down my back. The canoe rubbed against mangrove roots and protested loudly. I gripped the sides to steady it, although there was no danger of it capsizing: it was jammed in too tightly between roots and limbs.

I had to find the paddle or I was going nowhere. Dread of the men trumped the fear of the unknown. I put my hand over the side, searching in the reeds and the mess of roots for my paddle. Something splashed inches away from my hand. I jerked away and waited. Nothing. Cautiously I started searching again, barely touching the water, trying not to make waves and ready to fly back to safety at the first touch of anything but water. I couldn't find the paddle. I pushed the little craft farther out into the canal and began my search again. Just as my fingers touched the smooth wood and closed around it, something big broke the surface at the bow of the canoe.

CHAPTER 7

Fear shifts. Replace one kind of terror with something more horrific and it's a whole new game. Now I only wanted to get away from that thing in the water. I scrambled loudly, crazily. I didn't care about noise or dangerous men finding me. I pushed and shoved and pulled, all the while mewling in fear.

I broke free and hauled on the paddle, spurting forward. Head down, and panting through my mouth, I tried to distance myself from both the other boat and that thing in the water. The burst of speed didn't last. Couldn't last. Worn out, I rested on the paddle, leaning forward and taking long gulps of air. I looked back towards the gas bar. No light shone down the waterway, and there were no shouts of discovery. Only silence. Maybe I was safe.

For long moments I drifted, the light craft bobbing towards a reed bed on my left. My breathing steadied. I tried to judge how late it was. I was overcome with a longing for home and for Clay, so strong I nearly cried out to him. My promise, "I'll be home before midnight," laughed in my head. I shouldn't be here, that's what my brain kept saying. If I'd listened to Clay, I would have been home in time for dinner, and well before dark. It had all gone terribly wrong, but given another chance I would make it right and wipe away this night. Why had I gone to Miami? Now, sitting here all alone, I'd have given anything to be back at the

Sunset, kibitzing with the regulars and complaining about how hard I worked.

I wiped away my tears and picked up the paddle. There was only one way I could get home again.

The rusty roar of a bull gator sounded over the chattering chorus of insects and frogs, but he was far away, no threat to me. Not so the mosquitoes; they tormented me, feasting on every inch of bare skin.

My strokes were long and smooth now, but my left palm burned with each twist of the paddle. Already blisters had formed. I was focused on that pain in my hand when my paddle hit something hard. I jerked to the left, away from this new terror, sending the canoe rocking crazily. In the moonlight, an alligator surfaced. I clung to the rocking vessel, willing it to settle. To capsize now . . .

The gator seemed to hang suspended on the surface of the water, waiting for some unknown thing to happen.

The rocking of the canoe had brought me too close to the left bank. Branches poked me. I stretched out my arms, sank the paddle deep into the bottom and pushed the craft forward and away. Again it swayed dangerously. Tentatively I took another small stroke. The gator didn't react. With a deep breath, I dug deep and surged forward. I was safe. It didn't last long.

CHAPTER 8

In front of me, a black structure bisected the river of moonlight. Exhausted and barely able to take it in, I studied the object in the water and tried to figure out what it meant. And then it came to me. A dock was jutting out from the shore.

A dock meant people. Sanctuary. "Be careful," caution whispered. Telling myself not to let my eagerness for shelter jeopardize my security, I left the path of the moonlight and slipped through the shadows along the edge of the canal. Quietly and warily, I floated towards the dock, studying it and the open space it jutted out from.

In the clearing sat a low, flat house. A soft yellow buglight glowed over the back door of the pale house. Along the right side of the property, tall pole lights stood over a long shade house for plants. I'd reached the nursery.

On the left was a shack. The pole light threw just enough light to read the sign tacked to the shed's side: CANOE RENTALS. A scattering of red canoes, just like the one I sat in, littered the bank. Was this where Tito had come from? Likely. Quite possibly the men in the boat with the electric motor had come from here as well. And that meant they'd return to this place—probably sooner rather than later.

Go in or go on? There was a risk either way.

I needed help and I needed a phone. A house offered both of those. I could break in and call for help. That wouldn't take long. I'd be gone before they came back down the canal.

I calculated the timing. If they'd spent fifteen minutes searching at the station and then started back, how much time did I have? They'd make better time than me, but they'd search more thoroughly on the way back. How long would it take to break in and make a call? Minutes only. Was the house deserted? Was everyone out searching for Tito, or had they left someone behind? No car was parked in the yard. One thing was clear: I had no time for sober second thoughts. I had to decide. Caution and fear were overcome by exhaustion.

The bow of the canoe sliced into the soft sand of the bank. If I saw any sign of them returning while I was out of the canoe, I'd bolt into the brush edging the clearing in a flash. Unless they had dogs, it would be almost impossible for them to find me. I wished I hadn't thought of dogs. All country properties seemed to have at least one. I waited for the racket of that warning bark. Nothing. And nothing moved under the lights. A dog might be inside, but there was no sign of one out here.

The beach was too exposed. I backed off the sand, then lifted the soggy rope out of the bottom of the canoe and tied it to the dark underside of the dock. I slipped over the side to the shadows of the underbrush. Staying away from the open space, I came ashore quietly and slowly. The grass under my feet was cool and slippery. I realized I'd lost my other flip-flop. No matter. I hugged the deep shadows and stole towards the small outbuilding, tasting the very air for the presence of another human, listening for the hint of a breath.

At the edge of the hut, I reached out to touch the roughness of the board siding with my fingers and then slipped along its side. I dipped below the window and paused there, listening, before I dropped to my hands and knees and crawled forward.

The door to the shack hung open. There was a deadness to the place, a feeling of being deserted. That was fine with me. All I wanted was a phone. Surely if they were running a business out of it, the building would have a phone, a landline that would connect me to help. I studied the dark interior of the shed, trying to commit myself to going into it. In the blackness inside, there wasn't a rustle or a breath. I stretched out my arm. My hand crept along the floor and touched something soft. I jerked back. What was it? A jacket? Cloth for sure. Was there someone inside that bundle of material? Nothing stirred.

I didn't have time to hesitate. I needed a phone. I reached out again, inching towards the cloth and expecting to discover a hard lump of a body but finding nothing but a pliable bunch of fabric.

Slowly, slowly, I felt my way forward. The room was a box about eight by eight. As my fingers explored the interior, my eyes adjusted to the lack of light and broke the shadows into pale walls of unpainted wood, dark packs hanging off the walls—life jackets, probably—and, in the corner, a barrel of paddles. I could see a sleeping bag and a pillow crumpled on the floor, pale in the moonlight shining through the window. I stood up.

Examining the walls and a small shelf with my eyes and my fingers, I hunted for a phone. Nothing. I choked down my despair. I'd wasted time and gained nothing. I went to the door. From inside the shack, I studied the house. The light over the door called to me. Not much time left. I had to hurry now. Speed was more important than caution. I slid out of the shed and darted into the deep shadows of the scrub along the edge of the cleared land. I hesitated, unwilling to leave safety and cover the twenty feet or so of open space. "Go, go," my brain said, but my feet took their time listening. Finally, bent low but moving quickly, I scuttled to the house. Flattening myself against the cool metal siding, I sidled up to the window and turned my face to see inside. It was an office. The drawers to a filing cabinet stood open. Brown files were scattered among white pages on the floor, but on the old-fashioned oak desk sat a black telephone. I tried to open the window. It wouldn't give. I had to try a door.

Which entrance was safer, front or back? And which was more likely to be unlocked? The back—they wouldn't expect anyone to approach from the water. But first I had to be sure there was no one inside. As much as I wanted that telephone, I wanted to live more. I'd check every window, first to see if the room was empty, then to see if it would open. If all else failed, I would come back and smash this window. I waited for the bark of a dog, the creak of boards under the weight of a step, but there was nothing. I ducked down below the sill and headed along the back of the house, trying all the windows as I went.

At the back stoop I paused. Maybe there was another way to find a phone, a safer way. The shade house might have a landline. Was it worth the time and the risk to try it? If there was someone still here, they would be in the house and not out in the unlit nursery.

Crouching low, I darted across the open area between the structures. At the shade house, I paused. The pole lights along the front would make me a target if I went in that way. I'd try the back first and hope there were no alarms. Please, God, don't let there be a dog locked in there.

I ran around the corner and immediately tripped over a stack of clay pots. The noise of the clattering mess jolted me back to my feet and had me running for cover behind a giant oak. Precious minutes slipped by. There were two back doors in the shade house. I watched but neither opened. If anyone had heard me, maybe they just thought the noise was caused by an animal. I eased away from the oak.

The first door in the long narrow structure was locked, but the second one, a screen door, creaked loudly as I pulled it towards me. I slipped inside. A picnic table stood at the center of the room, and on the floor beside me sat a stack of wooden boxes. This screened room seemed to be a combination packing shed and staff room, and even though two of the walls were open to the outside, the smell of chemicals hung in the air. I felt along the wall to see if there was a phone. Nothing.

To my left was a door to another space. The door was unlocked and led to a plant room. The odor of damp earth and the cloying smell of flowers were overpowering. I eased myself inside, carefully closing the door behind me. Two steps beyond the door I trod on sharp shards. Someone had gone crazy in here. Broken pots and plants littered the floor. White blooms stood out among the carnage. I reached down and picked up an orchid. Placing my feet cautiously to avoid pieces of broken pots, I searched for a phone but again found nothing.

I went back to the screened room. The only option left was the end room with the locked door to the outside.

CHAPTER 9

Warily, turning the doorknob and pushing with only the tips of my fingers, I inched the door open. A warm rush of putrid air assaulted me, driving me back. I breathed deep and clamped my fingers over my nose, and then I pushed the door the rest of the way open.

The tiny office was well lit by the light outside, so I could see the destruction clearly. Papers littered the floor, and a chair had been overturned. I stepped into the room. The foul smell was even stronger. Pulling my blouse up over my nose and breathing through my mouth, I stepped around an overturned table. What I saw was worse than what I smelled.

In the middle of the mess was a man. He didn't move, didn't stir or jump up to protest my intrusion, didn't demand to know why I was there. He just lay there. Was he breathing? I inched towards him.

As I knelt down a cloud of flies flew up into my face. I brushed frantically at them before I sort of shook him and said, "Mister." His very stillness told me he was dead, but I touched the clammy skin of his neck anyway.

My probing fingers didn't find a pulse there so I searched for a beat on his cold wrist. Nothing. The man was beyond help. A quick look at the walls and the desk told me there was no landline. There might be a cell phone in his pants pocket or in his shirt. Patting his body down was difficult and disgusting. No cell, but it might be under the body.

I pushed my fingers under his side, feeling for his pants pocket. They didn't go in far enough so I grabbed his belt and turned the body over. The corpse made a noise. There was a new assault on my nose. I dropped him and ran.

Outside, I bent over and retched. I wiped my mouth with the back of my hand. I couldn't go back in there. I wanted to get as far away from the dead man as I could. I returned the way I'd come, down along the side of the building, past wooden crates, potted palms and stacks of clay pots, to the end of the shade house. I wasn't quiet nor was I careful. I was just trying to escape from the dead. At the house I hesitated. I looked into a bedroom window, lit from a hall light left on. It all looked so normal and inviting. I tried the window again. I still couldn't open it. After finding the dead man, breaking the glass seemed too big a risk. Easier to run than to break in and look for a phone. The men who were about to return to the nursery were playing for keeps and I'd exhausted my courage.

I ran across the open ground, past the upturned canoes and down the weathered dock.

At the edge of the water, where the air was fresh, I stopped and listened. The night seemed unnaturally quiet. I heard individual creatures instead of one loud cacophony. There was no human sound, no sound of a motor from a boat or from a car, just the ordinary things I expected to hear. I stepped into the canoe and looked down the ribbon of moonlight, searching the surface of the canal in both directions for danger. There was no boat coming towards me, but maybe it was pulled into the overhang of vegetation.

I untied the canoe and pushed away from the dock with my paddle, and then I dug in and stroked hard, wanting to put distance between myself and the nursery. The sound of the blade passing through the water seemed loud in the night that had suddenly gone quiet.

My hands, soft from my life running a restaurant, were blistered and raw. They could barely grip the wood. I adjusted my hold, trying to use only my fingers to protect the palms. It didn't work. I took off my gauzy blouse and wrapped it around my left hand to shield it from the head of the paddle. That was better. My foot was cut from the broken clay pot I'd stepped on. I tried to keep it out of the foul water in the bottom of the canoe but it was impossible. How long had it been since I'd had a tetanus shot? It was a worry for later. I fell into a steady rhythm of dip and pull. My shoulders ached.

It began to rain. The big round plops on my skin at first soothed me, but in no time they proved to be a false relief. Soon I was shivering. And then the rain stopped just as quickly and silently as it had begun.

No longer looking back, I pulled weakly on the paddle, my arms going through a numbing routine. How long? Ten minutes, fifteen minutes, maybe even a half hour, and then, over the stunted growth along the waterway, I saw the head of a loblolly pine, standing sixty feet above the brush. Strange and out of place among the stunted growth, it seemed like a beacon. I pulled over to the edge of the canal and considered it while I unwrapped my hand and shrugged my top back on.

The loblolly might indicate help. The fact that it was growing there signaled raised dry land and could mean someone was living nearby. Loblolly pines grow fast, so they're used a lot around new houses. But in my misery, this evidence of people seemed like a further threat. Everyone living in this swamp felt dangerous. I had no other choice. I couldn't go back, that was for certain. Forward was the only way. Could I get around the people living here without being caught? It was still dark enough that no one would be up—no honest people. But maybe I was worrying unnecessarily. A loblolly might just be growing there all on its own with no help from anyone. Sure, and I might yet be queen of the prom.

I eased towards the towering pine. I hadn't gone more than sixty feet when the brush disappeared and a chain-link fence replaced it. A tired-looking dog, lying in the dirt by the back door of a squat house, raised his head and gave a discouraged bark. He staggered stiffly to his feet and took a few steps towards me. A motion light on the back wall of the house came on, lighting up a red plastic slide into a child's pool. The brown dog gave another bark and flopped back down.

I slid by.

What I'd happened upon was a small subdivision of box-like houses with barren backyards enclosed by chain-link fences, the kind of place you'd be happy to live in if you were raising a family on minimum wage. In the middle of nowhere, with no services, and built as cheaply as possible, homes like these started to decay before the ink was dry on the sales agreement. This was a place not that different from the trailer park I'd grown up in, and it probably suffered from all the same problems, but it gave me hope. The people here would be people I understood—well, some of them.

I studied the dwellings, hoping to see something that would help me choose the right door to knock on to ask for help. The chain-link fences protected children and pets from gators, but how in hell did they protect themselves from the snakes?

There was no way to get into the backyards. The chain links kept out not only gators but me as well. I slipped by a half dozen of the pastel-painted structures before I came to a sloping concrete area for launching boats. I swung in but remained uncertain whether I'd reached shelter or more peril.

I needed a phone to call the cops. Okay, but which door should I knock on? Who could I trust? The risk of the unknown terrified me, froze me into inaction and sent wild thoughts buzzing through my brain. Cars were parked at every house, so there was access to a road. Maybe I could hitchhike out or even just take a long walk.

I had to do something, and I had to do it fast. I made my decision.

I pulled the canoe up far enough to keep it from floating away but not so far that I couldn't leave quickly if it all went wrong. Still I hesitated. There was a small, haphazard pile of bricks from a long-ago home improvement sitting off to the side by a fence. I picked one up, more for reassurance than actually believing I could protect myself. It was rough and painful to my blistered palm.

Creeping slowly and staying low, like I'd seen in a thousand movies, I went up the paved chute between the wire fences, checking out the backyards and trying to guess from the contents of each enclosure the sort of people who lived in the house. The houses on either side had a deserted look. The first house I'd passed after the loblolly tree, the one with a backyard filled with children's toys, seemed the most reassuring to me. Children indicated a woman, safety and caring. Maybe I was wrong, but I had to have some way of making a choice. I darted from one parked car to another. At the third house an unholy ruckus started up. A dog was going crazy inside. I crouched down on my heels and waited for it to end.

A light came on and then went off. The dog was silent. I started forward, past a white utility van, and saw a sight that lifted my heart. My red pickup sat before me like a gift. It was a surprise, but I should have known lightning-bolt man lived somewhere close if he went back and forth by canoe. Did Angie live here as well? She'd recognize me too. I looked around but couldn't see her car.

I scurried towards the truck, less cautious than I should have been.

The metal was cool and damp to my touch. I peeked inside. My purse was still on the floor where I'd thrown it. I tried the door, tugging on it again and again, but the conscientious thief had locked it. That was okay. I wasn't done yet. Marley, my best friend and the most organized person on earth, had made sure I'd never be locked out of my vehicle. She'd not only given me a magnetic key box for my birthday, she'd cut a key and stuck the magnetic box under the back bumper, knowing I never would.

I was on my knees, feeling under the bumper for the spare key, when I heard a door slam. I froze in a tight ball behind the truck. I heard the crunch of footsteps coming towards me.

CHAPTER 10

I stole a look around the back of the truck. Tito. He'd changed his clothes but I still recognized him. He was at the door to the pickup with a duffle bag in his hand. He tossed the bag in the bed of the truck and started digging in his pocket.

Still holding the brick, I jumped to my feet. He had the key in the lock and was turning to me in startled surprise, raising his arm to protect himself, when I hit him.

He went down but he was still conscious and moaning in pain. I hit him again. He covered his head with his hands and drew his knees up under him, trying to protect himself.

The key was still in the lock. Safe inside the truck, I hit the lock button and then reached under the seat to the little metal shelf Tully had installed and took out the Beretta. Working late hours at the restaurant and making bank deposits, Tully had insisted, over Clay's objections, that I carry a weapon.

Tito scrambled to his knees and raised his hands in supplication, saying, "Please don't leave me here." I pointed the Beretta at him. When he saw the gun his eyes widened in surprise and then he said, "No, no, no," over and over.

My eyes searched the houses to see if anyone was coming to his rescue. No lights came on and no one ran towards us. I started the engine.

Tito was on his feet and flinging himself against the truck door. "Please," he shouted. His arms were spread wide, begging. Blood streamed down his face from his forehead, spilling into his eyes and mouth.

I put the gun on my lap and shifted into reverse.

Holding onto the mirror, he said, "I want to go with you."

I pointed the gun right in his face. "After what you did?" A small part of me wanted to pull the trigger. "You've got to be joking."

I could see his fear, but he didn't back away. "It wasn't my fault."

I motioned with the gun. "Back away from the truck."

He stepped back a few inches, still close enough to lunge for me.

I rolled the window down about four inches. "You stole my truck and now you want me to help you?" My voice rose to a screech at the end of the sentence.

"I was going to return it."

My disgust was boundless. "Sure you were."

He lowered his head, beaten. "I needed to get away." He wiped his nose with the back of his hand, smearing blood across his face. "I always take a canoe home at night and back to work the next day. I don't have a car, easiest way to get there . . . to the rental place where I work. Tonight, my dad was drunk . . . uses me as a punching bag when he comes home that way. I went back to the shack." It all poured out in one unbroken string until he stopped and wiped blood and snot away with the flat of his hand. "I keep a sleeping bag there for when I have to stay.

"Those men came to the nursery with my cousin Angie's boyfriend." Fear enlarged his eyes. He wasn't seeing me anymore but something more frightening than a woman with a gun. He moved closer to the truck. "They beat Mr. Bricklin and then they killed him. I saw them and they saw me, but I got away. I paddled out to the service station where Angie works, but Ruben had already called her to find me . . . told her what they were going to do to me and that she should stay out of it. Angie wouldn't help me."

I could see that her betrayal still surprised him.

"That's why I stole your truck and got out of there." It seemed so logical to him, like he expected me to totally understand and forgive him.

"You left me there to get killed, and now I'm leaving you." I rolled up the window.

"Don't leave me here." His hands were on the window, smearing it with blood, his face close to mine. "Please help me."

"What the shit do I care about you? You aren't my problem."

He fell against the glass, crumpling into a heap of defeat and pain. "If you leave me, they'll find me and kill me."

"Still not my problem." But he was as scared as I'd been, and my own terror was too new for me to ignore his. "You stole my truck." I eased off the brake. I'd already wasted too much time on him.

He ran along beside me, holding on to the door handle. "Please." He started to cry. "There's no one else to help me." There were no sobs, just rivers of tears running silently down his face, mixing with the blood.

My rage left me. I braked. My shoulders slumped. "Okay."

He didn't hear me so I rapped on the window.

He looked up and I nodded to the empty truck bed. "Get in there and keep down."

In the rearview I saw him clear the side like an Olympian and disappear down into the bed.

I laid the gun on the seat beside me and spun gravel getting out of there. I took the turn too fast, the truck rocking and giving me hell before I got it settled. "Shit, shit, shit." I suddenly realized that when the men didn't find Tito, they would head here. I watched for lights coming towards me. Why had I taken him with me? I prayed I'd get clear before they came, hoped they wouldn't find Tito in the bed of the truck.

The little road came out to the westbound freeway entrance, leaving me no other choice, but two miles down the road, before I got to Last Chance Road, I spotted a turnaround for cops and service vehicles. I shot across the gravel path, warning myself to slow down, and rocketed onto the freeway headed east. There was no way I was going to cross the Alley to Naples with Tito in the back. All I wanted to do was find a place to drop him and forget I'd ever seen him.

I was doing eighty-five. The whole vehicle shuddered and shimmied. Any faster and the whole frame might fly apart. Still, I pressed on the gas. The speedometer hovered around ninety. I actually hoped to see a police car. Driving too fast and getting stopped by a cop would be a good thing. But there was none.

The hangover from terror had left me with only a fine thread of control. I took deep breaths, trying not to think any further than the road directly ahead of me. While there were few other cars traveling Alligator Alley, each set of lights felt like a threat. The problem was, I no longer knew what danger looked like. I was only too aware of my surroundings, watching the bed of the truck in the rearview and trying to guess where the next bad thing would come from.

Within ten miles, everything changed. In Florida you move from the raw, dangerous natural world to the man-made plastic world and back again. Florida is a paradox; wild nature fights urban growth, but development moves unrelentingly on.

Here on the edge of the Glades was the land of the weird, with no planning and no regulations. My panic had barely settled when the Everglades morphed into half-built subdivisions and billboards for tourist traps. A falling-down sign advertised Swamp-Man Pete's gator farm and airboat rides. When I was a kid I'd begged my dad to take me there, but he'd always said they were closed. Tully is the only person on earth who lies more than me, so there was no telling if Tully was fibbing or the sign was. It would serve Tito right if I dropped him in a pile of gators, but I needed an exit with an on-ramp to the westbound freeway. On we went.

Running along the highway on the right was a deserted housing complex, abandoned in the collapse of the housing market. I took another quick glance at the subdivision. It looked much like the one Clay and I were camping out in until he could sell it for the owner. As in our subdivision, the odd house still looked lived in, but most of the structures, in various stages of construction, were abandoned. Florida weather isn't kind to man-made things, and it's cruel to unoccupied buildings and equipment. Within months, houses can become unlivable, places you wouldn't want to reside in at any price.

The bulk of Clay's listings were in places like this, subdivisions the swamp was slowly reclaiming, along streets that were bordered by tall grasses with traffic signs and street signs poking out of them. The signs all had bullet holes in them, just like the signs where we lived. Failed developments all over Florida were being used for target practice and as garbage dumps. Some were also used for racing cars or landing small planes full of drugs. All of which made this a good place to get hijacked again.

I drove on. The next off-ramp offered a safer slice of civilization, nothing remote or lonely. I pulled into a strip mall at the junction of the main road and didn't even take time to find a parking spot, just slammed on the brakes and turned in my seat. The boy raised his head. I jerked my thumb over my shoulder and yelled, "Get out."

He got to his knees, searching my face with eyes that implored, waiting and hoping I'd change my mind.

"Get." I banged on the rear window with the flat of my hand like I could scare him away—the way you'd use a loud noise to drive off a wild animal. Still he was slow to go over the side. I lifted the gun.

When his feet and the duffle hit the pavement, I hit the gas. Looking back, I saw him raise his hand, saying goodbye. Or maybe it was the salute of the dying. I neither knew nor cared. I banished him from my mind.

I wanted a restroom, coffee and food, in that order. I also needed to take care of my broken blisters and raw flesh.

CHAPTER 11

Down the road was a cluster of fast-food businesses. Gold and red and orange, they were temples of normal, high art to me, and the everyday things I longed for most. Right now ordinary was as precious as air. There was comfort in knowing what to expect, knowing exactly how they'd be laid out, what they would serve and how much it would cost. I wanted the grease-stained cardboard box of fries, the paper packets for the salt and pepper, and the too-hot coffee, wanted to be back in the real world, away from danger I couldn't see and evil I didn't understand.

I wheeled in and parked as close to the door and its reassurance as I could get. I stretched my neck and had the phone in my hand, intending to report what had happened. I punched in the nine and the first one of the emergency number, and then I hesitated over the third digit. Calling the police meant interrogation. I needed food and coffee first. I'd eat and then I'd inform the police I'd been robbed.

But I'd gotten my truck back. Not much to report or to investigate. Still, I needed to tell them about the dead man. My stomach roiled at the memory. And it wasn't just recent memory that bedeviled me. Whenever I'd tried to do my duty as a citizen in the past, it had turned out badly. My inner self, always looking for the easy way, said, "Don't think about that now. You need to eat and get yourself under control. Besides, he's dead; you can't help him."

Later, I promised myself, I'll tell the police what happened, tell them about a dead man and the guy with lightning bolts in his hair. Already the whole thing was starting to feel impossible, like something fantastical that I'd dreamed.

I did call Clay. I barely got to tell him I was on my way before he said, "Fine," and ended the call. I folded the phone and tucked it in my bag. I paused for a second and then I put the gun in too. No way was I going anywhere without it.

I looked in the mirror before I went in. I was not a pretty sight. My eyes were bruised and blackened by exhaustion and red bites covered my face and arms. My blouse was soiled from the bottom of the canoe and dotted with blood from my hands. I was too tired to actually do anything about the way I looked, but I did run my fingers through my hair, clotted from the foul water in the bottom of the canoe, before I declared it good enough. I'd picked up my purse and started to slide off the seat before I realized I was barefoot. I remembered one flip-flop bobbing in the water at the station, but where had I lost the second one? I had no idea. Maybe it was at the nursery. It didn't matter.

I dug around in my overnight bag for runners, not really caring but aware that I already stood out. If someone came looking for me I didn't want the staff in the fast-food joint to remember me, and they would if they'd refused to serve me because I was barefoot, shoes being the minimum dress code necessary for service. I glanced at the brightly lit interior of the restaurant as I laced up the runners. Seeing as I was going to be the only customer in the place, it was unlikely they would refuse to serve me even if I came in naked. I wished it was packed with diners, a crowd I could disappear into.

I grabbed a baseball cap out of the back seat and tucked my damp hair up inside.

I jammed my keys deep in my pocket where they'd be safe, and picked up my purse, eager to be in the too-bright protection of the fast-food joint. As I turned to push open the door, the blood smeared on the driver's window made me hesitate, but only for a second. He wasn't my problem.

Inside, the smell of grease and stale coffee comforted me. The counter guy's face was filled with end-of-the-shift tiredness and boredom. He yawned when I stood before him. He didn't seem to notice that I'd been dragged through a ditch and eaten by an army of bugs. But then, working here, he'd seen it all. I could have been a walking zombie and it wouldn't have mattered to this guy. I even liked that.

I delivered my starvation order with saliva gathering in my mouth. It had been a long time since the conch fritters and sea bass I'd had for dinner. The coffee he shoved towards me was too hot, the full breakfast on an English muffin was too salty, but I adored it all. I wanted to stay there, out of harm's way and without the need to make any life-shattering decisions, forever.

I waited for my second coffee to cool enough to drink and stared out the window. With the passing of time my fear lessened, but not all of it. The night's events had left a residue of anxiety. Now it was over, and I was certain I would survive; I just wanted to put the whole thing behind me.

But there was a new worry buzzing in my head. Experience had taught me that it is a bad thing to be a witness to a crime. Not long ago, I'd witnessed a man die, a man some thought I could have saved, so I knew what to expect when you become a witness. Long interviews, going over the same material again and again, days of work missed for court time only to have it rescheduled—just the thought of the tedious and sometimes terrifying process had my face twisting in a grimace of distaste.

Worse than the inconvenience were the gossip and rumors that would start when it got out that I wasn't at the Sunset because I was in court. My past was colorful enough that volumes would be read into my involvement in another crime. Murmurs would start that there had to be more: *she must have done something to get mixed up in this*. Even my best friends would grill me on how and why. I didn't want to go through any of that again.

There was another thing. I didn't want those guys out in the Everglades to ever know I was there. Angie and the boy knew, but they had no idea who I was or where I lived. I could just slip away and never be connected to any of this. And really, what details could I offer? I had no names, no why, not even a when. The police would learn about the dead man soon enough, and the crime scene would say more than I ever could. This was one mess I didn't need to stir my stick in. I pushed my cold coffee away. I wanted to be home. I left the fast-food place eager to wipe out all memory of the previous night. This time I drove cautiously, not wanting to attract attention. When I hit Alligator Alley and civilization disappeared in the rearview, I was well within the speed limit.

Night was breaking up and the sun rose behind me. Clouds of ibis and white egrets flew up from their roosts in the Brazilian pepper trees beside the highway. I was alone on the road. I stopped gripping the steering wheel like it was the only thing between me and certain death. It was all right now. I took deep breaths and let my shoulders relax. And then I heard it, the faint scream of a siren. Were they coming after me? Surely not!

But the siren kept coming, and I was the only person crossing the Alley. Why were they chasing me? Had something happened to Tito after he jumped from the truck?

And then I was sure I knew why they were after me. The blood on the window, someone had seen it and reported it. I should have wiped it off before I went into the restaurant.

In the rearview, lights spun and flashed. Blinker on, slowing and pulling off to the edge of the pavement, I was already working on my story. I put the truck in park and slumped forward on the wheel and started to cry. I should have made that call.

A police car and then a line of fire trucks screamed past me. I jerked upright and watched them go. They weren't after me.

I took a deep breath. Carefully, I pulled back onto the highway and scanned the road ahead, expecting to come upon an accident, but before long I saw the reason for the emergency vehicles. Flames and a black plume of smoke climbed into the sky on my right. The nursery. I was certain the fire was at the nursery. It had to have started there, but it would affect more than just that property now.

Fires are part of the normal life of the Everglades, and the muck of the swamp is black from long-ago infernos, but a grass fire at this time of year was a catastrophe. In these drought conditions, a fire could burn for days, fed by the peat left behind when the water in the Glades dries up. A fire would consume thousands of acres and close down Alligator Alley.

"Please, not today." I didn't want to have to turn back because of smoke or, even worse, be stuck on the highway for hours, waiting for the visibility to improve so traffic could move again. Already, up ahead on the long flat stretch of highway, thick smoke was piling up. I rolled up my window and turned off the air, shutting it out as I drove into the cloud. More quickly than I thought possible, the road became enveloped in smoke. I thought I could smell burning meat. Ridiculous, I told myself, but the lecture didn't stop me from gagging.

I couldn't hear the sirens anymore. I slowed to a crawl, fighting to find the pavement and hoping no one had stopped in front of me, praying that anyone coming behind me and entering the thick wall of smoke wouldn't plow into me. I turned on the radio and searched for the Everglades information channel at 107.9. When I found it all I got was a loop of facts about the Glades and static, nothing to tell me what was happening on the road in front of me.

I drove on blindly. It was foolish but stopping felt more dangerous. Besides, if I stopped on the road in the truck I could get rear-ended. Pulling off the road wasn't an option either. No way was I going to hover on the edge of the tall prairie grasses with slithery things crawling up into the cab. Besides, sitting there the fire could reach me, surrounding me before I even knew it was near. I compromised by driving on the shoulder, half on the verge and half on the pavement. The feel of the concrete beneath my right tires was the only way to follow the highway.

I crept along until at last the smoke grew wispier and I could see the road again. On the opposite side of the road, a police cruiser blocked oncoming traffic. Another likely blocked traffic behind me.

I sped up, going home, going where I'd be safe.

CHAPTER 12

My business partner and life partner, Clay Adams, and I were living in a new development where only a third of the planned houses had been built before the economic crisis hit. Over the last couple of years half of those homes had been repossessed or abandoned. Living two miles from the Gulf of Mexico should have been wonderful, but this development was no longer anyone's idea of gracious living. Streets led nowhere and weeds reclaimed the scarred land.

We were there in splendid isolation in the burbs from hell because someone had defaulted on a brand-new house. At least with us living in the house and paying rent it would keep the vandals out. There had been more people when we first moved in, but one by one they'd lost the battle with a bank or a mortgage company and moved on. And then the builder of the subdivision had gone bankrupt, leaving unfinished homes where the weeds grew high and the plywood grew black. Piles of lumber meant for homes had been left behind to blow about when the next tropical storms hit us. Two-by-fours turn into projectiles with the forty-mile-an-hour winds that come with our summer storms.

Now, in March, our neighborhood was silent and empty and just too damn depressing. There was one exception, one good thing on our block. Every morning before work a man biked slowly by while his small daughter pedaled furiously behind him on a pink bike with training wheels and silver tassels flying from the handlebars. I watched for her glittering pink helmet and warned Clay that when she left, so would I. I'd rather make the hour-and-a-half drive out to Clay's ranch every night than live here without those silver tassels.

Clay was waiting at the open door when I pulled up in front of the double garage. Escaping down the canal, I'd become intensely aware of all the things that were important to me. At the top of the list was Clay.

I sat there with the engine running and considered his rigid body, trying to read what he was feeling. Beside him the pot of annuals that I'd planted with such hope back in January looked bedraggled and thirsty.

Normally, when Clay saw me his eyes crinkled at the corners, as if he knew the most delicious secret, but not today. There was no lifting of his mouth, not even a brow wrinkled in concern or annoyance . . . nothing but a silent mask of waiting.

Slim and muscled, Clay made women turn and take a second look when he walked by. His black hair and those black eyes over a hawk nose told of the far-off native ancestor who mixed with the English transplants back in Georgia before the civil war.

I stopped hoping he'd come to me. I turned off the engine and opened the door. Leaving my suitcase behind, I stumbled for him.

He didn't move towards me and didn't speak even when I stood in front of him. Trembling with exhaustion and emotion, I said, "Hi," before I reached out to hug him. His body was unyielding and as stiff as a store mannequin.

I didn't even try to break down his anger. I just said, "Fine," and walked past him into the house. I dropped my purse on the small half wall that divided the living room from the foyer. Behind me Clay quietly closed the door.

An enormous bouquet of red roses was on the coffee table in the living room. I turned away and walked down the hall to my right. Clay didn't follow.

In the bedroom, a tray of candles waiting to be lit sat on each of the night tables beside the king-size bed. The homecoming Clay was planning had been destroyed, but I was too whacked to give a shit about any of it. I just headed for the bathroom medicine cabinet and poured everything that might be the least bit antibiotic over the blisters that had broken on my hands. After I'd showered, I slathered them with more ointment. Then I went back to face him.

I seldom lie to Clay. I avoid telling him lots of stuff, but when it comes down to the line in the sand, he pretty much always gets the truth. He didn't like what I had to tell him about that final martini and where it had led. My story ended with heated words over what he called my "reckless behavior" and my "inability to plan."

I tightened the belt of my housecoat and turned away. "How is any of this my fault?"

His chair scraped back on the hardwood and he said, "Let me count the ways."

I threw myself on the couch and covered my eyes with my forearm. "It was just bad luck, being in the wrong place at the wrong time."

"That's exactly what I mean." He came to stand over me. "If you hadn't been there you wouldn't have been involved."

I lifted my arm from my face. "If you had come with me like

I asked you to, it would never have happened. So who's to blame for that?" Blaming someone else always seems like a good starting point for a defense.

He frowned before turning his back to me and saying, "I'll make you some breakfast. Then we can decide what you do next."

I raised myself on my elbows. "What do you mean, next?"

"You have to call the cops. You have to decide if you want to call the cops here or the ones in Homestead."

I stuffed another pillow behind my head. "I'll think about it." But I'd already made up my mind.

"So while you think, I'll cook." He headed for the kitchen without looking back.

When he returned he didn't wake me, just put a blanket over me and left me on the couch. When I awoke in the middle of the afternoon, my hands were swollen to double their normal size. Angry red and hot to the touch, they hurt like crazy.

Clay said, "You should go to the walk-in clinic and have them checked."

"Later," I said, not at all sure I was done sleeping.

"Later they'll only be worse."

"I'll put on some more salve."

His jaw hardened. "Call the police."

"I can't right now. I'm too tired."

He went to the front door, picked up his keys off the room divider and left without answering. The house was suddenly too quiet.

I thought about what that meant in the minutes before sleep.

Nearly the first thing Clay said to me the next day was, "Call the police."

"I don't need you to tell me what to do."

The snap of his newspaper accented the silence.

"Look," I said in exasperation. "What can I tell them? My truck was stolen, but I got it back. Where's the big crime there?"

He lowered the paper. "What about the dead man?"

"Oh, I'm pretty sure they know all about him by now. That fire was at the nursery, and they'll be sifting through the ashes. When they find those remains, they'll be looking for Tito. Maybe they've already got Tito and his cousin. Trust me, Tito will be singing like a little birdie."

"You've made up your mind." The paper went back up.

"All I can tell them is the man was dead and Tito knows something about the men involved. Not much help."

He stayed silent behind the paper barrier.

"I'm just getting over making the news." I stood and picked up our plates. "One more piece like that last one and the Sunset will be out of business. You know how people stopped coming in after that one ran. They blamed me for Ryan's death." I went to the sink. "Some people are afraid to be anywhere near me, like I carry some virus for violent behavior."

"Maybe you do." His muttered words were barely audible.

I wanted to go back to the table and smack the newspaper out of his hands, but that would only prove his point.

It was a scene that played out more than once between us over the next week. His line was always the same: it was my duty. Each time he brought the subject up, I came up with a new reason to delay. Along with lying, stalling is another of my specialties, and the harder Clay pushed for me to call the police, the stronger my resistance grew. There was a long stretch of silence and extreme politeness before Clay and I smoothed out the bad feelings between us and plastered over the disappointments and shortcomings we saw in each other.

I couldn't go back to work until my cuts and blisters healed, so I had lots of time to think. I'd come to a decision about our future, but I wanted things to go back to normal between us before I told Clay. I didn't want him to think I was using my change of heart to win him over.

What I thought about most, the thing that made me harden my jaw, was that I never wanted to be a victim again. Just how I was going to manage that I wasn't sure, but not setting myself up as a target by testifying against bad guys was a good place to start.

Doing nothing is easy. You just avoid the problem for a moment, an hour, a day and finally a week. Soon, doing something becomes a bigger problem than the one you're ducking. In time, if you open your mouth you have a whole new set of questions to answer, the first one being why it took you so long to come forward. So after a while it just became easier not to call the police and explain.

The weeks that followed the night in the swamp were a time of waiting, a holding pattern. Maybe, in the deepest part of my being, I was expecting more bad news. The hard part of fear is to know when it's over, to decide when you're out of harm's way and you can put it all behind you.

Whenever I was alone, I surfed the Internet for news. There was a report of the Osceola Nursery burning down and the death of the owner, a man named Ben Bricklin. The details on why it had started were vague. The news article only said that the fire department was looking for the cause of the fire.

In the end, three hundred acres had gone up in flames and

Alligator Alley had been closed for two hours. My pickup must have been one of the last vehicles to get by.

Two days after I read that article I checked back to see if there was any more news on the cause of the fire. What I read sent me into panic mode. Two more bodies had been discovered. The remains of Ruben Orlandez, twenty-three, and Angelina Martinez, nineteen, had been found in the ashes of the nursery. Ruben Orlandez had been an employee of the plant center, and Angelina, Angie to her family, was his girlfriend. Again, police weren't saying if their deaths were accidental or murder. There was a subtle suggestion in the news report that Ruben tried to burn down the nursery and got caught in the fire.

There was no mention of Tito. He was probably down in Miami or hiding out in the Keys. Either way, I was sure he'd gotten away. So unless the police found him, it was over. I didn't share any of this new knowledge with Clay. Except for the return of my violent nightmares, that horrible night was behind me.

CHAPTER 13

One Friday morning I was in the bar getting ready for the lunch crowd. Ella crooned in the background while overhead the giant fan turned slowly. It and the mahogany bar came from a private men's club back in the thirties. Black-and-white pictures of the early days in Florida cover the walls, and giant palms in clay tubs provide privacy for black leather club chairs and small silver tables. The bar of the Sunset is probably my favorite place in the world.

Tully strolled in and perched on a stool in front of me. His handsome rawhide face broke out in a big smile as he shoved his battered cowboy hat to the back of his head and said, "Good to see you, little girl."

My thirtieth birthday had come and gone more than a year before, but I couldn't stop my old man from thinking of me as a little girl. For a long time it had made me angry, like he was putting me down, but now it just made me laugh. I pulled him a beer and said, "What's happening, Tully?"

"Not much. Just thought I'd better come and tell you that Bernice is moving to California. Wanted to tell you before Ziggy gets his tail in a twist and rushes in here to worry you."

My hand stopped pulling the pint and I swung to face Tully.

He pointed at the half-full glass. "Jesus, girl, don't ruin my drink."

I looked back to the brown liquid and said, "So, how and when did this all come about?" Bernice was my ex-mother-in-law, a woman I hated but someone Tully seemed to care for. She and Tully had taken up with each other the summer before, and I'd practiced biting my tongue until the blood flowed. "You guys seemed pretty solid."

"We were . . . we are, but Bernice wants to be closer to Amy now that a grandchild is coming." There was the smallest hint of an accusation in his voice. He never got tired of telling me to hurry up and have a kid before he got too old to enjoy it, and I never gave up telling him to mind his own business.

I set the beer on a paper coaster in front of him. "I can understand that."

He reached out and pulled the stein towards him, his lips already pursing to welcome in the liquid.

"Did she ask you to move to California with her?"

He wiped his lips with back of his hand and said, "Yup."

"Why aren't you going?"

"Take me out of Florida, I'd likely die." He sipped his beer again. "'Sides, she wants to be with her daughter just like I want to be with mine."

I let out the breath I been holding waiting for his answer. "Ah, Tully, are you saying you're giving up Bernice for me?"

"Not exactly."

"Good. I'm glad you didn't try 'cause now I don't have to tell you how full of shit you are. My guess is, you got tired of Bernice and you're happy to see her go."

"Whatever you say, baby girl." He pointed the glass at me. "But I'm sticking with you."

I grinned at him and then I said, "Tully, I've got something to tell you." I told him about the night in the swamp. And then I told him about the other deaths, something I hadn't told Clay.

Tully listened without saying a word and then he said, "You think it's over?"

I turned away and reached for a bar cloth, saying, "Sure."

He knew I was lying, but he just nodded and picked up his beer.

Not long after my talk with Tully, there was a knock on my office door. I didn't lift my eyes from the timesheets I was filling out on the computer. I just hollered, "What?" and went on typing in numbers.

The door opened quietly. I heard it close but no one spoke.

I looked up.

Detective Styles stood just inside the door, leaning back on it with his hands folded behind him.

"Oh," was all that I could manage. I sat back in the chair, my hands settling out of sight in my lap as I waited.

Detective Styles was the cop in charge when my husband, Jimmy Travis, was murdered two years ago. Always holding himself in check and hiding any emotion, Styles was a man I'd thought of as gray and uninteresting—until recently. Then he'd become far too interesting.

Over the last couple of years our connection had changed, and we'd started dancing across dangerous ground, the advance and retreat of "Shall we wreck our lives by giving into a passing physical desire, or shall we pretend we're adults?" And then one night shortly before I ran to Miami, I saw another side of him, the face of raw and naked passion. It was a crazy experience we both were eager to forget.

We stared at each other, searching for danger—or maybe that thrilling excitement that had sent me into panic mode.

Styles's green eyes gave nothing away. The man I always called Mr. Bland, the man who always dressed in a plain beige suit, today had gone wild and put on a pink shirt with a navy and pink tie. He said, "Hi." And then he added, "I'm here on official business."

Well, that answered one question.

He walked slowly towards me, almost as if he was reluctant to get too close in case of . . . what? He stopped three feet away from my desk. "I had a call from Dade County police force. They found a young man murdered, executed by a shot in the head." He folded his hand into a gun and touched his temple with a forefinger. "He had your business card in his pocket."

If other things weren't distracting Styles, he would have caught the little start I gave, the sucking in of air. This was the moment I had dreaded. My guts were doing a rumba, but I managed to keep my mouth shut.

He pulled a photo out of his jacket and, leaning forward, laid it on the desk, pushing it towards me with the tips of his fingers.

I reached out a finger and slid it the rest of the way to me across the desk. Tito stared up at me. I pushed back in my chair, clutching my hands together in my lap to hide their trembling, and waited.

"Why?" Styles said.

"Why what?"

"Why did he have your card?"

It was because the ashtray in the truck was full of them. I lifted my shoulders and let them drop. "Someone must have given it to him."

"Why?"

"You're the detective. Maybe he was moving to this coast and was going to hit me up for a job—busboy, waiter . . ." I shrugged again, dismissing any knowledge of Tito. "Can't tell you."

He nodded in understanding but added just the same, "So you don't know him?"

"Don't think so."

"You didn't even ask what his name is."

"Okay, what's his name?"

"Tito Martinez."

I pretended to search my memory bank. "Still don't know him."

"Can't tell me anything about him?"

"Nope."

"He had eight thousand dollars in cash in his pocket."

"Then I sure as hell don't know him."

We both smiled.

"He'd just paid two thousand dollars for a used car. So how does a guy probably living on less than minimum come up with ten thousand cash?"

"If I knew a guy with ten thousand cash . . ." I stopped right there. It was a bad joke, and one I couldn't make. "Still don't know him."

"So I guess that's it."

"Looks like it." He leaned over and picked up the picture. He stepped back. Relief showed on his face. "Fine," he said.

What was fine?

His mouth lifted at the corners in a slight smile. "Just needed to ask."

"Anything else you want to know?"

It took him a minute. "Naw. I'm glad . . ." He didn't finish.

Was he glad I didn't know a murder victim or glad he could get the hell away from me?

"It's done then," he said.

I nodded. But it wasn't done. There was a whole lot more between us than an inquiry from Dade County. There was a cobweb of emotions, with a dangerous something squirming in the center that neither of us was going anywhere near.

"I'll tell Dade you don't know anything about this guy."

"Good," I said, looking back to the computer screen.

He started for the door and then turned back. "We have to talk," he said. "We can't just go on avoiding each other."

"Is that what we're doing?"

"It was only a kiss."

"Seen by Marley."

"It only happened because we'd been drinking."

"Yeah, lately too many things have been happening because I was drinking." I smiled at him. "I've drunk my last martini."

His forehead wrinkled. "Why . . ." Before he could finish, there was a brief rap on the door and Gwen came in.

Styles said, "Bye" and bolted out behind Gwen.

I was folding laundry on the kitchen table when I told Clay about Styles's visit and Tito's death. "Why did Tito have my card?" I asked. My hands smoothed a stack of towels, but my eyes searched Clay's face for reassurance.

"Didn't he say he was going to return the pickup?" Clay crossed his arms and leaned back against the counter. "Maybe he took the card because he felt bad and wanted to call and tell you where you could find your truck."

I pulled a pillowcase out of the pile. "Yeah, he said he was going to return it." This simple explanation was reassuring.

"Why didn't you tell Styles that you knew him?"

"But I don't know him." The cotton snapped as I shook it. "Except his name is Tito and he worked for the dead man, Ben Bricklin. The cops already know that." I smoothed the material, folding it in on itself. "There's nothing extra I can tell them about Tito." I picked up the stack of clean laundry. "I don't want to get any deeper into it. I don't want the guys that killed Tito coming after me."

"But maybe Tito told someone about you."

A pile of towels tumbled from my hands.

CHAPTER 14

The Sunset was packed with tourists hiding from the eighty-five-degree sun, but there were two extra servers on, so I wasn't totally on the run when the tall broad-shouldered man walked up to the bar and smiled at me. He was wearing a black tie with an orchid, hand-painted in white and mauve, on the silk. The outrageous necktie seemed at odds with the rest of him. In his early sixties, he was still fit and held himself with a confidence that said he was on top of life. Deeply tanned, like a man who'd spent his life on a golf course chasing pars, he had sharp blue eyes and stiff, wiry black hair that looked like it had an attitude to equal the guy himself. Even his eyebrows were thick and aggressive, but when he smiled I found myself smiling back at him.

A bartender quickly learns how to size people up, and I knew a few things right off. This man was different from the normal drinker who wanders in at lunchtime. This guy wasn't in the Sunset because he was thirsty for a beer; he was there to talk. I could tell because he stood right in front of the beer taps. If you want to talk to the tender, position yourself where they can't ignore you: at one of the work stations. I raised a finger and said, "I'll be right with you," then went to deliver the beer.

Coming back and watching him assess the room, taking it all in, I made another assumption. This was a man who was accustomed to being in charge—one who brooked no obstacle to his wishes.

My mind quickly processed the possibilities that brought him to the Sunset. It was one of those rare times in my life when I wasn't noticeably behind in my payments, so he wasn't there to break my legs or repossess something. And as far as I knew, he couldn't have been sent to find me by a rich uncle with money to give away.

Wait and see, I told myself as I came up to him. "What can I bring you?" I said, giving him my best customer-relations smile.

He pointed to a purple orchid sitting by the cash register. "A fellow orchid lover, I see."

My eyes followed his pointing finger before I replied. "Home Depot, the grocery store . . . I can never resist them." I set a paper coaster on the bar in front of him.

"It's a *Dendrobium*."

I tried out the name. "I'll have to take your word for it. I haven't got a clue about them."

His broad finger twirled the coaster. "It's the most common orchid in the retail market. There are millions of them grown every year in Florida. A billion-dollar business."

"No kidding." Already I knew where this was going, but I'm awfully good at playing dumb. Well, let's face it: it isn't much of a stretch.

He smiled, a self-deprecating and strangely boyish smile. "I go on a bit, don't I? Can't help myself."

"Do you grow orchids?"

"Nope, but my brother did."

That's when I knew for certain. I smiled and asked again, "What can I bring you?"

I drew the light beer while he spread hands the size of dinner plates on the bar and settled himself on a stool, still surveying his surroundings, taking in everything and judging. When I set the beer in front of him he drew it forward with a hand that knew how to work. Maybe I had him wrong, maybe he wasn't a rich golf lizard, but he wasn't in a hurry to set me straight. I filled a dozen orders while he drank half his beer. I'd go broke if everyone took as long to finish a beer as he did. He ordered a sandwich and didn't finish half of that either. An hour later he was still there.

He lifted his nearly empty glass.

I drew his second beer slowly, watching him as I asked, "What brings you to Jacaranda?"

"You."

I stared at him, hoping my face gave nothing away, and then, when the silence was becoming uncomfortable, I set the fresh drink in front of him. "That's a line I've heard before," I said, but I knew this wasn't a casual attempt at a pickup. This man had an agenda. I tried to grin, carrying on with the joke, but I didn't like where this conversation was heading. "I can quote you all the variations on that theme." I dumped the dregs of his first beer and upended the dirty glass in the rack. My night of horror wasn't over. I stood facing him, both hands on the bar, and waited.

"My name is Ethan Bricklin. My brother was Ben Bricklin."

So that was why of all the beach bars in Florida he'd walked into this particular one.

"I'm sorry," I said, faking confusion. "Is that name supposed to mean something to me?"

"Ben was an orchid grower over east, near Homestead."

"That doesn't help." I turned away and got a bag of lemons out of the bar fridge. "I still don't know him." I started slicing lemons.

"No, but you know the man who may have killed him."

The knife slipped and sliced my finger. "Damn." I wrapped a bar towel around my hand and pressed down hard, buying time. "You really know how to get a girl's attention."

"Sorry," he said.

When I had myself and the bleeding under control, I said, "Maybe you should start at the beginning and tell me everything."

"My brother, Ben, died in a fire, a fire that was deliberately set. A young man who worked for him, Tito Martinez, was suspected of the crime. The police think Tito killed Ben."

It wasn't hard to show shock. I'd only thought of Tito as a victim. Why hadn't I considered that Tito might have killed Ben? I concentrated hard on remembering what Tito had said. Hadn't he seen Ben Bricklin killed? Wasn't that why he was running away? And surely Tito had been with me when the fire was set, which made me his alibi for that crime.

I realized Ethan Bricklin had gone silent, waiting for me to respond. I looked at him with genuine confusion and said, "I'm sorry about your brother. Have the police arrested . . . Tito, was that his name?"

He nodded. "Tito. No, he hasn't been arrested." Bricklin was considering me like an eagle watching a mouse in the grass. "Because Martinez has been murdered."

"Murdered?"

He nodded. "When the police found him he had your name and address in his wallet."

"And you know this because . . . ?"

"Because the police told me. Your name was the only unusual thing on him."

That and eight thousand dollars, I thought, but I kept that observation to myself. "Okay." I nodded in agreement. "Now I know what you're talking about. The police came and asked me about someone who died with my business card in his pocket." I rubbed my forehead, searching for words. "I have no idea why he had my name, unless he was going to come here looking for work. I get a lot of people like that; a friend gives them my name." I turned away, unwrapping the towel and throwing it in the sink. I turned on the tap and let cold water splash over my finger and the towel below it. When the pink water draining away ran clear, I said, "We hire a lot of seasonal help. Someone who worked here last winter maybe told him it was a good place to work. Beyond that . . ." I shrugged any involvement on my part away and said, "I'm sorry about your brother."

"So am I. Real sorry." He tried a smile. "Regrets . . ." He looked away from me, his eyes searching the room as if he'd forgotten why he was in the Sunset. "You can't get back time. So sometimes all we are left with are regrets. Take my advice: don't leave things too long."

I nodded. "It's exactly what I've been telling myself lately." I dug a bandage out of the drawer and pointed down the bar to three newcomers who were pulling out stools. "I have to serve those guys."

"Sure." With one word, he made it clear he was in no hurry, had no plan to go anywhere and wasn't done with me yet. This man wanted answers he thought I might have.

When I came back down the bar again he leaned forward and said, "So it was just a freak thing he had your name?"

"That's the only way I can explain it."

He watched me with eyes the coldest shade of gray-blue I'd ever seen. This man really wanted to know what had happened to his brother, might even be looking for revenge. I was even more determined to stay silent and keep out of it.

"I can see why he had your card." His head was nodding, but his eyes, locked on mine, were searching for the lie. "I can see how it would work; he was looking for a job." He worried the inside of his cheek before he added, "But this Tito never came to talk to you, right?"

"Nope. As far as I know, he was never in Jacaranda." I couldn't help asking one question. "Why do you think your brother was killed?"

"Robbery—money for drugs probably."

I nodded. "It seems that most of the crime in Florida has something to do with drugs." I grabbed paper napkins and a bowl of nuts and went off to check on people at the bar whose glasses were still full.

Lunchtime was over and the customers had thinned out to a few diehards and latecomers, but Ethan Bricklin stayed on. Just seeing him, I would have bet he wasn't the kind of guy who would waste an afternoon hanging out in a bar, but there he was, chatting with Mathew Fine, a local lawyer who'd come in for a late lunch after a meeting in Sarasota.

I was giving them lots of space, but Ethan raised a hand, motioning me back, and then he pushed his half-finished beer towards me and ordered a coffee.

"Obsessions are dangerous things," he was telling Mathew when I brought him the extra cream he asked for. "They take us beyond reason, decency and even the law." He looked up at me and said, "Thanks, Sherri. I was just telling Mathew about the people who make orchids their lives."

Mathew grinned at me. "In here we're mostly passionate

about booze, right, Sherri?" His words cut too close to the bone for both of us.

"And thank god for that, or I'd have to find myself a new occupation." I cleared away Mathew's empty plate.

Mathew smiled and turned back to Ethan to ask, "So what made you get into orchids?"

"It wasn't just me." Ethan stirred his coffee. "My brother and I were both fixated on orchids, collecting them and breeding them. We came by it honestly. Our mother shared our enthusiasm and taught us well. She had a large assortment of native orchids she collected in the wild, from the swamps around where we grew up." He frowned. "She gave her plants to Ben before she died . . . every one of them. I felt . . . well, she could have shared them between us, but it was always Ben."

"Ah," I said, nodding in understanding. "The 'Mom always liked you best' sort of thing?"

His grin was sheepish. "Silly."

"Still hurts?"

He ducked his head and then looked up at me and smiled, the kind of roguish beam that brought out the sun.

I returned his smile and turned away, still listening to the conversation as I stacked fresh wine glasses on a glass shelf.

"To compensate for Mom liking Ben best, I drive the only Cadillac my father ever bought. I've owned lots of Caddies since, but it's the only one I ever kept."

Mathew said, "So did getting rich balance out not getting the orchids?"

"Who says I'm rich?"

"The Cadillacs that came after your father's . . . ?"

Ethan gave a soft humph of a laugh and said, "No flies on

you." He tilted his head to the side, considering the question. "Ben built his first orchid business from my mother's stock. It was a pretty extensive collection and it gave him a strong start, so he was first out of the gate in business. He began when he was just out of agricultural college."

Mathew caught my eye and pointed at his empty cup as Ethan said, "He was the largest exporter of orchids in Florida, with thirty acres of shade houses for bromeliads and orchids, but Hurricane Andrew wiped him out in 1992. He was massively in debt and had no hurricane insurance. He started over, but then he was taken out a second time by DuPont's Benlate, a fungicide that destroyed the last of his stock in the nineties."

"Jesus," Mathew said. "The poor guy."

"Ben had one piece of good fortune. His wife's grandparents left them a little bit of land over along the east side of Alligator Alley. Osceola Nursery was his last attempt to stay alive." Ethan's hands were clenched in fists on the bar, but his voice showed no emotion—*just the facts, ma'am.* Pity the guy who'd killed his brother when Ethan got his hands on him, and I was betting that he intended to find Ben's killer.

I poured Mathew more coffee, asking, "Were her grandparents Seminole?" I held out the coffee carafe to Ethan.

Ethan put a hand over his cup. "How did you know?"

"Not magic. Osceola is the most common Seminole surname in Florida, like Smith or Jones for us, and very confusing if you're trying to sort out the lineage of a Seminole. Do you know the Seminoles never signed a peace treaty with the United States government?" I set the coffeepot back on the element. "An old friend of my dad's told me that." Just thinking about Sammy, a wild man who survived out in the Fakahatchee swamp by hunting and guiding, had me smiling. "Sammy claims the Seminoles are still at war with the United States Army."

Mathew said, "Them and everyone else these days if you listen to the news."

Ethan pushed his coffee cup away from him. "Susan's mother was a Seminole, but her father was white. A real bastard."

"Well, none of us has a lock on those." I picked up the cup. "There've been a few bastards in my own family."

"Not like him. He beat Susan's mother something awful. She died in her fifties, and I always figured the old man was to blame for that too. It was supposed to be an accident."

Ethan wiped his hand across his mouth. "Anyway, she left Susan and Ben the land, and they started over for the third time."

"That sounds like the history of Florida—getting wiped out and starting over." Mathew downed the last of his coffee and pushed back from the bar. "I'd better get started or I'll get wiped out." He raised his hand in farewell. "See you later." He'd be back in a few hours, just like he was every night.

Ethan hardly noticed he was gone.

I added Mathew's cup and saucer to the rest of the dirty dishes. "Mathew's right about Florida. My daddy's family moved down to Florida in the thirties. If everything is timing, my family has none. Losers 'til the end." I dug a couple of jars out of the bar fridge and began to load a garnish tray with pickled onions and olives. "Turns out things were as bad here in Florida as they were back in the coal mines up north they were trying to get away from. When they got down here they survived by fishing, crabbing and hunting wild hogs, eating anything they could catch, just like Sammy is still doing."

The spoon I was digging out olives with stilled. I could almost see Grandma Jenkins standing at the stove, one hand planted on her jutted hip, madly stirring something cooking on the burner and telling the family history. Recounting how for years no one in the family had a new piece of clothing. "In those days sugar came in cotton sacks," she would say. "Empty sacks became pillowcases, towels and our clothing." When she got to the clothing, we always waited for the best story of all, how at a revival meeting a woman got the power and started rolling around on the ground. Her dress worked up her legs until the congregation could see, written across her cotton-covered backside, the slogan *Sweeten with Redpath*. No matter how many times she told that story, Grandma would laugh 'til she cried and we'd howl right along with her.

"Funny, all that no-account poor-folk food we ate when I was a kid, things like fried gator, is now the most expensive thing on my menu."

I raised a hand and waved to Paul Clarke and his real-estate partner as they left. "All except coon. Not much call for that."

Ethan grinned. "You never know, it might catch on. It's out of the ordinary and original, just like you."

"Oh, I'm not all that original. Down here, pretty much all of us have the same stories about the struggle to survive."

He pointed a finger at me and then at himself. "That's why I think you and I have a connection: a common background."

"What? I thought you were one of the lucky ones, born rich. Your daddy drove a Cadillac; mine was lucky to have a ten-year-old used pickup."

"Ben and I were raised on a ranch not that far from here." He lifted his hand and pointed in an easterly direction. "We were expected to work right alongside our parents, with no special concessions for our age. Later, I stayed on the ranch while Ben went to agricultural school over in Miami. It was a hardscrabble life, barely staying alive by working like hell, but then we started mining the land for phosphates." He rubbed his palms together, and his face twisted in an emotion I couldn't get. "Ben was younger than me and idealistic, wanted no part of phosphates. We fell out. It destroyed us. Only saw him once in twenty years, and that was at his daughter Val's funeral."

He went silent, staring down and away as he gazed into the past. "Ben never had any luck . . . except for Susan." He said her name like it was sweet toffee on his tongue. "I suppose she was enough luck for any one man." He flinched and then a wry grin lit his face. "Ben got Susan and I got rich."

"Rich sounds good to me."

"Hell, it's not so bad." A bark of laughter. "Do you hanker after money, Sherri?"

He watched me closely; there seemed to be a subtext to what he was asking.

"It would be a lie to say no. Like everyone, I want enough to be protected. Beyond that . . ." I shrugged. "Hell, I'm too lazy to be rich. I'd have to go out and spend it. You have to do things when you have money, join things and take part. I'm not a take-part sort of person, so I'll settle for safe."

He wasn't leaving it alone. "How much would it take to make you feel safe?"

"I don't even have to think about it. No mortgage, that's my happy place."

Both of his palms were flat on the mahogany and he leaned towards me. "So what would you do to be there . . . steal . . . kill even?"

"No." It came out way too loud and too emphatic. I was denying a bad memory of being willing to cross a line, to kill to protect myself, but that was a secret I shared with no one. Guilt turned me away from him and set me fussing and tidying.

"Ah, but sometimes," he said, his voice deep and soothing, like he was practicing seduction, "temptation is too strong to deny."

"Yeah, like having that last dirty martini."

"It led to something bad?"

I nodded. "Not a Hallmark moment."

He looked at me quizzically. "What's a dirty martini anyway?"

"About five ounces of vodka, or gin if you're a heathen, and the brine from a jar of olives." He'd hit my obsession now, and my hands were busy describing the process as I drifted towards him. "You take a martini glass out of the freezer, coat the inside with a little vermouth and then shake up the vodka and the brine and pour it in. Pop in a few olives, olives that are stuffed with jalapeños, and sail straight to heaven."

"Your favorite drink?"

"Nope, not anymore. I've given them up."

"Why?"

"Because I'm not good with temptation."

"Few of us are."

"Talking from experience?"

"Oh, yeah."

"But we learn from our mistakes, right?"

"Yup, and we probably have lots more to learn."

We laughed together, knowing we'd each met a fellow sinner.

CHAPTER 15

Back in the thirties, the building housing the Sunset Bar and Grill was a hotel. Now, the Sunset takes up the entire second floor, giving diners a clear view of the sun going down out over the Gulf of Mexico.

There are three commercial properties on the ground floor and one of them houses Clay's real-estate company. It means we can see each other during the day, for coffee, lunch or just because, and he never goes out to show a property without coming up to tell me where he is going.

Clay is old Florida. His kin have been here since the Civil War. They served in the legislature early on and led movements to pass laws designed to generally make Florida a better place. Coming from a family of Florida landowners and people who counted, his mind is an encyclopedia of who, what, where and when. I count on him to recite the social register when questions arise. So later, after Ethan had left and before things started to buzz in the bar, I asked Clay if he knew Ethan Bricklin. Clay had come in for an early meal before showing a property and now sat at the bar, eating scallops.

He carefully put down his knife and fork in the five o'clock position and raised his head. "Who?"

"Ethan Bricklin. Ever heard of him?"

"Sherri, he's one of the richest men in all of Florida. Everyone knows him."

"You mean everyone who reads the financial pages. Tell me about him."

He didn't even have to think about it; he just reeled the information off like he was reading a stock report. "He struck gold, or rather phosphates, on the family ranch and turned it into a multimillion-dollar industry. He used that to grow more wealth, diversifying into land and other industries, but phosphate mining is still his main business. There are big issues over phosphates now, but back then everyone wanted to get into the act." He grinned. "I remember my father asking everyone how you could tell if there were phosphates on our ranch." He picked up his utensils again. "He rode his whole thousand-acre spread on horseback, looking for a sign of them."

"Did he find them?"

"Nope."

"Bummer."

"Bad luck. Dad always thought fate had cheated him, but my mom just called him a fool for dreaming. The most practical-minded woman in the world, my mother."

"Guess you take after her, huh?"

He didn't rise to the jibe, but then he never did. I asked him another question. "So Bricklin would have no reason to hang around the Sunset, or look me up, except trying to find out about his brother's death."

"His brother?"

"Ben Bricklin, the dead guy at the nursery, was Ethan Bricklin's brother."

Clay looked doubtful, like I'd told him an alien had just

landed in the kitchen. "Are you sure these two guys are related?"

"Swear," I said, raising my right hand. "Ethan Bricklin came in today and stayed awhile."

"Ethan Bricklin came in here today?" he asked in a tentative voice.

"Yup. He was here for about three hours."

"Why?"

"The cops told him about Tito having my card. He seemed to think I was involved."

I watched him push a very fine scallop around the plate. I asked, "Can you think of any other reason he'd hang around except wanting to know how I knew Tito?"

He tilted his head to the side, thinking. "No, unless it's the obvious."

"And that is?"

"He wouldn't be the first man who got ideas being around you."

I planted my forearms on the bar and leaned towards him. "You mean the way you get ideas being around me, some real dirty ideas, some 'let's get naked and roll in the muck' sort of things. That's the kind of ideas you get, isn't it?"

He put down his knife and fork again, but this time he pushed his plate away. "Time for me to go."

"One day you're going to break, Adams."

He pointed at the sapphire-and-diamond engagement ring I wore, the one we couldn't afford, and said, "I thought I already had."

I watched him walk away. The guy had the best ass in town.

Later that night, I told Clay I'd made a really big decision.

He reached up and turned off his light. "Going to come clean with Styles?"

"God, no. Are you crazy? That business in the Everglades is over." I stretched my arm across his chest and covered his legs with mine. He pulled me close to his side.

"No," I said, "this decision is about us."

His body went rigid and he lay still, waiting without speaking for what was to come. It almost felt like he'd stopped breathing.

I reached up and stroked his cheek. "I was thinking perhaps we should move the wedding up."

"What?" He pulled away from me and reached to turn his light back on. Raised on his elbows, he stared down at me. "What's brought this on?"

I could have told him it was a reaction to facing death out there on that drainage canal. My life had changed that night, and there was no going back to where I'd been before that night in the Everglades.

Clay's brows were furrowed and his piercing black eyes were locked on mine. "You aren't saying this just to please me, are you? I know I've been bugging you to set a date sooner rather than later."

"Nope."

He still wasn't convinced. "What changed your mind?"

I started to lie, but it wouldn't work. "Fear," I said. "I didn't want to die and leave no one behind."

He beamed down at me. "I should have taken you out in the Everglades and dropped you there a year ago."

It was a busy Thursday the next time Ethan Bricklin came in.

Saying it was a surprise to see him back again hardly covered it. I picked up a tray of drinks and took it to the wait station, making an effort not to look at him or engage with him in any way, figuring if I ignored him as if he were an unwanted salesman, he'd go away. Turned out Ethan wasn't easy to ignore and he was more determined than the best aluminum-siding man in the business. He sat down in front of the beer taps, the same as before, crossed his hands on the counter and waited.

What the hell did he want with me? I was pretty sure it wasn't my sparkling conversation. Besides, I thought we'd discussed everything we had in common: redneck living in Florida, whose family was poorer and where to get the best grouper sandwich on the Mangrove Coast—besides the Sunset, of course. He waved at me to catch my eye. I nodded to him but went right on shaking martinis and filling the glasses on my tray. I carried the martinis to the wait station and buzzed Jackie and then went to Ethan. I placed a paper coaster in front of him and said, "What's your pleasure?"

He gave me a naughty grin and raised his eyebrows.

"Shit, not you too."

He laughed. "I'm still breathing, aren't I?" A little-boy-in-trouble grin teased his face.

I pointed my forefinger at him. "You do know that when you waggle your eyebrows like that, your ears wave too. Might want to think about that."

He ignored the jibe. "I brought you a present."

Now it was my turn to raise my eyebrows. Gifts from drinkers aren't a good idea.

He picked something off the stool beside him, then sat an orchid on the counter.

"Oh, it's so cute." I looked closer at the base of the plant. Yellow and brown, the flowers grew out from a large dried-out clump of roots that didn't look capable of sustaining life. "Wait a minute. It isn't dying, is it? The roots don't look so healthy." Suspicious and annoyed, I glared at him. "What kind of a gift is a dying plant?"

"It's a cowhorn orchid," Ethan said. "A slipper orchid, native to Florida and tough. It can live in the air or in water and in sun or shade. It reminded me of our conversation about people like us, who survive. There aren't many of these left in the wild and not many of us left either."

I pushed the orchid towards him. "If it's rare, then don't leave it with me. It will die for sure."

He slid it back towards me. "I told you it was tough, just like you. Now, how about a draft?"

I brought his beer but he didn't touch it, didn't even look at it when I set it in front of him. Instead he said, "I've just come back from Redlands."

"What's that, a music festival?"

He shook his head in despair at my ignorance. "It's an orchid show over near Miami. Orchidophiles from all over the world show up for it. It's a big deal. Florida does millions of dollars in legal orchid sales alone every year. If you add in illegal sales . . ." His shoulder rose in a little shrug. "There were hundreds of thousands of people at this show."

"God, maybe I should open a bar just for the show. Put little orchids in every drink."

He laughed but it didn't last. "There's a rumor going round that Ben bred a black orchid before he died, even sent out notices to people offering it for sale."

I turned the crazy-colored flower around, studying it from all angles. "A black orchid sounds pretty boring compared to this little darling."

He shook his head. "You don't understand. No one has ever seen a black orchid. There are some with black petals or black spots, but there's never been one that's all black. They don't exist. It's a matter of genetics." He spread his hands wide. "There are thirty thousand species of orchids and more than a hundred thousand hybrids, making it the most lucrative flower business in the world. Can you imagine if you were the only person in the world to own a black orchid, can you see what that would mean?"

"Money would be my guess."

He was leaning forward with enthusiasm, his eyes shining with excitement. "A black orchid is like . . ." He thought for a minute. "Like finding a Michelangelo in your attic. If you had a black orchid, had a new genus, it would be worth a lot of money, but more important than money would be the bragging rights."

"That's not more important than money."

"You'd have the right to name it." He spoke slowly, emphasizing his words by marking them off with his open palms. "Your name would be on it forever, making you immortal."

I moved aside so Mick could pull a pint. "You orchid people are all crazy."

"Perhaps you're right. People will do all kinds of things, legal and illegal, for an exotic plant. At Selby Gardens, up in Sarasota, they had a big problem with an illegal orchid that was brought in from South America. People ended up in court, a really nasty business. If people thought Ben had a black orchid, some orchid collectors would offer him a fortune for it and some would try and get it by any means. Even murder."

Fear shivered down my spine. "That's crazy. People don't kill for a flower."

"I think you're wrong about that. This gossip about Ben having a black orchid, even if it wasn't true, would make him a target."

"So how did the rumor start?" I asked.

"Apparently, it started with Ben. That's what I can't understand. He knew better than to make a mistake between a truly black orchid and an almost black."

"Has anyone actually seen this orchid?"

"He e-mailed a picture of the orchid to at least a dozen buyers and said he had one for sale."

And then it hit me. "Maybe your brother was playing a gigantic practical joke." Just thinking about him having all these fanatics running around, lustfully panting after something that didn't exist, gave me a giggle. "Man, that's my kind of funny. I think I would have liked your brother."

Ethan wasn't smiling. "Ben didn't have that kind of sense of humor."

"Could he have faked the picture?"

"Why would he do that? These were people he did business with and wanted to stay on friendly terms with. You don't do that by playing games."

"So he must have believed he had one." A second possibility hit me. "Or perhaps the e-mails didn't come from Ben."

"My tech person at the mine says they did." Ethan paused, watching me and waiting for me to respond, but I was fresh out of ideas.

"Well, I'll take real good care of this flower." I picked it up. "And when it's finished blooming I'll take it out to Clay's ranch in Independence and reintroduce it to its proper home, but you better tell me how to look after it and keep it alive until then."

Ethan hung around, drinking slowly, ordering stone crab he barely touched and waiting for me to come back for more conversation, telling me more than I wanted to know about raising and keeping orchids. He was right when he told me he was obsessed. I knew better than to ask people about their passions. It was always just too boring.

Over the next hour, drifting back and forth between mixing drinks, I got a college course on orchids. But there was an intensity about Ethan that said he wasn't idly passing time. I was ready to bet Ethan Bricklin never did anything without intent. But why on earth would anyone talk to me about orchids? And it was definitely orchids he wanted to talk about. For me, they were just pretty things that survived a long time on the bar—lots of bang for my buck. Man, I should put that on a tee shirt, I thought. *Lots of bang for your buck* . . . but then people might get the wrong idea.

When Ethan was through talking about orchids, he wanted to talk about the one thing I didn't want to think about ever again: the night of the fire. Hunting and searching for the words, he told me he had been a bad brother, not keeping in touch and not helping out when Ben needed him. Now he wanted to do one last thing to make things right.

"You can't change the past," I told him.

"No, but I can see that justice is done."

"Justice?"

"I know he was murdered." His calmness was chilling. "And I'm going to find out who did it."

His tone of voice left no room for argument, but I tried anyway. "Leave it to the police."

"But they don't understand orchid lovers. I do. Ben died

because someone thought he had a rare plant. They won't stop until they get it."

"That's why you think Ben died. It doesn't make it true."

"It's true."

The register pinged, telling me there was a bar order for the dining room. I read the order and pulled a Budweiser, saying, "Then it sounds to me like you should be over on the other coast, where it happened, and not here in Jacaranda."

CHAPTER 16

Clay came in. He leaned across the bar and kissed me. I introduced him to Ethan.

Two alpha males. Right away I could see them circling each other, sniffing like stray dogs who meet on the sidewalk, trying to decide if they were going to form a pack, fight to the death or head off in different directions. Making up their minds didn't take long. Soon they were talking about people and places they had in common, but mostly it was money and how to make it out of Florida land deals that set them on fire.

An hour later Clay watched Ethan leave the bar and said, "A man like that can do me a lot of good."

My hands were full of glasses but I hesitated before putting them in the tub and frowned at him. "How?"

His face was incredulous. "He can introduce me to people."

"You know lots of people." I just wanted Ethan to go away and forget about us.

"Not the people in his circle. Meeting Ethan may turn out be the most important connection I ever made." He stood up. "Ethan is optimistic about the economy. Says it's turning around and is going to start moving again." It was just what Clay wanted to hear—needed to hear.

"Still, I'd rather we didn't have anything more to do with

Ethan. Don't encourage him. He has an agenda, and it isn't to make you rich."

"Don't let your fears get the best of you."

"What do you mean?"

He took his time, picking his way around the minefield. "You've had bad things happen to you, starting with Jimmy's murder, and those things have made you . . . nervous. Even before the Everglades, you saw a killer in every shadow and jumped at every noise. You're stressed to the max, but you won't listen to anyone and get some help."

He was right about one thing. Since that night in the swamp, any hint of threat, any situation that might turn bad, had me going on high alert. More than one person had commented on how jumpy I was. I bit back my defense, trying to stick to facts. "Ethan's only interest is revenge. That's why he's here—he thinks I know something. I just want to convince him he's wrong so he'll move on."

"Pushing him away isn't the way to do it. Give him time and he'll see you have nothing for him." Clay shoved the barstool under the counter with more force than necessary. "Besides, this is an opportunity, and I'm not going to miss it because of your paranoia."

"Better paranoid than dead."

He stopped moving away and came back to the counter. In a voice you'd use for a child frightened by a clown, he said, "No one is trying to kill you."

"Maybe not now, but before."

"Exactly. Before. But it's over now. You need to get some help to understand that and put it behind you."

I didn't even take the time to argue with him, just stomped off to the kitchen to make someone else's life a misery. But there was some truth in what Clay said. The fear flowing out of events from my past had never left me. I always expected the worst-possible outcome from any situation, and sometimes I saw danger where there wasn't any.

When had I become so distrustful of the world? It was long before Jimmy died. Our life together had been one treachery after another, and I always looked beneath the surface, searching for the lie. My suspicious ways had begun with Jimmy's first betrayal and then multiplied when he was murdered along with Andy, his best friend.

Jimmy's death had nearly destroyed me, sent me scurrying away from involvement. Clay had to work hard to overcome my distrust and anticipation of duplicity. I still expected our life together to go wrong sooner or later.

I felt a connection to Ben Bricklin, a man who had lost more times than he'd won, and I figured my luck was about as lousy as his. Except for Clay. I thought of Ben and his Susan. No good could come from comparisons like that. I shoved the memory of the dead man into a dark corner of my mind, more determined than ever to drive Ethan away.

I didn't count on Clay working against me. Two days later Ethan dropped into Clay's office and said he was searching for more warehouse space for one of his companies.

When Clay came up to tell me about it, the normal, stoic guy I knew was gone. He was beyond animated, pacing up and down in front of my desk and waving his hands, saying, "It will be worth tens of thousands in commissions, more than I make selling houses in a year."

"You do all right now."

"I don't want to just do all right." Clay planted his hands on my desk and leaned towards me. "I want more than that for you and our kids. I failed once; I won't fail again."

"You didn't fail, the economy did."

His jaw set into a hard rock of determination. "This is my chance to make our lives better."

"Our lives are good enough for me."

I should have saved my breath. Avoiding Ethan was no longer an option. Every day, Ethan and Clay were together in the bar talking business, but, unlike Clay, I didn't think it was buying and selling land that brought Ethan through the door. My reaction to his presence was to revert to the good-time girl, always up for a party and never taking anything seriously. Just a dumb-cracker girl who wouldn't know enough to keep her mouth shut if she did know something about some dead people connected with a nursery. Playing ignorant and tacky is second nature to me—my default mode.

Ethan was like a rock star in Florida industry, so when word spread throughout the county that Florida's richest man hung out in the Sunset, businesspeople started showing up for drinks and meals. Maybe they were hoping to be noticed by the king of phosphates or were praying that some of his money would just rub off on them.

While I wanted nothing more to do with Ethan, I had to admit I liked what knowing him was doing for the Sunset. Soon we were turning diners away. Clay was already right about Ethan improving our finances.

And Clay was right about another thing. Ethan introduced him to people. Over the next week when Ethan dropped by for lunch, he brought interesting people with him, many of them orchid fanciers. One was Sasha Kranoff, a man Ethan introduced as a Russian immigrant and "one of the biggest collectors in Florida, with a special interest in exotics."

Sasha's silk sports coat was well cut, but it didn't hide his inelegant build. He had short pillars for legs and a long body with shoulders that rolled forward, but he was saved from ugliness by a handsome face with soulful brown eyes and long feminine lashes.

When Ethan introduced me, Sasha said, "So you're an orchid fancier," pointing at Ethan's gift.

"Not really. I just like them because they don't die within days of unwrapping them."

Ethan said, "Sherri has no interest in orchids. I've bored her to death with my talk."

Sasha shook his head and said, "You don't know what you're missing."

"Believe me, when it comes to orchids and me, there's nothing to miss," I told him and began working my way down the bar, filling tiny bowls with peanuts.

"Mick," I whispered to the other tender when I was out of earshot, "change stations with me so you look after those two guys."

Mick nodded and kept on moving.

When Sasha left for the men's room, I went back to speak to Ethan. "Your friend . . ." I began and then hesitated. How do you ask someone if his buddy is in the Russian mob? It wasn't just where he came from but his whole demeanor that made me uneasy. Ethan saved me from finishing my question.

"He's not my friend. He contacted me days after Ben died and asked if I had the black orchid."

"I remember—you told me black ones are rare."

Ethan couldn't keep the irritation out of his voice. "Not rare, nonexistent."

"But Sasha thinks Ben had one?"

Ethan glanced towards the men's room.

I added, "If he didn't, why would he be here?"

He nodded.

"Both Ben and Sasha thought a black exists." I worried the inside of my cheek, intrigued despite myself. "So what does that mean?"

"It means that if I made a list of people who might have killed Ben, Sasha's name would be at the head of the list."

"And you're drinking coffee with him?" It was my turn to glance over to where Sasha had disappeared. "I surely don't thank you for bringing him to the Sunset."

"He's rich, the kind of diner all restaurants want."

"Yeah, but how did he get rich?"

"Ah, good question. His father was high up in the Russian army before he left Russia. The old man brought tons of cash with him. It's a safe bet that if anyone knows what happened to the missing nuclear warheads from the old USSR, it's Sasha and his old man. They escaped with more than just money." Ethan pointed a finger at me. "Be careful. Sasha is very Americanized but still thinks like a Russian."

"What the hell does that mean?"

"It means rules and laws are for other people, not Sasha."

"Now I know I'm not going to thank you for bringing him to the Sunset."

"Maybe you should. He's on the board of a half dozen not-for-profit organizations. He'll bring the right kind of people your way. Don't worry, he has beautiful manners, and he'll always have someone attractive with him; he always does. Lately it has been an American model named Willow. A treat to meet." He laughed but I heard something more than amusement in his voice, something below the surface of his words. I wondered just what kind of amusement Willow handed out.

Sasha returned but he didn't stay. He spent maybe ten minutes with Ethan before he took a call and charged out, shouldering aside people at the door like he'd just learned his house was on fire.

Ethan didn't even watch him go. Taking his reading glasses out of his shirt pocket, he signaled for me to warm his coffee.

While I filled his cup, I asked, "What sent him off?"

His eyes rose to mine. "I don't know. I was talking about you. It seemed to upset him." His eyes went back to his Blackberry.

"Exactly what were you saying?"

He glanced up briefly and then his eyes went back to the device in his hands. "Oh, I just told him about the weird coincidence of Tito having your business card."

I wanted to hit him with the coffee carafe. Instead, like the good bartender I was, I said, "How about some lunch, Ethan?"

"I'll wait," he said, without looking up from the tiny screen. "Someone is joining me."

I started to turn away but then stopped and pointed the coffee carafe at his Blackberry. "Is that a list of enemies or friends?"

"Both. And some I'm not sure of yet." His granite jaw clamped down tight.

"Man, I wouldn't want to be on your enemy list. Just do me a favor and don't bring all of your enemies to the Sunset."

The woman who joined him minutes later was nearly six feet tall and severely undernourished. She had a long face with thin eyebrows that rose like mountain peaks over deep-set piercing eyes. The look of leanness about her was underscored by her upswept hair. A human wolfhound, her name was Nina Dystra.

I wondered if she was married to a lawyer named Dystra, the guy Clay had taken to court over a real-estate deal that went wrong.

I went over to take her drink order. Ethan and Nina were making plans for some kind of a fancy party. When I came back with their drinks, they seemed to have settled on three hundred dollars a person as the ticket price. I went away shaking my head.

Minutes after they moved into the dining room, Clay came in. He checked out the bar, searching for Ethan, before even saying hi.

"He's deserted you for another." I set a coffee in front of him. "But don't feel bad. She isn't nearly as cute."

CHAPTER 17

That was about the time I started to get the feeling I was being followed. Crazy, spooky feelings, but ones I knew well. I didn't tell Clay or anyone else; I kept it to myself because my sanity had come into question more than once lately. It wasn't just Clay advising me to get professional help. Even Tully, king of the wary, thought I'd crossed a line. Trauma, that's what everyone kept telling me I was suffering from. Seems it isn't only soldiers who suffer from post-traumatic stress; victims of crime have their own issues. But even admitting to one and all that I'd now danced around the bend couldn't stop the alarm I felt, the creepy sensation at the back of my neck that said I was being watched.

I knew it wasn't my imagination. If you've been stalked, you develop an extra sense, one it's best to pay attention to no matter how nutty your nearest and dearest say you are.

Be aware of your surroundings is what they taught me in the self-defense course I took after Jimmy's murder, and I had become a master at it. I started doing strange things—well, things that were bizarre for anyone but me. I wrote down license-plate numbers, noted unfamiliar cars outside the house and checked the parking lot for those same vehicles before I left the Sunset. I even took a good look through the glass doors of the grocery store or the bank before leaving, looking for a face or vehicle that kept turning up.

I began changing my schedule, never doing things by rote, making it difficult for a watcher to predict where to find me. Sometimes I got up early and went into the Sunset when Clay left for his office. I told Clay I was going in early to catch up on bookwork to explain why I was there hours before the restaurant opened. I wanted his protection, but more than that, I didn't want to be alone among all those empty houses. And when the staff questioned why I was leaving in the middle of a shift, I started coming up with various health reasons, anything other than telling them I was jumping at shadows.

I developed a new defensive routine. Every day when I got to the Sunset, I went immediately to the front windows and looked outside. I'd ignore the turquoise-blue Gulf of Mexico, the sea grass and the boardwalk and concentrate on the people. I was looking for that one figure that didn't fit in. Mostly I saw inline skaters, earbuds firmly in place, zipping along the sidewalks and forcing the rest of the world to step aside, dog walkers and tourists, heat rising from the pavement, and white ibises stepping in and out of the tall grasses, searching for food. Just another day in paradise on a street where everyone and no one belonged.

Later in the afternoon, after the drinkers playing hooky from life had left and before the serious drinkers had arrived, I'd be back there. The neutral time—that's how I always thought of this time of day. I'd stand at the windows for half an hour, searching for anything out of the ordinary, but it was the normal things that kept grabbing my attention, like a father kneeling down in front of a crying child to wipe away his tears. My heart did a somersault, my brain deep in a fantasy of the future I dreamed for Clay and myself.

One day, when I knew I would be coming home alone after dark, I sprinkled a little cinnamon outside the glass doors at the back of the house. Not a lot, not enough to catch Clay's attention, but just enough to show a footprint. I did the same outside the front door. Then I got in my truck and locked the doors before I opened the garage door. Like I said, I was well into the wacky and weird, playing hide-and-seek by myself and discovering nothing.

The spooky feeling wouldn't let go, jerking me around like a puppet to locate danger. But there was never a concrete reason for my discomfort.

It was the shower curtain that really set me on high alert. A shower curtain—how's that for something to pin your arguments on? Growing up in a trailer park, in a home covered in tin, we alternately froze and fried. In the summertime, at a hundred percent humidity, it was almost as wet inside as it was outside. With temperatures hovering around a hundred degrees and rain pouring down, mold grew everywhere. My mother fought mold like a true believer fights sin. She hated it, even though it was as much a part of our world as the heat. That didn't stop Ruth Ann.

She'd go on these campaigns, battles to eradicate the creeping black fuzz from our lives, and attack the black ooze growing around the single-paned windows with bleach so strong it made our eyes water. My job in this war was to pull all the shoes and purses out of my mother's closet and scrub away the gray haze inside with vinegar. That miserable occupation taught me to hate the black goo as much as she did.

But she saved her real fury for the slime that grew in the shower. To fight its spread, we pulled the shower curtain across the tiny enclosure at all times so that water would drain off the plastic, preventing black gunk from growing in the folds. Some things become a habit. I may be the world's worst housekeeper, but my shower is always wiped down and the curtain is always stretched wide to allow it to dry.

On this night I'd left the Sunset early, still changing up my routine, and the first thing I did when I got home was head for the shower. The shower was wide open. I was the last one to leave the house, the last one in the bathroom. I was sure this wasn't how I'd left it. But why would an intruder pull aside a curtain and check out a shower? Only the silliness of the idea kept me from calling the cops and telling them someone had been inside our house, but I knew it was true. I couldn't even tell Clay someone had been in our shower because it would prove I'd lost it and really have him on my case to get some help.

My insomnia came back big-time. I prowled the house at night, checking and rechecking locks, hunting shadows and hidden places where death could wait, never confident I was safe. Deep in my heart I believed it was just a matter of time before someone came for me. I didn't know who, and I didn't know why; I just knew it would happen.

Sick with fear. That's exactly how it feels, like you're going to puke. It's a never-ending thing sitting in your gut and gnawing away. You can't eat, you can't think of anything else, and you sure as hell aren't getting any sleep. There's just no relief from this kind of fear.

One night I was staring out into the night, trying to see any light or any movement, something that didn't belong, concentrating all of my being on the world beyond the slit in the curtain. Hands slipped around my waist. I drove my elbow back hard and whirled with the flat of my hand raised, ready to strike. Clay had already danced away.

"Jesus, Sherri, it's only me."

"Don't sneak up on me like that."

"I wasn't sneaking." His right hand rubbed his ribs.

It was true. He hadn't been trying to surprise me. It was just that Clay moved like a panther in the night. I never heard him, never knew he was there, until he touched me.

He stepped towards me, arms circling me and pulling me against his naked chest. "You've got to get some help, Sherri."

I laid my cheek against his shoulder. "We've been through this. I'm fine."

"You jump at shadows and see danger where there isn't any. How many times have you woken up in the night, sure someone was in the house? Or had Miguel check out strange cars in the parking lot? Asked him to walk you to your truck? You even have him follow you home and then sit there with the engine running until I open the door and you know it's safe. Do you think that's normal? I'm worried about you."

It was no time to tell him that I was too.

My fears were given credence when a friend who worked at our bank told me someone had been making discreet inquiries into our financial position. A credit check had been done, but there was no indication of why or who was involved. Then Gwen, the Sunset's hostess, told me about a man who asked too many questions and showed too much interest in me. Even Clay was aware of someone poking around in our lives, but it didn't rattle him. But I didn't like being in someone's headlights. It wasn't just what had happened out in the Glades that had me jumpy. There were way too many secrets in my past, and too many scary people who might want to get even, for me not to worry about a stranger poking around in my life.

While all of this was happening, Ethan Bricklin was becoming almost a regular. I was never surprised to see him come in and always enjoyed our conversations, and if I'd really paid attention I could have become an expert on orchids. It was just about his only topic of conversation.

One day he surprised me by saying, "I came to invite you to a party," adding quickly, in case I got the wrong idea, "you and Clay."

"What kind of party?"

"The Orchid Ball at Selby Gardens—it's a glitzy black-tie night. I'm on the committee with Nina Dystra, and it's my duty to buy lots of tickets." He smiled in a wry, self-deprecating way that took years off him. "Buying tickets is about all they expect of me so I'm making it a celebration."

"Woo, black tie! I'm not sure we're up for that." I threw a bar towel at the sink. "A hog roast with hillbilly rock is more my kind of social evening."

"C'mon. A masked ball—how can you turn that down? The theme's Venice," and then he added, "Italy, not Florida."

"Good thing you cleared that up. Our Venice is cargo shorts, with tee shirts that advertise Sharky's, not tuxedos and cummerbunds. Although I once saw a man in a tux dancing with a woman in shorts out at Sharky's tiki bar."

Ethan wasn't interested in local color. "This will be fantastic, good food with superb wines." His eyes glinted and he waved his hands in the air, enthusiastic and excited. "I'll pick you up in a limo so you can let yourself go without worrying about driving. Even better, I'll book you a hotel room." He added, "Did I mention there'd be fine wines?"

"Yes, I seem to have heard that."

"C'mon, say yes."

My brain was going over my wardrobe and finding it wanting. I shook my head. "We're beach people, not charity-events people."

"You'll enjoy it. And you'll get lots of new customers for the Sunset."

I shook a finger at him. "Appealing to my greed; good one. I'll talk to Clay."

He rubbed his hands together. "And I'll order your masks. Everyone is going to have something unique, something that represents them. I'll pick the perfect one for you." He bounced to his feet, eager to make things happen.

"I haven't said yes yet."

"But you will."

Ethan didn't wait for me to talk to Clay but went out to find him and convince him to join the party. I'm pretty sure it wasn't a hard sell to get Clay to agree, not as hard as it was for Clay to convince me.

The hunt for the perfect dress turned into my personal crusade to improve the finances of southwest Florida. After a new dress and new shoes came hair and nails. My mission to grow the economy was such a success that for once in my life I got it all together.

On the night of the ball I stood before a full-length mirror and turned this way and that. Damn, I looked good in a lock-the-doors-and-turn-out-the-lights sort of way. Elegant sophistication will always elude me.

After making sure everything was tucked into place, I swept into the living room, doing my best red-carpet posing and enjoying the tender kiss of silk on my skin.

Clay clutched his heart. "I think I'm having a coronary."

Stroking my hair back carefully, I lifted my chin and showed him my profile before I vamped towards him with my hand on my hip. "Do you like it?" I purred.

He picked his cell up off the table. "Shall I dial 911 now, or do you expect to do me more damage before we leave?"

"Best to hold off on that." I pivoted on the toe of my impossibly high heels that had cost a week's tips and showed him the back of the dress, or lack of it in this case. The back plunged to the crack of my ass in a gentle drape of silk. I turned halfway back and gave him a smile over my mostly bare shoulder.

"I see what you mean." He shook his head in mock dismay. "Lady, wearing that, you can do damage coming and going."

"Never mind the damage this did to my bank account. Why does free stuff always end up costing us a bomb?"

Clay was looking pretty fine himself. With his black eyes and sculpted jaw, he looked like he'd just stepped out of a magazine advertisement for an expensive men's cologne.

"Are you"—Clay made lazy circles with his hand and searched for words—"wearing anything under that"—he coughed—"dress?"

I picked up my silver purse with the jeweled martini glass on the side. "Well, that's a little mystery to be solved later."

Behind Clay, through the uncurtained window, I saw the limo make a wide turn and pull into the driveway. How strange that extravagant car looked in this subdivision of lost hopes.

Inside the limo, light indistinct music played in the background, the kind of music you wouldn't recognize if you ever heard it again, a melody meant to soothe and relax. While we settled ourselves, the chauffeur unwrapped the foil from a bottle of champagne and poured two glasses. Ethan had thought of everything.

We eased out onto the street. No one lived in the stucco houses on either side of us to be impressed by our luxury. Slowly, silently, we passed through the empty streets of tract housing, where vacant lots stood out like missing teeth on a homeless person. I turned away from the depressing sight and said, "I'm going to enjoy this night."

Clay lifted his glass in a salute. "To the future and our brilliant new life. All our bad times are in the past."

I grinned and clicked my champagne flute against Clay's. "Eat, drink and be merry because someone else is paying." I sipped my champagne before I asked, "Did you give Ethan our address?"

Clay froze, and then he set his glass down on the small pop-up table by the door. "No, I didn't."

"So how do you suppose he knew where to send the limo?"

Clay's eyes locked on mine. "You tell me."

"Ethan's a suspicious sort of man . . . and very rich. Maybe he just wanted to know more about us before he got too friendly." I saluted Clay with my glass. "I guess we know who's been asking questions."

"Maybe," he said, unconvinced. "But there's also Sasha."

If Ethan was making inquiries, okay, but the thought of Sasha sniffing around scared me silly. "Why would he go around asking questions?"

Clay's expression grew grim. "The same reason as Ethan: your business card tying you to the scene."

"Shit." I looked out the window so Clay couldn't see my face.

Clay said, "Maybe they were only checking out if they could

trust me enough to do business with me. If either of them had asked, I would have given them lots of referrals."

His faith in his contacts was touching and a little naïve. "I don't think they're looking for references, nor are they Chamber of Commerce sort of guys."

Clay considered that for a moment. "So, just what sort of men are we dealing with?"

My eyes found his. "The kind who cut corners and expect others to do the same."

"Ah," Clay said. "Know your enemies."

"Know your friends, but know your enemies better," I said, and then I lifted my glass.

Locked safely in the back of the limo, we shared our dreams. There were so many things about our lives together we'd never discussed, and suddenly we both wanted to rush at them and make decisions, building our castle in the sky and planning for a future full of dazzling, exhilarating things. There's nothing like a limo and endless champagne for making future plans in an ideal world where you're in control of your destiny. The world slipped by while we conspired and dreamed of pleasures yet to come.

The Tamiami Trail runs from Tampa down through Sarasota, along the west coast past Fort Myers to Naples and from there across the Everglades to Miami. The Tamiami is the lifeline of the coast and traveling on it now in this luxurious car somehow felt like a weird continuance of that journey I'd begun down in Miami.

Sixty miles south of Tampa, Sarasota sits astride the Tamiami Trail. A jewel of a city, overlooking Sarasota Bay and a group of barrier islands stretching along the west coast, its bay frontage has been turned into parklands and marinas, and its white sand beaches are among the best in the world.

Outside the limo was a world of luxury. Beyond a row of tall palms a windsurfer sped across the gulf. The red-and-white stripe of the sail made it look like a toy. Sipping champagne, we sped silently by a sculpture that looked like a crane had dropped a pile of I-beams that were leaning together to keep from falling down and then past a twenty-foot-tall sailor kissing a nurse. Tourists turned to look as the limo drove by. When the limo made a right onto a long drive bordered by tall waving palms, I readjusted the silk over my shoulders and said, "We're going to the Ritz-Carlton. Why is Ethan staying at the Ritz?"

"No idea." And then Clay added, "And don't you ask him. It's none of our business." Clay somehow had the idea that I was overly curious and not always tactful. I had no idea where it came from, and I couldn't disabuse him of the notion.

I leaned forward to get a better view out the window. "When I die, I don't want to go to heaven."

"That's a good thing," Clay said. "You won't be disappointed then."

"I don't want to go to heaven because I want to go to a Ritz-Carlton Hotel forever and ever, amen. There ain't nothing like it."

"When did you stay at the Ritz?" Skepticism was thick in his voice.

"My wedding night. Want to hear about it?"

"I'll pass."

I made a face at him and drawled, "You never want to hear my best stories, and you don't like it when I . . ." I didn't finish because we were at the front door of the hotel and the doorman was opening it for Ethan to come out. Ethan was followed by a bellman carrying an armload of gold bags.

"How did he do that?" I asked. "Come out the door right when the car pulled up?"

"I suspect it involves something called a cell phone rather than magic," Clay said. "But you'll enjoy the idea of supernatural abilities much more than reality."

Behind us the trunk opened. I turned to watch the chauffeur hurry to the back of the car. "Reality is for people who lack imagination."

Clay laughed. "In that case, you never have to worry about the real world."

After the packages were safely stored, the chauffeur opened the door for Ethan. When it had closed silently behind Ethan our driver went to the front of the car and placed a white flag, bearing a scarlet orchid, on the right fender.

Ethan saw me watching the chauffeur and said, "The flag on the car is to tell the man on the gates that we're on the guest list for a very exclusive party before the ball."

I clapped my hands. "A party before the ball; you are so talking my language."

We swept out of the Ritz turnaround, the orchid flag flying, and I said, "Let the games begin."

CHAPTER 18

Ethan put his champagne flute down on the tiny polished table beside him and took two packages out of the gold shopping bag at his feet. Wrapped in shiny gold-and-silver paper and tied with metallic bows, they were treasures in themselves.

Wary and cautious, I took the gift he offered me. "What's this then?" Ours was a lopsided friendship at best, and his gifts seemed to be piling up.

"Your masks. Each guest will have a different one and . . ." He hesitated and for a moment he looked unsure of himself, something I'd never seen in him before. "I thought I'd get something that represented you, at least in my eyes."

Inside the wrapping was a clear plastic box containing a black-feathered mask in the shape of a swan. The body of the swan fit over my eyes, and the neck and head swept up above my hair, dramatic and eye-catching. The wings covering my eyes were outlined in rhinestones. It was . . . well, regal . . . created for someone important.

I had to swallow several times before I could speak. "Thank you, Ethan. I like my swan. It's one of the nicest presents I've ever received."

He gave a small nod and said, "You're welcome."

As pleased as I was, I couldn't help making a joke. "Unlike some people, you see the true me, elegant and graceful."

Clay's mask was a plain metal façade in the lightest of material. The metal curved under his chin, covered his mouth and had no opening, and rose high above his forehead, like the helmet of some ancient knight. Totally unadorned yet somehow menacing, it made me uneasy.

"Why?" I asked, pointing at it.

Ethan answered my question with one of his own. "Do you know the story of the man in the iron mask?"

"No."

"A prisoner in the Bastille, he was made famous by Dumas. No one ever saw him without his mask, never knew his identity, but people guessed he was royalty. This mask is for a man who keeps his own counsel and remains hidden."

Ethan had captured the essence of Clay. No matter how well you thought you knew Clay, you really didn't. A part of him was always concealed and private. And, yes, there was a sense of superiority about him, an awareness that he was less prone to foolishness than the rest of us might be.

"Okay," Clay said, still holding his mask up in front of his face, "show us yours."

"When we get there." Ethan picked up his glass. "I'd much rather enjoy this."

Clay lowered his mask and said with a smile, "Then tell us about your other guests." He picked up his champagne flute but he didn't drink. Unlike me, Clay never drank much.

Ethan turned to me and smiled. "Who do you think I asked, Sherri?"

I shrugged before I remembered my dress was best worn by a mannequin that didn't move. I tugged the silk back in place on my shoulder and said, "I just figure you picked people for the Orchid Ball who like orchids. I don't suppose they buy their plants from Publix's like me and throw them out when they die." I frowned at him. "Honestly, Ethan, don't let anyone ask me a thing about orchids or they'll figure out how stupid I am. I'm depending on you to keep me out of trouble."

"Count on me," he said. "And you're right, they're all plant people." Ethan listed them on his fingers. "Sasha will be there. You've met him, Sherri. And Dr. Martin Faust and his wife, Erin, will be joining us. He's a man you can't call too many nice things. He's nasty, petty, self-important, misogynist and racist, but damn, the man knows his orchids."

I said, "Gee, all those things and clever too."

"Yup. And heavily into micropropagation."

I lowered the glass halfway to my lips. "Which I hope is something legal, not something disgusting he does with underage girls."

"Asexual reproduction."

My glass came down again. "Okay, now you're being crude. Aren't there any normal people at this party?"

"Define normal." He wrinkled his forehead in thought. "Of the eight at the table, besides you, Richard Dystra would likely seem the most regular person, mainly because he has the least money and can't afford to be too outrageous. He's a defense attorney." His eyes moved to Clay. "I believe you know him, Clay."

"Yes." Clay's voice was totally neutral. "Dystra was head of a real-estate consortium that I did business with. We ended up in court."

"Well, as I heard it, you won, so it shouldn't be a problem for you."

Clay stopped pretending to drink and set down his glass.

"Why are we here? How did we make it on the guest list? We don't collect orchids and didn't know your brother. I'm guessing that's another attribute your guests all have."

Ethan spread his arms wide. "You're here because I like you. I had to have someone at the table I like."

"That's a lovely sentiment." Clay's lips spread in a thin smile. "But we seem to be a little outside your group of friends."

"Which is perfect. They aren't exactly friends." He leaned forward. "I need you there, someone who is on my side, someone who didn't want Ben's orchid." Ethan seemed to struggle, about to say more, then shook his head and sat back on the leather seat and picked up the champagne bottle. "I want you to enjoy your evening." He topped up the glasses we'd hardly touched. When he got to mine, he started to pour and then lifted the bottle and said, "What do you think this evening is about, Sherri?"

I opted for a rare bit of honesty. "Except for us, each of your guests is an orchid collector. Even though you keep saying it's impossible, it seems your brother had a black orchid for sale, and these people were on the list of potential buyers."

He finished filling my glass. "And?" His eyes twinkled with amusement.

I lifted my glass towards him. "You're looking for the person who killed your brother. You think that person will be at your table tonight."

Ethan set the bottle in its silver bucket. "Yes." The smile was gone from his face and there was ice in his voice. Ethan nodded in my direction but spoke to Clay. "Beauty and brains. You'd best watch this one, Clay."

"Thanks, Ethan, but I figured that one out a long time ago."

Ethan crossed his legs and folded his hands on his lap. "So, Sherri, what do you think I'm planning?"

"I'm not sure." I studied him. "Maybe . . ." I stopped myself. Glancing out the window, I said, "Vengeance is a dangerous dish." My eyes went back to his face. "I hope you don't serve up more than you can chew."

He winked. "Don't worry about me. I have a very healthy appetite."

The limo stopped at the entrance to the Selby mansion. Wrought-iron gates, hung between white pillars topped with iron carriage lights, were opened by a man dressed in a black suit. We cruised silently over the circular brick drive, past a live oak dripping in Spanish moss and masses of red bromeliads, as the iron gates closed behind us.

We parked in front of a white-pillared house with dark green shutters. The front doors stood open, welcoming us, while on each side of the doors stood a man wearing a black half mask. "Very impressive," I said.

"There's a special reception here first for the directors and lead donors," Ethan explained. I wasn't listening. What held my attention was a pink Cadillac with extravagant fins, parked beside a carriage house to the left of the entrance. "Ethan, didn't you say you still had your father's Caddy?"

He followed my gaze. "Yes, that's mine."

A man in a suit opened the limo door.

"It's pink." I couldn't understand the shock I was feeling.

"I think of it as a test of manhood," Ethan said. "It takes a real man to drive a bubblegum-pink Cadillac from the fifties."

"You get my vote," Clay told him. "But you didn't need to

order the limo just for us when you already had a car here."

"I wasn't planning on driving myself. Crazy—I haven't driven Dad's Caddy since before Ben died, but I did today. I was here earlier to attend to a few last-minute things. I went out for lunch with some people and they dropped me off at the Ritz."

"Haven't I seen it before?" I glanced over at him. "Did you bring it to the Sunset one day?"

His lips stretched in a pleased smile. "That's right, I did. I'd forgotten that. You're very observant."

"I was sure I'd seen it before."

Ethan was the last one out of the car. When he emerged he was wearing a tri-cornered hat with a huge red plume, a cape and a devil's mask with red horns.

You have got to admire a man who boldly says he's the devil. While I was pretty sure he was exaggerating, I still pitied the poor murderer who had the devil after him.

As I started up the steps I suddenly felt strangely reluctant and fearful. It wasn't just a sudden case of social anxiety; I was terrified, really afraid. This was no longer just an evening of incredible celebration but a night fraught with danger. Ethan was on a track for truth and retribution, and I didn't want to get caught in the fallout.

CHAPTER 19

Clay clasped my elbow and drew me to his side. "Are you all right?"

"Jitters," I replied. "Now, take Cinderella to the ball."

And so we proceeded into the wonder of Selby House, into a luxurious but alien world, and out to the reception on the brick balcony overlooking Sarasota Bay where masked servers carried silver trays full of champagne or canapés. Dressed exactly the same and wearing black half masks, the waiters were totally anonymous and, to me, threatening.

Ethan greeted people and introduced us before we moved on. It was easy to see that he was the center of attention. Groups parted and people turned to nod and watch him pass. Suddenly, there was a man directly in front of us. Pugnacious in his walk and stance, everything about him presented a challenge. His eyes were firmly fixed on Clay.

Beside me, I felt Clay stiffen.

The man blocking our way held out his hand to Clay as if daring Clay to reject it. "Heard you were coming tonight."

It was the briefest handshake in history, and it was Ethan who introduced Richard Dystra to me.

Richard Dystra's eyes turned from Clay to me. His jutting jaw and squat build made him seem more like a gangster than a smooth-talking criminal lawyer, but from the pouches under his eyes to the blue-black of his cheeks where whiskers threatened to sprout, his hound-dog face was alive with character. "Well, well, well," he said as if someone were offering him a particularly fine and delicious dessert.

Dystra didn't settle on a mere touching of hands as he had with Clay; he enveloped my hand in both of his. When I tried to pull it back, he wouldn't release it.

I looked to the woman who'd come to stand beside him, Nina Dystra, the woman who'd lunched with Ethan. A cloud of flowery perfume surrounded her and tickled my nose. She was wearing a suit of stiff, crumpled material in a deep purple. It had a high stand-up collar with a low neckline that showed rather a lot of her freckled chest.

I turned back to Dystra. The pressure of his hold hadn't lessened. "May I have my hand back, please?"

He faked a moue of surprise. "Oh, of course. I was so taken by your loveliness, I forgot my manners."

I was tempted to wipe my hand and ask if the slime he oozed ever stuck, but I'd promised Clay I would behave. My eyes returned to the woman beside him. She hadn't smiled, frowned or said boo. "Hi, Nina," I said, offering my hand to her.

She looked at it and frowned. Knowing her husband had just touched it, I could understand why. I withdrew my hand and gripped my bag.

"Hello," she said. There was no smile, no inflection. It was like someone had prodded a mechanical response out of her.

Dystra said, "You know Nina?"

"In passing," I said, while she looked around the room for someone more interesting to talk to.

"Will you excuse us?" Clay took my arm and led me away from the crush of partygoers.

I looked back over my shoulder. Ethan was still talking to them, but both Dystras were watching us.

When we stood on the edge of the mass, I blew out a huge breath. "I feel I could use a shower."

"He has a reputation. You wouldn't be the first woman who had to fight him off."

"Oh." I nodded. "I understand, a pig in black tie. I hope I don't have to sit next to him at dinner or I may commit a felony."

After another glass of champagne and some hors d'oeuvres, we walked along a winding path beside the bay where mangroves grew and fish splashed. We watched a fisherman, up to his waist in the water, cast time after time while fish jumped around him.

Under the gumbo-limbo tree, we sat on a teak settee that overlooked Sarasota Bay and the arching Ringling Bridge to St. Armands. For a moment there was only us in the whole world.

It wasn't long before Clay suggested, "Perhaps we should get back to the party." He was already getting to his feet. "Let's go check out the auction items."

I looked back over my shoulder to see who he was trying to avoid and saw Laura Kemp, Clay's former girlfriend, leaving a small group of partygoers and bearing down on us. Her electric-blue fringed dress ended at mid-thigh, and below it her long, shimmering legs looked lethal.

"Very wise of you," I said, rising. My last meeting with Laura had not gone well. "Two felonies in one evening would be too much even for me to explain."

Clay took my elbow and hurried me along, at a speed nearly

impossible in spiked heels. The brick path led to two large white dining tents set up on the lawn under banyan trees. The roots of the banyans spread out at their bases like the swirl of a long, sleek ball gown from the twenties. In the shade of the trees, elegantly dressed people stood drinking champagne while tiny lights sparkled above them in the trees. It was an enchanted scene from a magical land.

Between the two marquees was a black-and-white-checked dance floor that ran the length of the tents. The orchestra was already playing. Laughter floated on the soft breeze, feathers trembled on shimmering gowns, and jewels flashed. Orchids were everywhere, hanging from trees and decorating every surface.

Across from the orchestra was a black-and-red gondola, raised on a cradle and transformed into a table for the silent auction. At each end of the gondola was a red-and-white-striped pole beside which a guard stood, watching the guests.

I pointed to where the silent auction had been set up. "Why the barber's poles?"

Clay turned a page in his program before answering. "Apparently, they mark a place to moor your gondola."

"Good to know. If mine sails by, I'll know where to park it. Is there anything here we can afford?"

"Nope," Clay said without raising his eyes from the program. "Unless you need a Cartier watch."

As we headed towards the display, I kept my eyes on the rent-a-cop in front of us. He had his hand on his gun, and his uneasy eyes were checking us out and then going right and left before coming back to us. His eyes never settled as he analyzed the grid for danger and raiding pirates. "Man, that guard is serious," I whispered to Clay. "I've spent time in some pretty low-life bars and felt safer. Who knew fine living could be so dangerous?"

Clay whispered, "Walk slowly or he might shoot you."

"At the first sound of gunfire I'm going to dive under the boat and pray the thing doesn't crash down on top of me."

"Whatever you do, don't make any sudden moves."

"Tell that to this dress. Without sudden moves I'd be naked." In an attempt to be the sexiest girl at the ball, I was risking indecency and humiliation, and every step was cause for an adjustment. It would be a miracle if I made it through the night without flashing the revelers. Once again I'd taken things too far.

Joining the crowd of shoppers, I glanced behind us to see if Laura Kemp had followed. She wanted Clay and wasn't about to give him up. Maybe I could figure out a way to get the guards to shoot her and put her out of her misery.

Inching past the array of things for sale, I understood why the guard was uneasy. There was a diamond bracelet valued at twenty thousand dollars, and a Chinese vase at thirty-five thousand.

At the far end of the gondola, Clay met a contractor who wanted to discuss a new development. Leaving Clay to talk business, I headed off in search of alcohol.

With a glass of wine in my hand, I wandered to the koi ponds. The orange-and-white fish rushed to my feet the moment my shadow spread out on the water. They hovered there with their mouths opening and closing, begging for food.

"Ethan tells me you are interested in Ben's orchid."

"What?" I looked up in puzzlement and saw Nina Dystra standing beside me.

She said, "Maybe we should talk."

I looked around for Richard Dystra. "I thought your husband was the collector."

The sound she made was dismissive and disgusted. "He has his enthusiasms but they aren't plants." She moved in so close that her nose was practically touching mine. I leaned back as far as I could, away from the intensity that burned in her eyes and the essence that made me want to sneeze.

"If you have Ben's orchid, I'll pay you one hundred thousand dollars for it."

My enthusiasm for the number she quoted must have shown in my face because she held up her hand and said, "Provided you can guarantee me that it's the only single one."

For a hundred thousand dollars I'd tell her anything she wanted to hear, including that I didn't think she was a repulsive bitch.

I glanced over at Richard Dystra, who was talking to a beautiful coffee-skinned woman with silver bracelets around her upper arms. The woman must have felt my gaze because she raised her eyes to mine. "Will Richard mind you spending all that money on an orchid?"

Nina didn't hide her contempt. "Why would he mind? It's my money. Do you have the orchid?"

"If I find one, I'll be sure to get in touch." I dug out a business card for the Sunset. I had only this minute decided that everyone under the banyan trees was doing business but me, so I figured it was time to catch up. I handed her my card. "Bring your friends by the Sunset sometime. Our food gets rave reviews in all the best magazines."

As I swayed across the lawn, attempting to keep my heels from digging into the turf, my dress from falling off and my wine from spilling, I tried to figure out how I could dye an orchid black.

Ethan intercepted me. “There you are.” He took the glass from my hand and put it on the tray of a passing waiter, replacing it with a full glass of champagne from the tray.

As he handed it to me, I said, “You didn’t tell me it was the wife in the Dystra family who was the collector.”

“You didn’t ask.”

“So why did you tell her I might have the orchid?”

“Just to get up her nose.”

“I knew there had to be a good reason she didn’t like me. Thanks.”

“You’re welcome,” Ethan said. “She’s also afraid you might cut into her fun.”

“And what amusing little thing would she be into?”

“Young men, very young men, not-old-enough-to-vote young men.”

“Well, she’s safe from my interference on that one.” I studied Nina’s progress; she said hello here and there, but barely paused in her prowl of the garden. “She’s the one with the money, right?”

“Inherited tens of millions, while Richard only has what he can earn.” Ethan made it sound like failure, as if a man who was a defense attorney and real-estate investor lived hand to mouth. It indicated how wealthy Ethan was—and how he judged people.

“So, if she’s so rich, why keep him around?”

“Maybe he keeps her out of trouble, either paying off her mistakes or strong-arming them. He’s ruthless, and he knows where to find muscle when he needs to. I suspect Nina wouldn’t last long without him to fix things for her. Besides, they each get to indulge their sins and enjoy her money. It works. They’ve been together a long time.”

I saw his face change.

"Ah, Liz," Ethan said to someone behind me.

I turned to see a petite woman in her fifties. Sleek as a cat and radiating pent-up energy, she had caramel-colored hair cut short in an angled bob, which set off unforgiving feline eyes of steel blue.

Ethan held out his arm to welcome her. "This is my oldest friend, Liz Aiken."

She looked up at Ethan, who towered a foot above her, and raised an eyebrow. "Perhaps you could rephrase that."

"Oh, sorry. This is Elizabeth Aiken, a friend from childhood."

She tilted her head to the side and gave him a searing glance.

He hurried to smooth this latest gaffe. "I'm much older than her, of course. Liz grew up on the ranch next door, and I've known her since she was a baby."

"Much better." She held out her hand and said, "It's true, we grew up together. Mrs. Bricklin, Ethan's mother, taught me about orchids, gave me my first one for my sixth birthday." A swift glance at Ethan. "Remember how she used to take us swamp walking in search of orchids?" She didn't give Ethan time to respond. "We'd be in water up past our waists, following her where no white person had ever been before."

"Weren't you afraid of getting lost?" I asked.

"Never thought of it." A swift turn of her head towards Ethan. "Did you?"

"No."

That was all he was allowed to say before Liz went on. "Mrs. Bricklin always seemed to know where she was and where to find orchids. So did Ben."

The mention of Ben Bricklin stopped her for a second before she started to describe an orchid show she'd attended the day before. Now Ethan was allowed to join in.

Their conversation went on like they'd been saving it until they were overflowing with talk, had to get it out before they exploded. I listened to the rat-a-tat of their gunfire exchange, but I was way out of my depth. Every few minutes one of them would turn to me with some tidbit for my enjoyment. I had no idea what they were talking about, but I nodded anyway. Then I went back to checking out the dresses of the other women while their conversation wrapped around me.

Suddenly, Liz turned and asked, "What particular type do you collect, Sherri?"

"Oh, I don't collect. Actually, I don't even understand your passion. Is the attraction that they're rare?"

"Oh, my dear, they aren't rare. They're one of the two most common flower species in the world. Only some of them are rare."

I threw up my hands in surrender. "I'll never understand."

She laughed. "That's all right, I'm not sure I do either." She bounced up on her toes in her animation. "All orchid collectors are a little out of control."

Ethan handed her a glittering package. She took it from him but she hardly looked at it. She just continued talking. "I still have that orchid Mrs. Bricklin started me with, a *Tolumnia bahamensis*. I named my island after it: Dancing Lady Island. They are almost wiped out in the wild, thanks to overdevelopment."

"Dancing Lady Island. Lovely name," I said.

"But the flower has a nasty smell." She turned back to Ethan. "I just got back last week from Moyobamba."

He took the gift out of her hand and started to unwrap it as she explained to me, "It's an orchid town in Peru." She didn't wait for me to respond but went back to telling Ethan about her trip and what she had found there.

Ethan held out the present he'd unwrapped. "Try on your mask, Liz."

Liz's face covering, in black leather, was the face of a cat. It rose above her forehead into pointed ears. She put it on and became strangely menacing and ominous. "How do I look?" she asked.

"Beautiful," I told her. Which was true, but it also made me want to ease away from her. I added, "And bewitching."

Already pulling it down, she nodded and waved at someone behind us. "Excuse me," she said, patting my arm. "We'll talk later."

I watched her go, wondering if Ethan realized she hadn't thanked him for the mask or offered any parting words to him.

Liz greeted a woman with slicked-back hair and a face totally tattooed in a pattern reminiscent of a South Sea Islander. The tattooed woman wore a long-sleeved glittering black sheath, completely molded to her body and reaching the floor.

I couldn't take my eyes off her. "Are those real tattoos?"

"Well," Ethan replied, "the last time I saw Myra she didn't have them, but there's no telling with her."

I turned to face him. "I like Liz."

He was frowning and studying Liz's back.

"Why a cat?"

His eyes stayed on Liz and his answer came slowly. "Liz has that quality, slinking and secretive. Her mask represents a special cat, an Egyptian cat." His eyes followed Liz through the crowd. "The ancient Egyptians' religion centered on the worship of animals, especially cats."

"And?" I prodded when he went silent.

"Cats killed snakes, like cobras, and were the ancient symbol of grace and poise. There were two cat goddesses: the lion-headed goddess Mafdet represented justice and execution, while the other cat goddess was the deity of protection, fertility and motherhood."

"So which one does Liz represent, the nurturing one or the one out for vengeance?"

When he didn't answer, I reached out to touch his hand.

He gave a small jerk and said, "Sorry, I was lost in thought."

"About Liz?"

Instead of answering, he asked, "Do you know her story?"

"I just met her."

Ethan took my elbow and led me farther under the banyans, out of earshot of the other guests. "I thought you might recognize the name."

"Why, is she famous?"

"Sort of. She killed her husband."

CHAPTER 20

I swung around to stare at the small middle-aged woman, now deep in conversation with an elderly couple. Her mask was in her hand as she waved her arms about, describing something with great gusto. The couple she was speaking to burst into laughter.

"A murderess? How's that possible?" I asked.

"Liz's husband beat her. She ran to Ben and Susan's to hide. Her husband, Kurt Aiken, came after her, and when he found Liz in Susan's kitchen, he beat Liz so badly that she miscarried their child. In the struggle, Liz stuck a knife in Kurt."

The possibility of that tiny dynamo killing a full-grown man seemed ludicrous. Liz seemed to feel my eyes burning into her. She glanced over her shoulder and then raised a hand in acknowledgment. It wasn't hard to smile at her.

I said, "It was self-defense then."

"Unfortunately, she stuck it in his back. Liz was charged with his murder."

"Did she go to jail?"

"Everyone knew she'd killed him, but the jury voted to acquit anyway. They figured the bastard deserved to be knifed."

"I would have voted the same way."

"Well, it worked out for her in the end. She became a very rich widow. Aiken owned car dealerships all over Florida. She inherited millions and turned them into a lot more millions. She's very smart, and when she sets her sights on something, she gets it."

"And you think she wanted Ben's orchid?"

"I suspect she may have got it."

"Did she ever marry again?" Her sad story deserved a happy ending.

"No."

A crush of people moved towards us, pushing us farther back.

"It was more than Kurt's death that kept her from remarrying. It was always Ben for Liz. I think she married Kurt because she knew she was never going to have Ben, but I thought they might get together when Susan died."

"There you go. If she felt that way, she'd never hurt Ben, would never steal from him."

He frowned. "Liz's had a tough life. It's made her hard. I don't think there is much she wouldn't be capable of. Her old feelings for Ben might not be enough to overcome her desire to possess the rarest orchid in the world, to propagate it and have it named after her. Naming a species is a way of making yourself immortal."

He'd already told me this. "Immortal." I tried the word. "If that's true, why would Ben sell it? Wouldn't Ben want a perpetual monument by putting his name on the orchid?"

"Ben couldn't afford that luxury. He needed money."

Someone backed into me and jostled my arm. Champagne washed my hand. I turned, and a glamorous presenter from the six o'clock news smiled at me.

"Oh, excuse me." Leah Woods took the glass from me and held out a napkin. "I'm so sorry." She was even more beautiful in person than she was on television.

I shook the liquid off my hand and took the napkin she offered. "No problem." I dried my hand and moved aside to put the crumpled napkin on a small table.

Ethan followed me, and I asked, "Liz could afford to have her name on the black orchid?"

"Like everyone at the table tonight."

"Except me . . . and Clay."

"But you could be acting for someone else." His voice was light and reasonable, not as if he was accusing us of anything but rather pointing out the obvious. "Clay buys and sells property. A black orchid is just another form of property, and it would be worth hundreds of thousands of dollars to a breeder, to say nothing of the glory. So anyone can get into this race, and you do have some connection to Ben."

"No, I don't. I never met your brother, never even spoke to him on the phone or exchanged an e-mail with him."

"Still, there's a link."

He must've seen my puzzlement because he added, "Your business card."

"Ahh, I'd forgotten about that. Right, someone had my card." I smiled at him, genuinely relieved. "I intend to give them out all night. If one of these people turns up dead tomorrow with my card in their pocket, how much am I going to be able to tell the police about their deaths?"

His smile was real now. "I see your point."

"Look, just to put your mind at ease, I'll tell you one more time: I never heard about a black orchid until you told me about Ben's, okay?"

He looked deep into my eyes, as if he could read the truth there. "And you have no interest in a black orchid?"

"Jesus, yes. Nina just offered me a hundred thousand dollars for one. Believe me, if I knew where to look, I'd be out there digging one up."

"You don't dig them up." He couldn't help correcting me. "They're air plants. They hang in trees and on other plants."

"Whatever." I brushed aside his lecture. "Since I'm never going swamp walking, I'm not likely to ever see one in its natural habitat." I stepped back and adjusted my gown. "One more time, just so you know—no one sent me anywhere, at any time, about an orchid. And if I knew where there was one, you think I wouldn't be all over it? I'd sell it immediately to Nina Dystra."

The tension went out of his face and he laughed. "Okay, I never really thought you were involved. I've just got a disbelieving nature. But if you find one, call me first, okay?"

"Agreed."

He was determined to find his brother's murderer and no one was exempt from suspicion. A man with few friends and not many people he trusted, he'd be watching me intently, and at the least hint of me being involved with Ben's death, my credibility would fly away like a flock of terns on the beach.

It was definitely time to change the subject. "Now, are you going to ask me to dance or what?"

Ethan smiled and led me to the dance floor.

The orchestra was playing big band music, and Ethan was a wonderful dancer, easy to follow and light on his feet. We stayed on the dance floor for a second number before we joined the throng spilling into the marquees for dinner. As we made our way through the dancers to our seats, I saw a tray of used glasses on a folding table against the wall. Among the debris of crushed napkins and half-eaten hors d'oeuvres was Liz's cat mask.

CHAPTER 21

With the scraping of chair legs, the swishing of satin and laughing voices calling out to friends, the diners settled in for the first course. The clamor reminded me of the night sounds in the swamp, a chorus of chatter that blended into a whole refrain. Occasionally a bellow of laughter rose above the babble, like the roar of a gator in the swamp.

Ethan's table was on the edge of the dance floor, the best table in the tent. Overhead, a giant crystal chandelier sparkled.

The theme of the ball continued with black tablecloths draped to the floor and a napkin folded like a tuxedo on each white plate. In the center of the table sat a silver bucket full of white orchids. On each silver-gilt chair was a bidding paddle with a number on it to use in the auction. I planned on pushing mine way under the table so I didn't end up buying that diamond-encrusted watch by accident. Above my place setting was a card with an embossed medallion and my name in the center. Inside was the menu in Italian and the wine list.

Two people had entered the marquee ahead of the rest of our party and were already seated. They didn't rise to greet us, just sat there looking somehow mulish and discontented. Even when Ethan made the most pleasant of introductions, Dr. Martin Faust neither bothered to rise nor offered his hand. He did, however, nod slightly in my direction while his fingers remained firmly laced over his basketball of a belly. Just below his fingers, one stud on his shirt front had given way, showing a slice of pale, hairless skin. This was matched by a pancake of baldness on the crown of his head, giving him the look of a cranky priest from some ancient monastery.

Ethan thrust a handsome package in front of Martin's face.

Martin frowned. "What's this?"

"Open it," Ethan said. "It's your mask."

Martin pulled off the wrapping without enthusiasm, revealing the largest and strangest mask in the room. Black and rigid, it had a long ferocious beak, like some vicious bird of prey from a nightmare. "What's it supposed to be?" Martin grumbled suspiciously, turning the hideous thing around in his hands.

"It's a Medico Della Peste."

"What's that exactly?" Martin's voice was full of misgiving, and he held the mask away from him between the tips of the fingers of both his hands.

"A plague doctor's mask." Ethan jabbed at Martin's shoulder with a fist. "Get it . . . Dr. Faust."

Martin's face pinched up in disgust. "Well, obviously I get it, but do I want it?"

Ethan's enthusiasm was undefeatable. He beamed at his own cleverness. "It was worn in the seventeenth century by doctors treating plague victims. Put it on."

The masks Ethan presented to the Dystras were even more telling. Hers was a . . . well, basically a two-faced presentation, smiling on the mauve side and frowning on the purple side.

Ethan said, "Nina is on the Orchid Ball committee, and she's on the board of the theater. I chose her mask for her love and commitment to the theater and the arts."

Nina's face said she didn't believe him, and neither did I.

Richard Dystra held up the image of a scarlet goat with long curved horns. He only positioned it in front of his face for a second before he lowered it. He wasn't smiling, but I was.

Ethan handed Sasha his gift last.

"Ah," Sasha said with relish. "I've been looking forward to this." Sasha threw aside the wrapping paper, looked down in the box at the mask and bellowed with laughter. He threw his arms wide, embracing Ethan's description of him with joy. "The trickster," he said. "Yes. That's me." He gently lifted a sparkling creation out of the paper and put on a Harlequin mask with diamond shapes in bright colors—oranges and greens and reds and blues, all sparkling with sequins. Sasha's pleasure in his gift was evident, and he threw himself into the party with gusto, entertaining us with stories and setting the whole table laughing.

Sasha's voice was deep and it carried. Around us, people turned to look. Sasha seemed quite unaware of the glances coming his way and was so animated that anyone passing by would have mistaken him for the host. Ethan sat back quietly and watched.

Charming and entertaining, but with an aura of contained violence about him, Sasha was a man who would always compete like his life depended on winning, whether it was for an orchid or for riches beyond my imagination. He was a man who'd do well in the turmoil of war, and perhaps his drive to conquer everything around him had made him thrive in the commercial world, but it was a little overpowering in a social setting.

At Sasha's side was the model Ethan had told me about, Willow—no last name, just Willow. She was a goddess. Thin and flawlessly beautiful, she was the kind of woman who made all other women feel inadequate. She was exotic, almond-eyed and coffee-skinned. Every woman in the room instantly hated her on sight and every man wanted her. I almost could feel pity for Willow. Almost. She was wearing a brown rag. Well, at least that's what it would have been on anyone else. The iridescent silk jersey dress clung to her in erotic delight. It was all too clear she wore nothing beneath it, so there were two of us in danger of shocking the ensemble. Her mask was of gold filigreed metal, light and insubstantial, and represented nothing. Perhaps Ethan didn't know her well enough to make a statement about her, or maybe it was his strongest judgment of all.

While the original seating was fixed by name cards, Ethan's plan was to have his male guests change seats with each course. It was my misfortune to be seated next to Martin Faust for the beginning of the dinner. Florid of face and pugnacious in attitude, he sounded like he was challenging me to argue with him even when he was just passing on innocuous information. I soon decided that he, along with Richard Dystra, was a dinner guest I didn't want to know. But whether or not I wanted to know about Dr. Faust, he told me anyway. "I'm cloning ghost orchids," was his reply to some mild question of mine about his interests outside of work.

"That's nice."

He frowned. "I'm helping preserve wild orchids by propagating them and spreading them among orchid lovers. As the swamps disappear in the natural world, this may be their only hope of surviving." He paused as if waiting for my applause. When no clapping came from me, he continued. "Clamshell orchids and crooked-spur orchids are almost gone from the Fakahatchee swamp near Naples, so I'm also specializing in those."

I was looking around for the promised food and wine, so I didn't reply. It didn't stop him from talking.

The waiters were all busy delivering the soup course, so I smiled at Ethan and pointed to my wine glass. If I was going to spend part of my evening with the man beside me, I needed a whole lot more alcohol.

There was a strange pause, and I realized I wasn't keeping up my side of the conversation. Really, I didn't care if Faust spent the rest of his life in a swamp, making it with plants, but to be polite, I said, "Ethan explained the new rules of collecting. Do the new laws stop your work?"

His hand waved. "Stupid law. All wild orchids are endangered, and it's illegal to take them out of the swamp, so they are just left there to disappear under the blade of the bulldozer. I'm sure even you can see how ridiculous that is."

"Ah." I nodded in understanding. "Your collection is illegal."

He pressed towards me, spitting out the words. "My collection is very old and dates back to before the regulations on taking natural material out of Florida swamps were put in place."

"How nice for you." Where was my wine? Faust was working hard at spoiling what should be the most exciting event of my year.

Erin Faust, "the wife," as Martin called her, leaned forward from the other side of him and said, "Martin and I are pariahs here tonight."

"Excuse me?"

She made a moue with her mouth and fanned herself faster with her bidding paddle. "You mean Ethan hasn't told you?"

"No."

"Martin has been charged with theft. He's been stealing orchids from all over the world for years, obsessed and trying to collect every rare orchid there is, but he finally got caught smuggling in one from Thailand. It got him fired from the Sutton Botanical Gardens." Her smile of satisfaction was broad. "Pariahs," she added. "You won't see too many people stopping by the table to say hello, not with us here." Her mouth was a thin line of satisfied venom.

I looked from husband to wife and back again. Dr. Faust looked like his head was going to explode, while she smiled in a sly, pleased sort of way.

Erin Faust was a woman who disappeared into the background, a woman who long ago gave up on life and reneged on sex appeal. About fifty, she wore the comfortable, drab clothes and sensible shoes of a seventy-year-old. Still, she was delighted with her silver mask and its feathers flaring out like a Plains Indian chief. She became all coy when she thanked Ethan. Coyness didn't suit her. The mask, covering the upper half of her face, glittering with purples and reds and golds, did suit her. When she put it on she changed, no longer the faded frump in lavender but a regal presence growing in stature, dominant and forceful.

Martin Faust said, "You look ludicrous." He pushed away from the table.

She lowered her mask and watched her husband as he left the table without excusing himself. Her eyes followed him as he pushed past the people at the edge of the dance floor. The expression on her face startled me. Hate and loathing were not the looks a wife normally gave her husband.

I searched for something to say. "Do you help in your husband's orchid business?"

She nodded, her eyes still following her mate. "Martin is out collecting much of the time and going to shows and judging. He isn't home much." She didn't add, "Thank god for that," but it was there in her voice. Her eyes turned to me now. "I do the propagating and fill the orders."

"So he was interested in Ben Bricklin's orchid."

Her nostril curled. "He'd go to any lengths to have his name on an orchid, he wants it so badly." Her laugh was spiteful and mean. "He just doesn't seem capable of making it happen."

Around the marquee, diamonds glittered in the light from the chandeliers, flickering like fireflies at twilight.

"Do you collect?" she asked.

"Yes."

She waited for me to say more and when I didn't, she added, "What exactly do you collect?"

"Drinks." I gave a limp flutter of my right hand. "I like the ones with little umbrellas best."

Standing beside me, Ethan reached out a hand to me. "Dance with me, Sherri."

"God, yes," I replied.

"Lovely couple," I said as Ethan guided me from the table, his hand on my elbow.

Ethan led me into a slow dance. "He's a brilliant taxonomist."

"What's a taxonomist when he's at home?"

"He's the guy that gives a new plant discovery a name from its appearance or characteristics, like how it reproduces."

He swung me around, and I felt silk slip from my shoulder. "Exciting." My left hand tugged the silk back into place. "He actually looks like the kind of guy that would find plant reproduction thrilling." I leaned back in Ethan's arms so I could look into his face. "Oh, please let him be the one," I said. "I'd like you to take him out." I smiled. "I'm thinking it couldn't happen to a nicer guy."

"You think that's what I'm planning?"

"Absolutely, and he deserves to be the subject of your vengeance."

Ethan smiled. "Now, my dear, you can't take this personally. We don't always get what we want."

When we returned to the table, Liz and Clay were deep in conversation. She held Clay's left hand tightly in hers, bouncing their joined hands up and down to underscore her words. Clay laughed and then rose, offering Liz his hand. As they passed my chair, she leaned over me, her breath tickling my ear as she whispered, "Be careful, my dear. The black swan always dies."

I jerked away. What the hell was she talking about? Was it a threat? I didn't get a chance to ask. With a smile and a lift of her eyebrows, she was gone. I watched her athletic strut as she led the way to the dance floor, a woman who was still fit and able, with a body that wasn't giving anything up to age.

I felt a hand on my bare shoulder and turned.

"Dance with me." Not a request but a demand. Sasha took my hand and pulled me to my feet without waiting for my agreement.

CHAPTER 22

Sasha drew me to him and led me into a fast gliding step, closer to ballroom than any dancing I'd ever done. He was a natural dancer, which made following him easy, although there was a certain aggression to his performance. The dance floor was crowded, but the elegant press seemed to part for Sasha. He charged around the dance floor at speed, expecting others to make way for him as he hurled himself into the thickest pack.

The music was too fast for conversation, and I was concentrating on following my partner and staying decently covered while he spun me until the world twirled in front of my face. Damn, I hadn't thought about dancing in a dress designed for standing perfectly still. Still, I'm the kind of girl who will do anything not to be ignored, so I danced under the stars with Sasha and let the silk take care of itself.

When the music ended, we made a dramatic dip in front of the orchestra and then Sasha led me into a slow dance.

I wanted to enjoy the dancing, and the only plant I wanted to think of was the one that put the wine in my glass, but Sasha's thoughts were still on orchids. "Mrs. Faust enjoyed telling you all about her husband's sins, didn't she?" Sasha said. "Their nursery has been illegally growing and shipping orchids for years, and she was part of it, but she likes to blame him. The Fausts used to be one of my best sources for exotics but not anymore. I think that's what she resents: losing business."

"All this fuss just for a few flowers."

"Oh, you heathen," he said. "Controlling life and creating something new—collecting is an act of a god."

I drew back in his arms. "Of a goddamn fool, if you ask me."

He laughed and we twirled again, until I was sure my whole dress was going to slide off my body and end up in a puddle on the checkered floor.

"You dance like Fred Astaire," I told him.

"It's all about timing and lightness of touch, just like in business—or making love." He placed his cheek against mine. "*A Carnevale ogni scherzo vale*, as they say in Italy: at Carnival, anything goes." His cheek nuzzled mine. "And life is a carnival."

Back at the table, Sasha told Martin Faust that he wanted his chair. Martin made a face but didn't argue. Then Sasha sat down beside me and turned his chair to face me, turning his back on Erin. Wine had been poured. He handed me my glass, and I noticed he wore a gold pinky ring with a crest. How many Russian families would flaunt a crest?

He picked up his own glass and bent towards me, his forearm on the table. "I want to know all about you. How do you know Ethan?" His eyes were fixed intently on my face. He'd picked a strange place to start in my life's story, but he really seemed to care about my answer.

I shrugged. "I don't really know him. Clay is hunting for some property for Ethan, or something like that, and I own the Sunset Bar and Grill over Clay's office."

"Ahh, that's right, you're a businesswoman."

"More like a bartender with pretentions."

"So, unlike the rest of us, you don't spend your life surrounded by orchids?"

"Nope. I spend my life surrounded by a riffraff of drinkers—not very flowery or exotic, but fun nonetheless." And the conversation at the bar of the Sunset was sure more interesting than any at this table, enough to make me yearn for it, but I kept that thought to myself.

"Ethan told me you knew the boy who worked for Ben Bricklin."

"No, I didn't. He had my business card." I pointed to where a card lay on the table. "Just like that one."

Sasha didn't let the subject drop. His questions turned into an interrogation rather than a conversation. He wanted to know all about Ethan. Somehow he was convinced that I was in Ethan's confidence. I denied it over and over, but he kept digging. His intensity was wearing.

"How did you start collecting?" I just wanted him to stop grilling me, and I'd already discovered that asking an orchid collector about his prize possessions was akin to asking a new mother about her baby. Just ask the question and then have a nap while they blather on. Sasha was no exception.

"I started collecting when I moved to Miami from New Jersey. Florida is the place for orchids. I started my collection late, so I have to hurry to catch up. I want them all, and I want them now."

"So you bought from Ethan's brother."

He gave me a look that said maybe I'd crossed a line.

I shrugged and then grabbed my dress before it slid away. "Ethan told me Ben was one of the biggest breeders in Florida."

"Ben Bricklin made me an expert on orchids. I was at the nursery in the days before Ben's death."

He looked past me to Ethan, sitting on my left side. Ethan wasn't bothering to hide his interest in our conversation.

"But of course you knew that," Sasha said to Ethan. "The police must have found my check for fifty thousand dollars in Ben's desk."

Ethan frowned. "The house went up with the shade house. There was nothing left to find."

"Ah." Sasha smiled. "So I needn't have explained about the money."

"What were you hoping to buy for that much money?" Ethan's voice was light, but his fingers rolled into fists on the table.

"It was just to encourage him to take my offer for the black orchid seriously." Sasha might have been talking about getting his car detailed. "But really, money was no object." He gave a brief wave of his hand, dismissing silly ideas of cost. "I would have happily paid him double that."

Alcohol was making my tongue work faster than my brain. "How did you get to the place in life where money is no object?"

Behind me, Clay said, "Sherri," outraged at my social gaffe of talking about money.

Sasha wasn't a bit put out. In fact, he looked pleased. "I did it the hard way: I earned it."

"But doing what?" I asked.

Clay's hand dug into my bare shoulder.

Sasha laughed and waggled his hand back and forth. "A little of this and a little of that."

"Let's dance," Clay said and dragged me to my feet before I got any ruder.

When we returned to the table, the conversation had turned to more interesting things. With a table full of Type A personalities, each with an agenda and each out to dominate the others, conversation was fast and deadly, each person trying to win points. Ethan played the game like a master. When I'd first met him, he had pretended to be a good old boy made good. He'd told me he had never been to college, unlike his younger brother, but the cracks that quickly appeared in this simple "just one of the boys" façade grew wider every time we met. He was more erudite and informed than he pretended to be, dropping knowledge like another man might shed dandruff, and when he was interested in something he'd shake it like a terrier until he owned it. That was the thing he shared with Sasha: intensity.

Their discussion was interrupted often, as one important person after another stopped by to say hello to Ethan. If I'd been in any doubt about Clay's early assessment that Ethan was one of the most important people in Florida, I no longer was.

As Ethan rose once again to shake someone's hand, I looked around the table and considered the people Ethan thought might be responsible for his brother's death. He'd brought his list of suspects down to these few, all important in their own right. One of them had killed Ben Bricklin. Oh, none of them would have done it personally. They all had the money and the resources to hire someone else to do their dirty work. Nina Dystra was married to a man who dealt with criminals every day, and Clay's experience showed Dystra was more than willing to cut legal corners.

Martin Faust had been arrested for smuggling orchids into the country—again, someone who wasn't hung up on right and wrong, someone who would do anything to get his name on an orchid. And then there was Sasha. If he was part of the Russian mob, there wasn't anything he would stop at.

Liz . . . I couldn't go anywhere with that. I just couldn't see how she could kill a lifelong friend, but then, going on my past experience and tendency to trust the wrong people, my not suspecting her could be a strong indicator that she was guilty.

It was a strange situation to find myself in, glamorous and exciting on one hand, and terrifying on the other. But then, maybe none of them had anything to do with the deaths at the nursery or with Tito's death. Across the table from me now, Liz had her eyes on me, cold and calculating. Damn, but I needed more wine. I looked for a waiter.

After the prosciutto and melon with fresh figs came a salad with thin slices of nearly raw tuna. When the plates were cleared for the next course, all the gentlemen rose to change places. Clay now sat beside me. We held hands under the table, like teenagers.

Willow laughed, a sound like rippling water that caught the attention of everyone at the table. We all turned to look at her. Man, she was beautiful! Just shoot me now. She held up her gold mask with one diamond tear below the left eye. It was mounted on a gold stick that rhinestones twirled around. She turned to show Martin Faust. I looked at Clay, followed his eyes to Willow and elbowed him hard.

Clay gave a humph of pain and then said, "Shall we dance?"

"Perhaps we'd better."

The orchestra was playing an old Whitney Houston hit. I turned to face him and said, "I'm so pleased you're enjoying the view across the table."

"Don't tell me you're jealous."

"Of course not, but did I ever tell you about Tully shooting up our trailer when Ruth Ann brought home a new man?"

"Many, many times."

"Good. Just remember I share some of my father's finer characteristics. I catch you with another woman, you won't be able to run far enough or fast enough."

"Yes, ma'am." He drew me to him. We swayed together as the band played, and he sang softly along to the song, "I will always love you." When his hand settled on my behind, I smiled. It isn't often in life that you're totally happy.

When the next song began, Clay held me close and said, "Just one more." Then he added, "Do you notice a bit of tension in the air around our table?"

"Tension? I'm just glad there are no steak knives on the table." I gave a dramatic quiver, well aware of what it did to the thin material grazing my body. "I wish I'd worn a Kevlar vest instead of silk."

"I enjoy this so much more without the vest."

"You start enjoying this much more and we'll be asked to leave."

He pulled me closer. "Being kicked out would suit me just fine."

CHAPTER 23

When the song ended I went off to the ladies' room, and there was Willow, sitting on a wicker chair before a long mirror-lined vanity. Elegant beyond belief, she was using a straw made of gold to sniff up the white powder on the counter.

Shocked, I glanced quickly around. We were alone, but I still whispered, "What are you doing?"

She blocked one nostril and sniffed deeply before she answered. "Well, I'm not dancing." She held her forefinger under her nose to keep herself from sneezing.

I took a deep breath, trying for a sophistication I didn't feel. "Don't you know that coke is so yesterday?"

"I'm an old-fashioned girl."

I laughed. You just had to. She so didn't care. Right out in the open, she was doing a line of coke and daring the world to do something about it, telling the rest of the human race to piss off.

She wiped her nostrils delicately with her fingertips. "Sasha likes you."

I waited, knowing something else was coming.

"Are you and Clay and Ethan . . ." She wiggled three fingers in the air.

"No . . . hell no."

"Pity. I thought you two might like to party with Sasha and I. Clay is very fine."

"And so is Sasha. Have you known him long?"

"A bit." She tilted her head to the right and then to the left, checking herself out in the mirror.

I opened my bag and started fixing my face. "Where did you meet?"

She licked her long, glamorous finger and wiped up the remains of the coke, then put her finger in her mouth. "Paris."

"Ah, Ethan said you were a model. Is that what you were doing in Paris? Were you actually walking down a runway? That's so exciting."

She was unimpressed with my keenness, just stared up at me and said, "Honey, don't go pumping me for information. I know nothing. It's safer that way."

"I was making friendly talk . . . you know, a little change from talking about the weather."

"Yeah, it sure is hot down here. How do y'all stand it?"

"Y'all? Your roots are showing."

She laughed. "I must get them touched up." She lifted her hair and let it cascade back down over her shoulders. "People are always pumping me for gossip about Sasha. When it comes to Sasha's life, I don't know and I don't care. All I care about is surviving, and the way to do that is to stay deaf and dumb."

"Yeah, I know what you're saying." I ran my fingers through my own hair and patted it in place. "I used to be brave. That was before I found out how much it costs."

She smiled and wagged a finger at me. "Girl, I think we hoed some of the same rows and know how to stay alive." She smiled at me and said, "We're just two girls looking out for themselves."

I pointed at the faint powder residue. "We all have different ways of doing that."

I went into a cubicle. When I came out she was still sitting there, relaxed and at ease, floating in a dream all her own.

As I dried my hands, she smiled and stretched lazily to her feet. "We gonna be good friends." She linked her arm in mine and we left the ladies' room.

Strolling down the brick path, under the trees and across the end of the dance floor, each of us tried to out-slink the other.

When we passed Clay, talking with someone at the entrance to the tent, he grabbed my arm, stopping me in mid-stride. He said, "Your daddy would call you two Heartache and Trouble, and he wouldn't be wrong."

If he only knew; heartache and trouble was only the start of it.

At the table, Sasha sat talking earnestly to Liz. Neither one of them took any notice of us, but they were the only ones in the room who didn't.

Twilight came, and with it, the fairy lights in the garden twinkled, lighting up this enchanted world and making anything seem possible. The smell of perfume and flowers and food filled the air with promise, and even the guests from hell seemed tolerable.

Ethan called the waiter and had him bring glasses of champagne for everyone. He stood and said, "Let's raise our glasses to my brother, Ben Bricklin. I wish he could be with us tonight."

"To Ben," we said and drank, but before we put our glasses down, Liz piped in with, "And here's to the black orchid, wherever it may be."

"There's no such thing as a black orchid," Martin Faust said. "I'm beginning to think Ben was just playing a nasty trick on us all."

Across the table from me, nerves jumped beneath the skin of Ethan's jaw, like snakes roiling in a gunny sack. He said, "My brother didn't play tricks, nasty or otherwise." He caught himself, straightened his jacket and said, "C'mon, everybody, let's all dance." He turned to Liz on his left and offered her his hand. She took it and they started for the dance floor.

No one followed.

"Please," she said. "This is a party. Let's dance."

Clay put his glass on the table and took my hand.

The Fausts protested. They'd already sat down. "We don't dance," Martin said. Of course not—dancing necessitated being close to each other.

Liz said, "Ethan has gone to so much trouble to make this a special night." She held out her hand to them. "Please. Humor me."

Martin's mouth pursed and then stretched into a straight, hard line, but he got to his feet.

Erin followed like she'd been asked to clean the urinals.

Two by two we left the table. Clay and I followed Sasha and Willow. Heads turned as Willow sashayed by.

On the dance floor, Clay said, "My, my, that woman . . ."

I waited while he searched for a description.

"Walk," he said. "She sure can walk."

"Sex on the prowl," I agreed, but I was thinking of food and watching a masked waiter place something on our table. Beyond booze, my one true love is food, and so far we'd just played at dining.

When the music ended and we went back to the table, the world had been revolutionized and even I forgot about eating.

CHAPTER 24

All hell broke out. There was a moment of shocked silence, followed by a collective gasp, then an eruption of noise from guests babbling and even shouting over one another, arms flailing and hands raised. The excited voices drew attention from all around, attracting more people to our table. There were lots of questions but no answers.

Martin Faust could deny the existence of a black orchid no longer. There was a fresh new orchid among the white ones. This one was totally black.

People were jostling us, shoving and pushing, to try and see what was on the table. The entrance to our tent turned into a bottleneck. Hands shoved me from behind, and elbows dug into me. There was no way to escape. The edge of the table was cutting into my thighs. Desperate to keep my dignity, I held the bodice of my dress tight against my chest to prevent it from being ripped off in the melee. The cloying scents of dozens of perfumes were increased by the heat of the packed bodies. I started to sneeze.

Across the table I saw Ethan. He'd frozen in the act of pulling out Liz's chair. Pale and shaken, he looked like he was having a stroke. He was going down, except bodies were packed so tightly around him there was nowhere to fall. And then I saw Liz's face.

She was watching Ethan. I couldn't read her expression. Delight or horror? Her eyes left him and swept the table, checking the reactions of the other guests. Her eyes reached me, saw my face turned to her and smiled. Delight, that's what I was seeing. She was enjoying watching the emotions the orchid was causing. Her eyes went on by me, assessing the others. I did the same.

Richard Dystra displayed the least passion, while Nina's face was flushed with an emotion I could only describe as lust, desire and ecstasy to the point of orgasm.

Erin Faust was pressed up against me in the crush. "It should have been mine," she growled through clenched teeth. Her face full of rage and resentment, she pushed roughly past me, trying to get closer to the orchid.

I leaned toward her and whispered, "Looks like you were wrong."

She pulled her stare away from the orchid and looked up at me. "Wrong?"

"You were mistaken when you said no one would drop by our table."

It took her a moment. Her eyes changed, meaner now.

I said, "Martin won't be lonely after all."

"Did you do this?"

"God, no."

She studied me with her hard stare, judging me. Finding me wanting, she turned back to gaze with naked longing at the flower, dismissing me from her sphere of interest.

Behind me, a woman elbowed her way into the scrum like a linebacker, fighting her way closer to the table. When she burrowed past me, I tugged on her sleeve. She paused and looked up.

I said, "Has anyone checked to see if it's plastic?"

She gave a startled squawk.

"Well, it might be. Now that would be a neat trick." I was grinning like a fool, but on her face there was only alarm. I half expected her to launch herself onto the table and squat there, examining it to see if it was natural or man-made.

Clay took hold of my wrist, dragging me away.

"What's the matter?" I yelled to him over the racket. "Aren't you interested in the latest news in horticulture?"

"You'll get trampled in the crush." He cleared a path for us away from the table, and we fought our way out of the marquee onto the dance floor. "That's a lot of fuss for a flower," he said.

Free of the squash of bodies, we turned back to watch in disbelief as flocks of diners flew by us from the other dining tent, fighting to get close to the latest wonder in the plant world. Things were out of control. Someone could get seriously injured in that mob. A magical evening had just morphed into the state of the bizarre.

Clay said, "Are all of these people crazy?"

I shook my forefinger at Clay. "You and your obsession to be rich. Let this be a lesson to you. No matter how much you do have, there's always something you can't have." It was a discussion we'd had often lately. I eased my dress back onto my shoulder and smoothed the silk over my hips. "Just look around you. I thought we were going to get stomped to death."

"How do you suppose it got there?"

"My guess is a waiter." And then, after a beat, I added, "Or waitress. They all look alike . . . all wearing the same black masks. They'd just have to come out of the kitchen with a covered dish and put the stem in among the others. No one would pay any attention to what they were doing."

"Maybe we know what the detail was that brought Ethan

here this afternoon. He probably brought it over and paid one of the waiters to sneak it onto the table when everyone stood up to dance." Clay looked around. "But which waiter?"

"Ah, now that's the question. Whoever actually put it on the table was well paid and is going to keep their mouth shut." I worried it around. "But I don't think it was Ethan who paid them. I caught Ethan's face when he saw it. I would swear it came as a complete and total surprise to him. Of the faces around the table, Ethan's was the most shocked."

"So who?"

"Only Liz took it in stride."

"Doesn't mean she knew anything about it."

"You two were having quite a talk."

"About my dad. She served on ranchers' organizations with him." Clay still watched the table. "My next question is, why would anyone do it?"

I considered the matter. "To shake someone up, or maybe to tell potential buyers there is still a product to be sold?"

"The problem is, everyone at our table wants the flower for themselves. They wouldn't want to sell it."

I studied the crowd around the table. "You're right. No one there is desperate enough for money to let go of something unique. Except us."

"Jesus," Clay said, "I hope they don't think we did it."

"I'm afraid that's exactly what will happen."

I felt Clay's hand tighten on my arm. I looked at him. "What?"

I could barely hear his whispered words. "If one of them killed Ben Bricklin for that orchid, maybe he or she just wanted to brag, just wanted everyone to see they had it without having to answer questions about how they got it. Maybe we're dining with a murderer."

"Or a murderess. Don't underestimate those women." I glanced around to see if anyone was close enough to hear, but we had slowly edged away from the stream of gawkers at the far end of the dance floor and were next to the band, on our own. "You're right. If you couldn't show anyone or brag that you had a black orchid, half the fun would be gone." But there might be another reason. A little idea was stirring in my brain.

When we got back to the table, one of Ethan's fellow directors was there, shaking his hand. "This is the best thing that ever happened to us. I hope you and Nina can come up with another event like this." He patted Ethan on the arm. Like everyone else crowded around the table, he believed Ethan was responsible for the black orchid appearing.

But Ethan's face didn't look smug or pleased the way it would have if he had pulled off this huge surprise. Instead, it showed distress . . . maybe anger and a little panic as well—confusing and dangerous emotions.

The madness had delayed dinner. People still stood around our table, blocking the entrance and refusing to move so that the waiters could serve the main course. When we were at last able to be seated, everyone at our table sat and stared at the black orchid. No one spoke. It was as if they'd used up all their energy and were totally drained.

"Can it be used to propagate more like it?" I asked.

My question was met with incredulous looks; it was Dr. Faust who set me straight. "There are no roots, no back bulbs, no keiki, no seeds . . . there aren't even leaves. How would you suggest it be propagated?"

The others at the table stared at me as though I might actually have an answer.

CHAPTER 25

I was hungry enough to eat the flowers, no matter how much the black one was supposedly worth, and finally the waiters came along carrying large silver platters.

I tasted the lobster ravioli in a cream sauce delicately. It set me purring. The food and the wine were every bit as wonderful as Ethan had promised, but I was the only one at the table who was hungry. The excitement had taken away their appetites. Probably my healthy appetite was a sign of my plebian origins, but I wasn't letting a drop of this nectar go to waste. "I need this recipe for the Sunset. Do you think we can sneak into the kitchen and ask for it?" I dipped my finger in a drop of sauce left on the plate. "I think there's nutmeg in it." I stopped short of licking the plate, even though I wanted to. "Aren't you going to eat that?" I asked, pointing at Clay's plate. He shook his head. I exchanged my empty plate for Clay's.

Almost everyone else at the table sent back their plates untouched. Not mine. After the lobster, I ate Clay's tiramisu and gelato.

Before the bidding on the auction items began, the director of the gardens took over the microphone to make an announcement. She called Ethan up to join her and then announced that he had made a million-dollar donation to the gardens in memory of his brother, Ben Bricklin. The money would be used to build a new laboratory to propagate orchids.

Everyone at our table stood and clapped along with the rest of the partygoers. But not everyone was excited by the news. Martin said, "You notice it will be called the Bricklin building." He wasn't even trying to keep his voice down. "Not the Ben Bricklin building, but the Bricklin building."

"What are you getting at, Martin?" I asked.

"Trust me, by the time it opens, it will be the Ethan Bricklin building."

"Is that so bad?"

"Yes." Martin's statement was flat and final.

The wild evening rocketed over the top. What goes beyond crazy? Whatever it is, that's what ensued. The noise was incredible. A mob of well-dressed revelers, jacked up by champagne, an incredible flower and now a million dollars, made a noise that had me covering my ears. It was hard to get people to settle down for the auction, but when they did, they started bidding like they were using play money.

When the auction was over, Clay led me back onto the dance floor, but we didn't really dance. We just clung together, swaying back and forth and letting the surge of dancers flow around us.

Clay said, "Are you through showing off your stuff?"

"What stuff would that be?"

He checked out my cleavage and then turned me slightly to peek behind me. "All the bits on display."

"Oh, that stuff. So, do you think maybe it's not just my easy-going disposition that all the boys like?"

His eyes crinkled in a smile. "Maybe."

Suddenly I saw how bone-weary he was. Why hadn't I realized it? He'd been putting in eighteen-hour days, and here I was, expecting him to dance all night. "Have you had enough fun for one evening?" I stroked his cheek. "Ready to check out?"

He looked around the room. "I think we should, before the cannibals really take over."

We went to say good night to Ethan. "Take the limo," he said. "I have the Caddy and I'm staying in town tonight."

Waiting for the car; I asked Clay, "Do you think Ethan and Liz are getting together?"

"Nope. She hates Ethan."

"I didn't get that impression," I said.

"I saw her watching you and Ethan dancing. The look on her face . . . well, if you can describe hate as pure, that's what it was. Pure hatred."

There could have been another target for her malice. Maybe Clay had made a mistake and it had been directed at me, but why would she hate me? Jealousy? If she was interested in Ethan and a younger woman cut in . . . I trembled in the night air and remembered her whispered words. *The black swan always dies.* It hadn't made any sense, but I'd met enough crazy people in my lifetime to know what was possible.

I hadn't told Clay about Liz's comment and didn't tell him now. He'd say I was paranoid, but I was going to stay well clear of Elizabeth Aiken.

The limo pulled up in front of us. I clung to Clay and whispered, "Now comes my favorite part of the evening."

Clay didn't wait for the chauffeur to get out and open the door. "What's that?" he said.

“Making out in the back seat with you.” I stepped into the car and slid across the seat to make room for Clay.

Clay stepped inside and his arm went around me, pulling me close. “Ah, and there’s that little mystery to be solved.”

CHAPTER 26

Sunday morning, Clay went out for croissants and the papers. Croissants, with Plant City strawberry jam that Marley had made, freshly squeezed orange juice and the papers—a perfect Sunday morning.

Clay took the front section and handed me the rest. I picked out the local news, and right there on the front page was a picture of the Orchid Ball. The photo had been taken just after the discovery of the black orchid. Everyone in the image was looking at the black orchid, except for one couple at the center back of the picture: Clay and I were smiling into each other's eyes. We looked mighty pleased with something. I just hoped none of the people at our table thought it was because we'd arranged for the blossom to end up there in the center of the table.

A few hours later, Cinderella was back behind the bar, checking the stock and loading up the beer wells, when Tully walked in. Dressed in jeans, a Stetson and his normal cowboy boots, he was the last of the wannabe cowboys. I started pouring his coffee before he even reached the bar.

"Well, how was the big evening?" he said as I set the mug in front of him.

"Like a night on a psych ward with everyone off their meds."

"Now that sounds like fun." He settled onto a stool in front of me and said, "Don't leave a thing out."

In the after-lunch lull I was working on paying bills when Clay stuck his head around the door of my office and asked, "Want to go on a little road trip?"

"To where?"

"I just figured since Ethan checked up on us, it's time we returned the favor. Let's go see this empire of his."

I grabbed my purse out of a drawer and shot my office chair backwards. "My vehicle or yours?"

It was a silly question. Clay hated my red pickup with a vengeance. It had belonged to Jimmy, my long-ago husband, and was one of the few things Clay and I fought over. The more he pushed me to sell it, the more determined I was to hold on to it. Really, I didn't know why I bothered except that it was the last thing I had of Jimmy—well, except for the tattoo on my ass that said, *Jimmy's*. I'd like to get rid of that bit of ink, and I'd get rid of the truck too, but I just didn't want anyone telling me to. Not Tully, not Marley and especially not Clay.

I went out through the kitchen to tell the staff that I was leaving for a couple of hours and then ran down the stairs to where Clay was waiting.

Going down the highway, waves of heat rising in front of us and the guy I loved beside me, I felt as joyous as on the last day of school. I stuck my bare feet up on the dash and started singing along with the radio.

We went up the interstate to Bradenton and then headed east towards highway seventeen. The roads along the coast were insanely busy, but out here, a little bit inland, it didn't feel all that much different from when I was a kid. On the horizon, sunshine shimmered on metal. The metallic light grew bigger, becoming a vehicle before it whished by us, leaving us alone again.

Pretty soon Clay started singing along with Lyle and me. "She hates my momma, she hates my daddy too."

If you live in ranch-country Florida, you live under a blue dome that covers your world like a giant cake lid. You can see for miles towards the horizon, and the earth truly seems pancake-flat. The fields beside the road hardly have a hump higher than my ankle, defiantly flat, so I don't know where this strange idea that the world is round started. Some beliefs I'm just not willing to give up on.

We drove through acres of oranges trees and fields of long-horn cattle towards Poke County, in the Florida Highlands. It's a real pretty part of the state. I stared out the window, enjoying it all.

Pine Lake sits between Tampa and Orlando. The sign at the edge of town says three hundred and fifty-two souls reside there—not people, just their souls. The only building in the place that doesn't need painting and fixing is a giant white Baptist church, sitting on an acre of green irrigated grass at the center of town. A lot of money and care have gone into maintaining the church. Right away, you know Pine Lake is a place where religion plays a big part in daily life, so it's best to watch your tongue.

Other than its manicured house of worship, Pine Lake has nothing to recommend it. The weathered houses were built of concrete blocks and painted in faded pastels. On the edge of town there is a giant railcar-repair business, with a half dozen cars sitting idle on a siding, and some kind of an industrial plant with no name on it.

In a minute, the little place was gone. We drove on, past what seemed like miles of trees bordering the road. The line of trees was thin, just enough to hide the mining operation behind it. Big signs that marked the property on both sides of the road said, BRICKLIN MINES. The only thing to be seen of the mining itself were huge stacks of material with pipes for venting sticking out of them. Over a fence we saw the bucket of an enormous piece of equipment. You could pop Clay's Ford Explorer inside that big boy and there'd be room left for my truck.

Clay pulled over to the side of the road. "I knew they used big machines, but that's just awesome."

"You men. It's all about size. What's it for?"

"The earth with the phosphates in it is fifteen to fifty feet beneath the surface. The bucket strips the soil, and then they dig out the stuff they want. Then they have to clean the material they take out with water."

"How do you know so much about it?"

"I looked it up after you left for the Sunset this morning."

I stared out the window and asked, "How big do you think this mine is?"

"Ethan told me this facility is over four thousand acres, and it's about mined out."

I turned to look at Clay. "And he told you this because . . . ?"

"He's looking for new land to mine."

"I thought you were hunting warehouse space for him."

"That's what the man said the first time we met."

"And now?"

His mouth twitched. "Now he seems a little more interested

in raw land." He looked out his window and away from me.

"Does he want you to buy up land for phosphate mines?"

Elbow on the open window, his chin resting on his hand, he watched the dragline dip out of sight. "I'm not sure. He started out talking about warehouse space but ended up talking about ranchland down in Charlotte County. He wants to accumulate about thirty-five thousand acres."

The figure took my breath away. Now I knew why Clay was staying close to Ethan.

Clay glanced at me and then looked away and spoke to the steering wheel. "If they start mining the lower Peace basin, they'll draw water from the Peace River to wash the material from the mine." He rubbed his forehead. "It will be a big problem."

I studied him. "Remember the first time we canoed down the Peace?"

He looked at me and smiled. We'd both got eaten alive by fire ants when we pulled our canoe onto a bit of sand. We'd ended up jumping in the river, clothes and all, to drown the ants.

His mind was still on the future of the river. He said, "Phosphate mining takes a huge amount of water, about a hundred thousand gallons a minute."

"So that's a problem." I pushed the hair back from my face. "Can't they reuse the water, or just put it back in the river?"

"It's polluted with phosphates."

"There goes that watercourse."

Clay nodded. "The plan is, after it's used, the water will be dumped out into Charlotte Harbor, bypassing the river."

"And then there goes the harbor along with the fish." Suddenly this road trip wasn't as much fun as it had been when we set out. "Are you going to do it . . . find more land to mine?"

"It's a legal business. Seventy-five percent of the phosphates used for fertilizer sold in the US comes from Florida. It's a case of get on board or go home."

"It's always that way, isn't it? Sweet fruit with a pit and a worm inside."

"I can't stop it happening."

"Maybe we can if enough of us care."

Clay started the engine. "There's nothing more to see here." He put the vehicle in drive and pulled back onto the road.

"This isn't right, Clay."

"Are you an environmentalist now?"

"No, just an angry redneck. Why don't we get a say?"

We drove about a quarter of a mile before we had to stop for a train, loaded and heading north, carrying away more of Florida and leaving behind poisoned water and barren land.

"You know what the crazy part is?" Clay said.

I was counting railcars and didn't answer.

"When I looked it up online it said this area is called Bone Valley. The ground is full of prehistoric creatures like saber-toothed tigers and mastodons. That's what they are mining."

"Great. Maybe next they can mine human graveyards."

The last car clattered by, and Clay said, "Let's head back to Ona. Ethan is looking at property there. Apparently, Ona is on a large deposit of phosphates."

We drove past mile-wide fields stripped of trees and planted with vegetables, past raised beds of strawberries growing in what looked like long black bags, past fields crowded with bent-over workers wearing broad straw hats. Everywhere you looked, irrigation nozzles sprayed water six feet in the air.

"I've seen the enemy and he is us," I mumbled.

"What?"

"Pogo was right. We're all responsible for this." I waved at the fields with their long lines of thick green plants. "This is what it takes to feed people, phosphates and water."

We drove past Bartow and the wet boggy area that was the beginning of the mighty Peace, past Mexican food stores and a crazy falling-down place, made up of advertising signs, with tables full of knickknacks for sale, a sort of permanent garage sale. I stared out the window at the New & Used sign on the tumble-down structure, a true symbol of my Florida where everything was for sale.

"You know what's bugging me?" I said.

"You might just as well ask me about the secrets of the universe as to figure out what goes on in your head. I couldn't begin to guess."

"Why you? There are plenty of big real-estate companies; why would Ethan ask you to buy up land for him?"

"Because I'm small-time and no one will suspect that I'm working for Bricklin Mines. If they did, the price would go up. I wouldn't be surprised if Ethan didn't have a dozen agents out there buying land for him; cheaper that way."

"It makes sense, but wouldn't you think he'd have someone else oversee the buying of land? Another layer of secrecy between him and the deal."

Clay tilted his head to the side, thinking about it. "He's all about control and he's accustomed to being in charge. Plus, I get the distinct impression he doesn't trust too many people. He'll want to make sure he's not getting ripped off."

"Do you really want to be part of this?"

Something in my voice made him glance quickly at me and

then back at the road. He said, "I'm tired of being scared of losing everything. The real-estate market isn't ever going to be what it was. I can't secure our future one house at a time, and the Sunset barely pays you a living wage. This may be my only opportunity for that one big hit, to get out from under, and I'm not going to miss it."

I still felt Ethan had an agenda, one to do with his brother's death, although these days I thought everything had something to do with that night in the swamp. I kept those thoughts to myself. No need to give Clay more reason to think I needed therapy. "Well, Ethan's a smart man, and he'd only hire the best," I said. "He's got that in you."

He grinned at me and said, "My little cheerleader." Even though Clay was opposed to the idea of mining in Florida, he'd still buy the land for Ethan. He said it was for our future, but the truth was that Clay had long ago decided he wasn't ever going to be poor. These last few years of the recession had only deepened that conviction, made him more resolved to be one of the haves instead of the have-nots. And like he said, if he didn't do it, someone else would. But Bricklin Mines wasn't in any of my dreams for our future.

CHAPTER 27

It was two days later and the end of the luncheon trade was heading out the door when Willow walked into the Sunset. A communal gasp of pleasure rose from the drinkers still at the bar, a shared sigh of helpless adoration. You gotta love a woman who brings out the worst in men.

She was partially dressed, wearing impossibly high heels and miniscule white shorts below a halter top, an ensemble designed to rip the heart out of the weak. She gave me a little wave and a smile and slinked towards me in a long-legged-model walk that had the guys struggling for air. She dropped a giant leather shoulder bag on the counter and breathed, "Hello."

"Good god, woman, the air conditioning is on. You're going to catch your death."

She laughed and lifted one nearly bare cheek onto a bar stool. The regulars were going to be fighting over that seat when she left. "How come no one ever says you're going to catch your life?" she said.

I tilted my head and thought about it before throwing my hands up in defeat. "Too deep for me. But I do know if you plan on hanging out in the Sunset the natives are going to have to hike their blood-pressure medication. You can cause a lot of damage with shorts like those." Her pupils told me she was already really high on something, but being a good bartender, I still asked, "What are you drinking?" She had a daiquiri and began charming the other patrons.

Between my serving people we chatted, as girls will, having a bit of a laugh. The laughter ended when Sasha came into the bar searching for her. I was delivering a tray of drinks to a table so he didn't see me behind him, but I saw how cruelly his fingers dug into Willow's arm as he jerked her towards him and hissed something in her ear.

When I was back behind the bar, he ordered me towards him with a crook of his finger. He ordered a scotch, but first he asked me some rather pointed questions. I kept it simple, explaining I had no idea how that black orchid had ended up at the Selby ball. His eyes drilled into mine, looking for the lie as I denied any knowledge of it.

His questions took a new tack. "Were you ever out to Ben's nursery?"

I looked him straight in the eye and lied my ass off.

After he had considered my words, he gave a small jerk of his head. Either he was finally convinced I was as ignorant as I claimed, or he was willing to let it drop for the moment. He flicked a business card at me. "If you have an orchid to sell, call." He grabbed Willow by the arm. I saw her wince, her body slumping towards him and her hand going to his fingers before he yanked her off the stool. He strode from the bar with Willow stumbling after him in her stilettos, trying to keep up.

An hour after they left, I got a call from Willow. She couldn't talk, she said, but she wanted to meet me, needed to get together with me.

"I'm working; come here."

"That isn't a good idea. I need to meet you . . . somewhere we won't be found."

"Sorry, Willow, I can't."

"Please," she said.

"Willow, it's not happening. We're busy and I'm short-staffed."

"Please." The pleading resonance in her voice couldn't be created by anything but fear. "You're my last chance."

"Shit." I'd let too many people down in the past to try rescuing anyone again. I said, "I don't want to be anyone's last chance."

Silence stretched between us until she said softly, "Please, Sherri."

"Okay." It was a halfhearted and weak commitment. "Where?"

She told me about a bar, deep in ranch country, a half hour east of Jacaranda.

It was raining, bucketing down, when I pulled into the pot-holed parking lot and backed into the space closest to the exit. I wanted to be able to leave quickly if things went bad.

I stared out the window. All I could see were beat-up sedans and muscle trucks, none of which looked upscale enough for Willow. I wasn't overly concerned that Willow wasn't there. She wasn't what I'd describe as a socially responsible person, and I was guessing that punctuality wasn't something she concerned herself with. It was likely normal for Willow to be a half hour late or even change her mind and stand people up.

I huddled down in the truck, watching the potholes fill with rain. It was the last place I wanted to be. Sasha's glare was still fresh in my memory, and I was sure Willow's frightened state was linked to Sasha. He wasn't to be messed with, and that's exactly what I was doing if I helped Willow. But there was something in the way she'd said please that kept me there, staring through the wall of rain at the falling-down joint called Zizzler's.

Why had she picked this place? Carved out of scrub on a back road to nowhere, it was rough and decrepit. You almost had to be a local to know it existed, and it sure didn't match the face Willow showed the world.

Beside the passenger door a creaking sign swayed in the wind. Rain pounded on the roof. I worried about who might show up with Willow and decided that inside was a safer place to be than alone in the parking lot. I jumped over the rush of water running into the storm drain by the pickup and ran through the rain.

Outside the entrance to Zizzler's, three smokers with cigarettes clamped between their lips clustered under the overhang. They watched me run towards them. Their shoulders were lifted to their ears to keep out the rain and their hands were stuffed in their pockets. When I reached the heavy funk of nicotine and the carpet of butts outside the entrance, one of the men reached out and opened the battered door.

Inside, the place felt familiar, although I'd never been through the door before. It was recognizable only because I'd been in a million dumps just like it. It smelled of beer, grease and the musk of male sweat.

Over the bar hung a picture of Ronald Reagan, the color fading to pastel-grayness. The picture likely had been new with the building.

Optimistically, Zizzler's could be called a sports bar, although there wasn't an athlete in sight—unless lifting a glass had become an Olympic event. Televisions hung off of every wall so there was no possibility of a diner doing something crazy like starting a conversation. Conversation was not encouraged in a place like this.

As the door shut behind me, the bubba-brained peckerhead behind the bar turned to see who had come in. The face he turned to the door said, "Please, give me a reason to boot your sorry ass back out," but that quickly changed when he spied me. He had no plans to kick me out. No, ma'am. He planted both hands on the bar and bent forward. While his eyes crawled up and down my body, a reptilian tongue flicked over his dry lips.

Lust is an easy emotion to read. Like the tavern itself, he was all too familiar, the kind of guy I'd been evading and fighting off my whole life. I avoided meeting his eyes and checked out the rest of the place. There were two other men in the room. At the bar sat a guy wearing a yellowed button-down shirt, guaranteed wash and wear. His jowly hound-dog face lifted without hope at the sound of the door, and then he went back to studying the puddles of beer on the counter and rededicated himself to the serious business of drinking. The obese mess of a man sitting to the right of the tender was savagely attacking a plate of grease and barely noticed my arrival. There was no Willow, unless she was in the ladies' doing a line. I was pretty sure she was too smart a girl to go back there alone.

I walked across the sticky floor and slid into a booth that also wanted to hold on to me as I worked my ass along it. When I'd settled, I pulled the gummy laminated menu out from behind the ketchup bottle. Everything edible, and a few items that weren't, came encased in a batter guaranteed to leave an oily residue on everything it touched. I put the menu back and waited. Careful not to make eye contact with the barman, I fixed my gaze firmly on the parking lot.

Ignoring him didn't keep Bubba away from me. When I heard the access to the counter bang open, I swung to face him. He ambled out from behind the bar, his flabby breasts jiggling beneath a black tee shirt that advertised a bottle of beer in front of mountains. While he might be out of shape, there were still some serious muscles behind the fat. Lifting tanks of beer and tossing around tons of frozen food kept him in the game enough that I wouldn't think of wrestling him. My well-honed instincts told me that a certain kind of wrestling was just the type of pastime he had in mind. He strode towards me with his watery eyes focused on me like I was a piece of raw meat thrown to a starving carnivore.

"I'll wait to order until my friend comes," I said before he could ask.

He chewed on this for a moment. "How be I bring you a little drink on the house?"

"I'll wait." I tried to smile, hiding how much I wanted him gone.

He did something with his mouth, making it disappear and then reappear a couple of times in disapproval or annoyance. He wasn't happy with my answer.

My grandma's voice echoed in my head, saying, "You want to make friends with someone, don't fart in their face first." I tried out my drawl, always a winner with guys like this. "I surely do thank you for the offer, though." I tried to smile.

He chewed on this some before he nodded and ambled reluctantly away.

I stared out the window and waited. With each passing second my apprehension ratcheted up a turn. A new and terrifying thought had just hit me. What if Willow was setting me up? I knew nothing about her except that she was totally under

Sasha's control. She'd betray me in a heartbeat and toss me to the wolves if Sasha ordered her to. It was a distinct possibility that she'd brought me out here to the boonies because this was where Sasha wanted me.

I so didn't want to be here, not with these men and not with the man that might show up with Willow. So why was I hanging on? I owed her nothing, needed nothing from her. She was late. It would be her fault if I was gone when she came. Still, I waited.

The door opened and the smokers came trailing in one after another, each taking a good look at me to see what might be on offer. I looked away and fixed on the world outside the window as they passed my table. I heard whispers, could feel their eyes caressing me as they took their places at the counter.

I didn't like the situation. Just me and six bottom feeders I trusted even less than I did Willow.

Outside, the neon from a beer sign shone on a slick of wet pavement. I watched it wink off and on as I waited. Country music wailed from the speakers. The Dixie Chicks were singing "Goodbye Earl." When they got to the line that said Earl had to die, Bubba killed the music. In the silence, I turned my head to see what was happening. Bubba was hunched over the bar and staring at me, a hungry dog drooling over a steak.

That was it. "Goodbye Earl," I whispered and scrambled out of the booth.

"Hey," Bubba yelled, his arm flying up like he might reach out and stop me, but I ran out the door and splashed through the rain to the truck without looking back.

With the doors locked and the engine running, I still hesitated. I wouldn't have hung around another second except for that *please*.

She meant that . . . and Willow was never a girl who had to say please. But what if Sasha had been standing over her, making her beg me?

Clay was right: I had an overactive imagination. I turned on the radio, but the music was drowned out by the noise of the rain pounding on the roof. I switched it off and waited, my fingers tapping the steering wheel impatiently.

I didn't wait long. I may be slow but I do catch up in the end. The thought that sent me blasting out onto the highway was, it might not be Sasha who showed up. No way I wanted to be alone in a parking lot when some dude with Russian prison tats showed up looking for me.

Speeding down the road I wondered why it had taken me so long to get out of there. I blamed it on Ruth Ann. My mother's insistence that I put myself out for others was a real deterrent to my peaceful enjoyment of life.

The rain ended suddenly, a tap turning off on a typical Florida day. The bright sunshine had steam rising from the pavement in no time. When I hit Tamiami Trail just south of Venice, the first thing I noticed was a car dealership, Aiken Pontiac. I must have passed it hundreds of times, but the name never meant anything to me until now. The apron in front of the building was empty, and there was a For Sale sign out front. I wasn't the only one struggling in this economy, but then, maybe Liz was one of the lucky ones who bailed long before the crash.

CHAPTER 28

I was grateful to be back in the sanctuary of the Sunset, although my delight in being safe didn't last as long as happy hour. I kept watching the door, sure that Willow would sail into the bar, full of casual apologies. It didn't happen. The possibilities for what had kept Willow from meeting me had me as jumpy as a meth addict in withdrawal. The longer I went without word from her, the more worried I got. It didn't help that I couldn't figure out why she'd organized the whole thing.

Liz came through the glass doors just when the regulars were settling in for the drink that would take them home. She was dressed in a white linen pantsuit worth one of my mortgage payments, with an Hermès scarf tied casually around her throat. Closing her dealerships hadn't hit her too hard. No need to feel sorry for Liz.

She placed her quilted leather Chanel bag on the bar. "I've just left Clay," she announced, settling herself on a stool in front of me.

"Are you trying to poach my guy?"

"I would if I could, and that's the honest truth." She threw back her head and gave a raucous roar of laughter and then said, "No, honey, I realize only too well my days of stealing a man are over." She leaned forward and pointed a finger at me. "But there was a day I would have had you really worried."

She took a smokeless cigarette out of her bag and rolled it between her fingers. "No, it's practical matters I wanted to see Clay about. I want to sell Dancing Lady Island. That's why I came to see him." She clamped her teeth down on the metal cigarette and inhaled deeply. A thin stream of vapor dribbled through her half-open lips.

She was watching my face for a reaction. When she got it, she raised one eyebrow and nodded a yes.

Dollar signs danced in my head. How much was an island in the Gulf of Mexico worth, and what would Clay's commission be?

She reached over and dug a couple of olives out of the garnish tray. "He's down there right now, figuring out the asking price and a marketing plan. I thought I'd come up here and have a drink with you while I waited."

"The drink is on the house. Maybe I'll even stretch that to two if you're very good; it's time to celebrate."

While we waited for Clay we slashed the reputations of the people we'd dined with, cutting and tearing the evening to bits. Liz had known everyone at the table and wasn't above sharing their faults. "Nina Dystra is an acclaimed botanist. She's written two books on orchids," Liz told me.

"I didn't know that, but Ethan said she could write a book on fifty shades of young lovers."

"Oh, that too. Once, when we met at the Redlands show, she described how she liked to have them pierced." Liz grimaced and reached for another olive. "Even told me how much she paid them to go have these very private piercings. It was a staggering amount. Nina was quite proud of her generosity."

"Crazy comes in all sizes." I pushed the tray towards Liz. "I'm a little worried about Willow."

Liz sat perfectly still, an olive halfway to her mouth, and listened while I told her about Willow's call and the way it made me feel.

"You don't think it was just a moment's . . ." She shrugged, unable to finish the thought.

"There was real desperation there, maybe even fear."

"Jesus." She stared at her glass of wine, her mind going somewhere I couldn't follow.

I took a couple of orders and filled the bowls of nuts along the bar while Liz sat slumped over her folded hands, staring at nothing.

I went back to her and lightly touched her hand to get her attention. "Hey," I said. "I didn't mean to upset you."

She didn't look up. "My husband beat me." She concentrated on her hands.

I covered her hands with mine. "I'm sorry if I brought back bad memories. Ethan told me your husband abused you. I should have thought before I told you about Willow."

She pulled her hands away and picked up her glass. Her eyes rose over the rim to find mine. "Did Ethan tell you about my arrest for Kurt's murder?"

"Yup."

She sipped her wine and set the glass carefully back on the center of the coaster.

I picked up the bottle of Merlot. "I would have done the same. I'm glad you got off."

Her voice was strangely wistful as she said, "But it wasn't true."

My hand hesitated. Our eyes met over the tilted bottle.

"I didn't kill Kurt."

CHAPTER 29

I lowered the bottle and waited.

"Susan killed him."

I let out the breath I'd been holding.

"I'd left Kurt before but always went back to him. This time I wasn't going back. I couldn't. It was more than just my life now."

The hand she lifted to the scarf at her throat was trembling. It wavered there and then she lowered it to her other hand, clenching them together. "I was in the kitchen cutting up beef for a stew. Kurt found me there. I should have realized he'd know I'd run to Susan and Ben. I had before."

Her voice was heavy with pain and loss. I crossed my arms over my chest, ignoring the guy waving an empty glass farther along the bar.

"Kurt was a brutal man." Her teeth bit down on her lip. She drew in a deep breath and straightened. "A functioning alcoholic, he was out of control at home but never set a foot wrong outside of the house. People couldn't believe Kurt was beating me. I don't really think Ben and Susan understood how bad it was when I told them."

She raised her fist in front of her mouth to block more words . . . or perhaps a sob. It had happened years ago, but she wasn't free of the memory. I left her to recover and went to serve the people waiting down the counter.

When Paul Hanson slipped in behind the bar and signed onto the register, I went back to Liz. She'd finished the wine so I refilled her glass.

I thought Liz would have been ready for a change of subject, but it wasn't like that. In control of herself now, Liz began her story where she'd left off. "When Susan came into the kitchen and saw Kurt punching me, she just went crazy. You see, her father beat her mother. I guess she'd never been able to protect Hazel, but now she was a grown-up and she was going to save me. She picked up that carving knife and stabbed Kurt without ever saying a word, no 'Stop' or 'Don't.'" Liz made stabbing motions with her fist. "She just picked up the knife and jabbed it into his back. I didn't even know she was there until he fell to the floor."

Liz's eyes were watching a screen of memories. "And then . . ." Her mouth worked. She couldn't finish.

I poured myself a glass of the Merlot and waited.

"Susan knew I was pregnant, understood that I was miscarrying before I did. It was Susan who called the ambulance."

Gently, not wanting to close her down completely, but not wanting to have her dredge up the horror again, I said, "Let it go. It's over."

She pounded her clenched fist on the mahogany. "Never." Along the bar, faces turned our way. Liz didn't care. "That's what people don't understand." Rigid with emotion, she hissed, "It will never be over as long as I live."

I frowned at the drinkers who were eavesdropping. For Liz, we might just as well have been alone.

She said, "I miscarried, right on the kitchen floor beside my dead husband, my blood mixing with his and our baby's on the linoleum. By the time the police arrived, it looked like a slaughter-house in there."

I had no words to make it better. She was beyond comforting remarks.

"Waiting for the ambulance to come, I made a decision. Sue had a young daughter, and I had brought this trouble to her family. I wrapped my hands around the handle of the knife to cover her fingerprints, and when the cops came I told them that I killed Kurt. Susan didn't want me to do it, but I made her promise to keep our secret."

She scrubbed at her face with her hands, smearing her mascara but wiping away the past, putting it back in its box, done with it for now. "I don't know why I told you that, except that it no longer matters now that everyone is dead. I've kept it to myself all these years. Not even Ben knew the truth." She thought about it for a brief moment and then corrected herself. "Unless Susan told him, but if she did, he never mentioned it to me."

"It was my telling you about Willow—sympathy, that's what brought your story out."

"Perhaps." But her face said it wasn't true. Something was happening with Liz that I didn't quite understand. She asked, "Do you think there's anything we can do for Willow?"

"Nope." The truth was, I didn't want to do anything, didn't want to risk anything I hadn't already. I changed the subject. "Why Clay? Why did you choose Clay to sell your property?"

She started to smile, and I could see a joke coming. I waved it away. "Oh, I know all about his physical assets. That's why I chose him, but why did you?"

"Dystra. Clay could have kept his mouth shut and walked away from that fiasco with a fistful of money. Instead, he went to bat for his client. Honest people are hard to find these days. I want one on my side for a change."

Down the bar Paul was run off his feet, but I stayed right where I was. "Clay is honest," I agreed, "but . . ." I bit down on my lip.

"What?" Liz said. Her eyes were locked on my face.

"I wish he'd just be happy selling one house at a time and not look for that one big deal."

"You're worried about his connection to Ethan, aren't you?"

Her insight was startling. I started to brush her words aside, but this wasn't a woman to bullshit. I just nodded and changed the subject. "Were Ben and Ethan close?"

"God, no. They didn't even get along as kids."

The register pinged with a bar order to be filled, but I ignored it. "Ben called everyone at our table for the ball about the orchid, didn't he? They were all potential customers."

"Nope. He didn't tell Nina he had the orchid. He only told Faust and, of course, Sasha and me."

"Why not Ethan? Surely he'd tell his own brother."

"They haven't talked in years."

"Why?"

She shrugged. "Family stuff. Ben thought Ethan cheated him out of his share of the ranch, and he hated the family homestead being turned into a phosphate mine." She smiled. "Ben and Susan even stood out on the road picketing the Bricklin Mines. Not a good way to promote brotherly love."

Clay came in. He hesitated. He glanced from Liz to me, knowing something was going on.

I smiled at him and started filling the dining room order, while he continued towards us and took the stool next to Liz. He laid some papers in front of her. "I've got some comps for you to look at, although there isn't anything close to Dancing Lady Island."

"Good." Liz smiled at him and he returned it.

I could see him relax. Whatever the situation was between Liz and me, he knew it wasn't going to harm his business. At the moment, that was the only thing that mattered to him.

It was a busy night, but as I drew pints and mixed drinks I waited for Willow to call or come in, still sure I'd hear from her.

Clay and Liz had dinner at one of the small tables in the bar. Liz never looked up from the papers on the table in front of her, just ate dinner and left with no more than a hand raised in goodbye. Sometimes people regret the things wine makes them confess, or maybe she was just over her brief rehash of her history. Liz was tough. She hadn't survived all she'd been hit with by giving in to grief.

Clay walked Liz to her car, and when he came back, he wore a big grin, the kid who'd guessed the correct number of jellybeans in the jar.

I couldn't share his pleasure in his good fortune at getting this commission. I could only see that kitchen—and the blood.

"We've been invited out to Dancing Lady Island," he said and slid onto a stool.

"I don't like this, Clay."

"Why?" I could see he genuinely had no idea what was bothering me.

"I don't like being involved with these orchid collectors. I want us to keep our distance from them."

"This is about real estate, not orchids."

"Maybe, but there're just too many people circling around me like sharks; I want them all gone."

"That's silly. Why can't you just see this as something good coming out of something bad?"

"It's just that as long as you're doing business with Ethan, that mess in the swamp isn't over. I want out of it, Clay. These people will destroy us without a second thought."

He brushed the back of his fingers across my cheek. "Don't worry."

"That's all I do with you hanging out with Ethan."

He sighed. "Look, you were the one who didn't want to go to the cops. When you made that decision, it was over, end of story."

"Ethan wants to know what happened and he'll keep digging."

"You're overreacting. I understand. With the things that have happened to you in the past, you're bound to be jumpy but—"

I interrupted him. "Or maybe I've just developed very good survival instincts, better than yours."

He slid off the stool. "I'm meeting Liz tomorrow at her lawyer's with the contract. And this weekend we're going to the island, so pack your bikini and bring your tennis racket. She has a court."

"Whoopie."

His face hardened. "I'm going down to work on those contracts. Don't wait up." Not hanging around for an answer, he headed for the door. Clay could smell money and he'd fallen under the spell of its perfume.

Willow never did show up.

CHAPTER 30

Liz's story ate at me while I pulled pints and delivered drinks. Over the last few years I'd heard dozens of similar stories about women being beaten. Most of those women went running to friends for safety just as Liz had. But what if you didn't have friends to take you in? Willow might be just such a woman. Doing nothing seemed wrong.

Slowly the night wore down and all the tourists paid their bills and left. Despite my vow not to get involved in someone else's life, about eleven o'clock I went into the office and dug out the card Sasha had given me. I dialed the number.

"Sherri," he sang, all cheerfulness and light, the nasty side I'd glimpsed at the Sunset well hidden. "I'm so glad you called. Have you got something wonderful for me?"

"Ah, that would be a certain flower, wouldn't it?" I sat down and pulled my chair up to my battered desk. "Well, I'm sorry to disappoint you. I wish I had the orchid—I could use the money—but I'm just calling you because I don't have Willow's number."

"Why do you want her?" His happy voice had turned to one of suspicion and distrust.

"Shopping. That girl has taste, and I could use a little of that."

"I'm sorry, but Willow isn't available." He was no longer glad I'd called.

"Oh, I'm disappointed, but let me have her number, and we can find a time to get together. I'm willing to hold off on the shopping spree until she's free."

"That won't be for some time."

"Why?"

"You're a very pushy woman, aren't you?"

"I've been called worse. Look, Sasha, I need to know that Willow is all right. I talked to her earlier today. She was supposed to meet me. I just want to speak to her for a minute. You can listen in if you like."

He sighed. "Willow isn't available because I put her in rehab in Tampa. Her little habit was getting out of control."

"You put her in rehab?" It was like he'd put his dog in a kennel.

"We've been through this before. This time, when she's clean, I'm done."

"For real?"

"Maybe."

"What's the name of the rehab place?"

"Why?"

I laughed. "I may have need of one myself. It's been suggested I may be drinking a little too much."

"Was there anything else you wanted?"

"Why Tampa? I thought you two lived in Miami."

He said, "Mind your own business" and hung up. Another person I wasn't going to get a Christmas card from.

I leaned back and thought about it. How do you find a woman you know only as Willow, in an unknown facility in a city the size of Tampa? And, my doubtful mind added, I only had Sasha's word for it that she was in Tampa. She could be anywhere. Besides, even if I found the right place, they wouldn't give out information on one of their clients. I did the only sensible thing: I got someone else to look for her. It took a little pleading, a little telling Styles how dangerous Sasha was, and then I outright lied and told him she'd been kidnapped from Jacaranda, from his territory. He didn't believe me, but our history was on my side. In the past, his not believing me had brought down a load of trouble on his head. He never knew when I was lying, so the little worry that I might be telling the truth brought him around.

It really didn't take him long at all. What a clever man he is. He called the next morning while I was on my way to the Sunset.

"Wilma McKenzie, AKA Willow, is in the Harbor House Rehabilitation Center in Tampa."

"Well, shut my mouth."

"I wish I could. Is there anything else?"

"Not at the moment."

He hung up without saying goodbye. I didn't get a chance to tell him I was going out to a barrier island, a place I was reluctant to go, with someone I didn't trust. Later, I wished I had.

I was fighting a cold, with a head that felt double its normal size and teeth that ached. I would have stayed home if I could have found someone to take over the bar for the first shift. Instead, there I was, watching a guy two stools away pull out his phone, holding it way out in front of him to make out what it said because he was too proud to put his cheaters on, and wishing I was dead.

Ethan came in and interrupted my study of stupidity. Sad and morose, he acted as if something had been taken away, as if someone had blown out a little flame. Maybe he was regretting giving away a million bucks. Giver's remorse. Perhaps that's what he was suffering from; I would be. Or maybe he realized he'd never know the true story of his brother's death.

I don't know if I was trying to cheer him up or just making trouble when I said, "Liz was here yesterday."

There was no sign of interest on his face.

Blame it on the head cold, but I didn't let it go. "She said you and Ben didn't talk much."

"Nope." Now he really looked sad. "I wish I had a chance to make up for a lot of things. Don't leave things too long, Sherri, or you may never get a chance to put them right."

"A lifetime wouldn't be enough time to make up for my mistakes." I dropped a couple of cold tablets into my hand and poured a glass of water. "Did you know Liz might be selling Dancing Lady Island?"

"No."

"We're going there this weekend. Clay may have the listing. Are you in the market for an island?"

"Why do you ask?"

"Because you're the only truly rich person I've ever met. Maybe Clay will share his commission if I find a buyer."

"My experience with women tells me you'll get your half even if he doesn't share his earnings."

"Nice to see you have faith in the female sex."

"Have you been to the island before?"

"Oh, yeah."

It was an island I'd spent time on as a kid. Tully used to take Marley and me out there to play pirates and shipwreck when it was his turn to play parent. He'd drop us there and then anchor a few hundred yards offshore to fish. It had been a magical time and place. Later, when I was a teenager, I went there with Jimmy to swim and make love under the stars.

Uninhabited, it was an island I'd always thought of as belonging to all of us. One day, one of our last times together as a couple, Jimmy and I went out there to try and retrieve a little of the magic. We were shocked to be faced with a big sign saying, PRIVATE PROPERTY—NO TRESPASSING. It was a pretty good description of how things were between Jimmy and I, a symbol of our dead marriage. Two things I'd never thought would happen came together that day: I'd never thought Jimmy and I would ever break up, and I'd never thought that island would be lost to us.

That night I was up front working as hostess because it was Gwen's night off. Nina Dystra walked in. I hoped she was there to have dinner and not for anything to do with orchids.

After brief and insincere pleasantries, she said, "May I talk to you?" and walked away, sure that I would follow her. I got someone to cover for me and went outside, where she had lit a cigarette and was dragging furiously on it, like she was about to inhale the whole thing right down to the glowing tip.

"Have you found it?"

She didn't have to tell me what she was talking about. I let out a big sigh, annoyed and impatient. It had already been a long day, and a stuffed head wasn't soothing my intolerance for idiots. "That's the same thing everyone asks me. One more time: I never heard of this orchid until Ethan walked into my bar. He explained about the orchid and told me about his brother Ben being dead." That's when I remembered Liz had said Ben didn't get in touch with Nina. "How did you find out about the black orchid anyway?"

Her eyes narrowed calculatingly as she considered me. "I went over to see Ben about Christmas." She threw the butt over the railing. "Ben had a guy working there from some place in El Salvador. That guy had smuggled in some interesting plant material in the past. I'd bought a small . . ." She thought better of revealing more. "I wanted to see if anything new had shown up." She opened her purse and dug out a fresh cigarette. "I got the strong feeling there was something more, because Ben had this animation about him. He was onto something good. I could feel it." She lit the cigarette before going on. "That's when I met Tito." Her tongue flicked out over her lips, a cat licking cream. "He was a little treasure in more ways than one."

Nasty. I edged away.

"I paid Tito to watch Ben and find out what he had, but then one afternoon over in Homestead, Ben accidently saw us coming out of a motel. He was furious with me." Her eyes opened wide. "Said he'd never sell me so much as a blade of grass, said I was dead in his eyes. Why was he so angry? Tito was nearly eighteen." She looked genuinely confused and hurt.

"But you found out about the black orchid anyway?"

"Tito heard Ben talking to someone on the phone. I couldn't believe he had a black orchid, but I gave Tito ten thousand dollars to find it. I told him I'd give him another ten thousand dollars when he delivered it. I never saw him again."

A couple in their thirties climbed the stairs. "Good evening," I said as they went by us. When the door had closed behind them, I said, "But that wasn't the last time you spoke to Tito, was it?"

She shook her head. "Tito called late the night Ben's nursery burned down. He was in trouble and wanted me to help."

"And?"

"And what? Tito said he didn't know where the orchid was. He was no use to me anymore."

"So you never spoke to him again?"

"Boys are a dime a dozen. I didn't have anything to do with Ben's death, and I didn't want the cops or anyone else looking in my direction."

"And that's all you know about Ben and his precious plant?"

"Except Sasha was there just days before Ben's death. They had a big argument and Ben told him to get out. I called Sasha after Ben died, but Sasha said he didn't have Ben's orchid."

"Do you believe him?"

"I don't believe anyone, not even you."

The bitch not only insulted me, she didn't even stay for dinner.

I went back to seating guests, smiling and handing out menus, while my brain worried the question of why all of the people from the ball were showing up at the Sunset and asking me questions. It was Erin Faust's call that set me straight.

After I told her I had nothing to sell, I asked, "Why come to me?"

"Our only chance of getting Ben's orchid is if you have it. The others won't sell it; they don't need the money. You haven't any money, so you'll sell it if you have it. That's why I'm calling. Please don't get rid of it until you talk to me."

So there it was. Everyone had come to the same conclusion. I was the weak link in the chain, the only one likely to do a little deal. And I'd given everyone at the dinner table a business card from the Sunset, convincing them I had something to sell besides food and booze. "If I trip over this orchid, how much are you willing to pay for it?"

I could almost hear her brain humming as she calculated sums and decided just how cheap I was. "I'm prepared to pay fifty thousand dollars if you can guarantee me it is the only one."

"Nina offered a hundred thousand."

"I'll match it."

"Is this a great country or what?"

"Have we got a deal?"

"I don't have that flower. You better talk to Ethan. It was his party and his black orchid."

She made a sound of disgust. "Ethan didn't stage that entertainment. Ethan wouldn't sell the black if he had it. The person who arranged that little show had all the big orchid buyers gathered in one room. They were showing off their product to find a buyer. Like I said, my only hope is if you have it."

"Then I guess you're screwed, aren't you?"

But the woman wasn't listening. She said, "I expected to hear from you before this. You haven't sold it already, have you?"

"Let me say it one more time. I haven't a clue when it comes to orchids." I reached out to Ethan's orchid, now sitting on the podium in the foyer. "I only have one orchid, and I only have that one because Ethan gave it to me."

She made a clicking noise. "Playing dumb might have fooled Martin, but you don't fool me. Here's my cell number." She rattled off a number, but I didn't waste time writing it down. "Get back to me and not Martin. He doesn't need to be involved."

The dining room had pretty well cleared out when Clay came in. His eyes were shining. "I just optioned my first piece of property for Ethan."

"Nice," I said. "Try the seafood lasagna for dinner. I want to know what you think about it. I feel it's a little bland, but Miguel says it's perfect."

He wrapped his arms around me and pulled me in close. "You are real impressed with my abilities, aren't you?"

"Some of them." I leaned back in his arms. "I'm just not excited about the people you're working for."

He released me. He wasn't smiling or looking enthused anymore. "I'll eat in the bar."

At the door he turned back and said, "I'll try the seafood."

How could I make Clay understand that what he saw as an opportunity I saw as a big deep well we were about to get lost in?

CHAPTER 31

The day before our trip to Dancing Lady Island, I went into the office to get the mask Ethan had given me. I wanted to have it framed in a shadow box to put behind the bar. The Sunset was slowly turning into a repository for bits of my life and was barely still on the side of tasteful, but there was room for one more treasure, especially one as beautiful as the black swan.

As my hand stroked the black feathers of the mask into place, I saw a small package on my desk. I set the mask down, took scissors from a cracked mug and cut across the top of the bubble wrap.

Inside was a pink flip-flop. No message, just the colorful rubber footwear with a red hibiscus on the instep. The shoe dropped to the desk as I sank down onto my chair and stared at it. What the hell did it mean?

Tully came in without knocking and I jerked back in startled fear, shooting the chair into the walnut bookcases behind me.

"What?" he said and stopped.

I was unable to answer.

He walked towards me. "What's happened?"

I swallowed and pointed at the thing on my desk. "I was wearing that when I went to the gas bar."

He reached for the flip-flop, turning it over in his hands. "What's it doing here?"

I shook my head.

"You must have some idea how it got here. Did it just appear on your desk?"

I pointed to the empty envelope. "It came in the mail."

He picked it up and looked at the postage stamp before he squeezed the envelope open and stared inside. Then he went to the door, glancing up and down the hall before closing it firmly. He came back to the desk. "Is it a threat?"

"Maybe. I lost one at the gas bar, but I don't remember what happened to the other. It doesn't matter. They know I was there. It was sent by someone who was also there that night."

He dragged his fingers through his hair. "Jesus, Sherri, what have you got yourself into?"

I gave a choked laugh. "You know how many times I've heard you say those words?" I followed this with "Don't tell Clay, will you?"

"Why?"

I couldn't really say why I didn't want Clay to know except that he was happy, excited about the future and our life together. I didn't want to screw things up for him. What was I thinking? I'd already done that.

Tully collapsed on the chair across from my desk. "He has to know. He has to be able to protect you."

The defiant part of me wanted to say I could look after myself, but it wasn't true. It's one thing to protect yourself from an enemy when you can identify them, but just who was I trying to protect myself from now? I tried to figure out why my flip-flop had been sent back to me. The only thing I could come up with was it was a ploy to make me do something. If I had the orchid, this definitely would make me get rid of it.

"Tell Clay," Tully said.

I made a face.

"And I'm following you home." He raised a hand to stop me from arguing, but I'd only been going to say, "Thanks."

Clay was already asleep when I got home. I didn't wake him.

My cold was still hanging on when I awoke to the sound of a lawn mower. Clay, determined to be the best little suburbanite ever, was mowing the sand that sprouted random blades of grass, but mostly weeds, in our backyard.

I checked the time. It was shortly after seven. I hadn't fallen asleep until just about four. Not quite enough sleep for me, but no way was I going to get more with that annoying racket. I headed for the shower.

The coffee was finished dripping when Clay came in, grass clippings clinging to his jeans and sweat plastering his white tee to his chest. It was already in the high seventies and almost a hundred percent humidity. It was going to be a scorcher.

His hair was rumpled and his face was flushed from beating back nature, almost cute enough to stop me from telling him a few home truths about how much I liked being wakened by a lawn mower.

He lounged against the counter and drank his coffee without comment while I expanded on the theme.

My anger ran down, and I refilled my coffee cup and went to stand beside him, staring out the window at the unfinished house behind us. Clay had mowed neatly to the edge of the tall jungle. Behind that, the concrete-block walls of the house had blackened with mold, and the bare plywood on the roof was discolored and lifting. The holes left in the blocks for windows stared back at me like unseeing eyes. The next builder who came along would probably knock the whole structure down and start over.

"I got a present in the mail yesterday," I said.

I turned my head to face Clay. He lifted his eyes to me and waited.

"Aren't you going to ask me what it was?"

Slumped against the counter, one hand on the granite and the other holding the mug, he lifted his shoulder and said, "You wouldn't have brought it up if you weren't going to tell me."

I've always figured conversation is a give-and-take kind of thing, but with Clay it was often a delivery of information from one person to another, and nothing more. He never felt it necessary to put in the extra morsel of chatter, the normal bits and pieces of everyday dialogue, so he just waited and listened until I dumped it all out there.

"Someone mailed one of my pink flip-flops back to me."

This time I got a reaction. He jolted to his feet, no longer detached. He stared at me and then looked out the window for a minute before turning back to me. "But you have no idea who sent it, right?"

"Of course I don't know who sent it." But that wasn't true. "Yes, I do." I set my mug in the sink. "The guy who killed Tito sent it."

"When did you get this package?"

"Yesterday."

"And you're only telling me now?"

I winced and folded my arms across my chest. "I was shocked, and I wanted to think about what it meant before I could talk about it. Besides, you were asleep when I got home."

"You . . ." I could see he was searching for a nonconfrontational way to say what was on his mind. "Well . . ." He smiled. "You have a pretty active imagination."

"What happened out in the Everglades wasn't my imagination."

"I know," he soothed. "I know you were scared and it's made you panicky and jumpy."

"Only a fool wouldn't be nervous, given the circumstances." I took a deep breath and forced myself to speak calmly, to bring my voice back in the register where humans and not just dogs could hear it. "Doesn't the fact that someone sent me that shoe say something?"

His thumbs rubbed back and forth on the smooth surface of his coffee mug as he stared straight ahead at the skeleton of a house.

"What?" I asked.

He shrugged.

And then it hit me. "You think I sent that thing to myself?"

He turned to me. "I think you're angry because you believe I don't take this as seriously as you'd like me to. You'd like some proof that it isn't over, that someone out there is watching you and waiting to pounce . . . something real to account for the way you feel."

"That's just crazy." Which was exactly his point. I sucked in air, struggling for calm. But how do you prove you aren't crazy? "Clay, listen to me. I did not put that thing in the mail. Someone else did."

"Why would anyone do that?"

"I don't know, but it proves it isn't over."

"Ahh," he said and nodded as if I'd just confirmed what he was saying. "When you decided not to tell anyone about Tito stealing your truck, it was over. That was your choice. And that put an end to it. Don't keep trying to show there's still something going on."

He really believed I'd put that flip-flop in the mail. I was so shocked I couldn't look at him, couldn't tell him he was full of shit. Big tears began to run down my cheeks and drip off my chin.

"Come here." He tried to turn me around to face him, but I went rigid.

I put my hands on his chest and shoved him away. "I'm not lying to you." I wiped away my tears with the flat of my hand.

"Okay. Call Styles and tell him everything. Turn it over to him, like you should have done weeks ago."

While Clay went to shower, I called Styles. I got a message that he was out of the office until Friday. I was given a number to call if it was an emergency. This was Thursday, and we were off to spend the night on Dancing Lady Island, so Friday was the perfect time to talk to Styles. Besides, it let me put off a nasty task a bit longer. Avoiding difficult things has always worked for me.

CHAPTER 32

We were leaving for Liz's after lunch, so I headed into the Sunset to make sure everything was in order. It wasn't. I called two suppliers and let them know exactly how unhappy I was with their delivery system, and then, feeling mean enough to chew horseshoes and spit tacks, I called a kitchen employee who was an hour late and told him not to bother showing up—ever.

I wasn't done with my very bad mood or the orchid party yet. I was stocking the bar when Martin Faust came in. He stopped just inside the door and looked around with a slight curl of contempt on his lip. My temper went into overdrive. The son of a bitch had the nerve to look down his nose at my bar, the best one on the Mangrove Coast—right there and then my patience ended.

When he got in front of me, I growled, "Doesn't matter what you want, I ain't got it. Get out."

He jerked back in astonishment. "What?"

"You heard me. I don't want you in my place—not you, not your wife, not any of your friends. My bar is off-limits to you."

Faust's stunned surprise nearly matched my own, but I'd already put up with enough shit for a lifetime.

His commitment to his quest was greater than my nastiness. He said, "I don't want a drink."

"That's good because you aren't getting one."

The guy sitting on a stool to my left, pretending not to listen, let out a snort of laughter. Faust didn't even blink. "I want the black orchid."

"I don't have it."

His eyes narrowed and he studied me.

"Beat it." I said it louder this time, in case he was deaf.

He didn't move. It seemed neither rudeness nor anger was new to him. He said, "I'll pay you well."

"Didn't you hear me?"

"Why were you at the Orchid Ball? You're the only one who would pull a stunt like that, putting the orchid on the table." He jabbed a finger in my direction. "It was you."

I turned away from him, went to the door of the kitchen and pushed it open. "Miguel, come here for a minute." I started to turn away but pivoted back to add, "And bring your attitude adjuster; there's a guy out here in need of it."

Martin Faust may have been a smart man, but he knew nothing about angry women fighting a head cold, bartenders or a Mexican chef who grew up in a really tough neighborhood.

Miguel came through the door with a meat cleaver in his hand, looked around the room and then at me. Miguel raised his eyebrows, asking a question.

I pointed at Faust. "Him."

"Oh," Faust said, bouncing on his toes with anxiety. "Oh," he said again before he scurried away like a rat fleeing a flooding ship.

"He wasn't much fun," Miguel said.

"Yeah, don't you hate it when people don't live up to their potential?"

Miguel grinned and went back to the kitchen while the three

locals at the bar, finishing their two-martini lunches, clapped and cheered. They had one more story to add to their Sherri chronicles. A girl can get a real bad reputation without even trying.

I dug in my purse for more aspirin.

I'd just unlocked the pickup when a voice behind me called, "Hi there."

I turned to see Ethan coming towards me. "Hi yourself."

"I was heading in for lunch, but it looks like I won't have anyone to talk to. It makes my day to lunch with you."

I smiled. "Sorry, today's the day we go out to Liz's island." I threw my purse onto the passenger seat.

"Ah," he said, nodding. "I forgot about that." He bent over a little, gazing up into my face and studying me. "You don't look too excited about it. Don't seem happy at all."

"Head cold." I slid behind the wheel. "Not much could excite me today."

He laughed, started to say something and then caught himself. "Have fun." He walked over to a Cadillac Escalade, digging out his keys. Obviously it took more than the best pastrami on rye in town to make him hang around.

My cell rang while I was packing. I threw my black bikini at my bag, not caring if it made the trip or not, and answered the call without checking the caller ID. The phone is my lifeline to the Sunset, and I pretty much never duck a call.

Sasha said, "You've been checking up on me."

I flopped backwards onto the bed. "Nope, only Willow. I just wanted to know she was okay." I watched the ceiling fan slowly turn. "Do you mind?"

He took his time answering. When he did, he surprised me by saying, "Bossy, concerned and pushy, just like my mother."

"Oh, shit, I don't want to remind any man of his mother."

He laughed. "Have you found the orchid yet?"

I swallowed a curse and put my forearm over my aching head. "I'm not looking for it."

"Like hell you aren't. Why are you hanging with Ethan?"

"He and Clay have business."

"And how did that come about?"

Did I owe him an answer? Not really, but the sooner I convinced him I knew nothing about nothing, the sooner he'd bugger off. "Ethan came into the Sunset and met Clay, or maybe he met Clay and then came into the Sunset. I don't know. Ask Ethan if you're so curious."

"Like I thought, Ethan came looking for you, and the only reason he'd do that was because he thought you had the orchid."

Or because he thought I knew Tito. Best to keep that to myself. "Look, instead of wasting my time, just call Ethan and ask him to satisfy your curiosity."

He gave a harsh laugh and said, "It's all the same to me how you got in the middle of this. I just want the black orchid."

I sat up, making the room swirl. "Trust me, if I had that stupid flower I'd sell it to you in a second just to get rid of you all. Everyone at the ball has called, or come by, looking for it. If I knew anything about the freaking thing I'd have sold it already and be on the way to the bank with the money."

Silence. Finally he said, "Who are you working for?"

I bit back a string of obscenities. "Not buying, not selling, not working for anyone. Cross my heart. Ben got in touch with you and tried to sell it to you, right?"

"Sure, that's no secret. Half the people at the Orchid Ball were on Ben's list . . . except Ethan. Ben would never sell to him."

Or Nina, but there was no need for me to tell Sasha that.

Sasha said, "The orchid was going to the highest bidder. Ben told us that from the beginning. This was the owner's chance to get his name on a new species; immortality, that's what we were all buying. And Ben was looking to clear his debt."

"So maybe Ben got an offer he couldn't refuse and sold it before he died."

"I thought about that. If Ben had a really good offer, he would have called us all back and tried to get us to up the price, but he didn't. That means he still had it, was still collecting names and deals. Trust me; he was going to turn it into an auction with the black going to the highest bidder."

"So then, it went up in the fire with him."

"If that's true, there's no use looking any further. You were my last chance."

"Sorry to disappoint you. Goodbye."

"Wait, wait," he said before I could put the phone down. "It couldn't have gone in the fire. There was that bloom at the Orchid Ball. How do you explain that?"

"I don't."

"Are you certain Ethan doesn't have the black? If Ethan has it, no one will ever see it again."

I sighed. "Ethan didn't know it existed until after Ben died."

"Not quite true," Sasha said.

"What do you mean, not quite true?"

"Ethan knew Ben had a black orchid."

"How?"

"I told him. I called Ethan three days before Ben died. Ethan told me he knew nothing about any black orchid, said he and Ben hadn't talked in years. I checked around after I talked to Ethan and he was telling the truth. The brothers had a nasty breakup, so it was unlikely Ethan knew what was happening at Osceola Nursery. All the same, once I told him about it, he would have checked it out."

My head, already swollen with a virus, couldn't take it in. "Ethan lied?"

"If he told you he didn't know about the black until after Ben's death, he lied." His laughter had a spiteful, grating edge to it. "I'm positive Ethan didn't know about the plant until I told him. I thought he was going to stroke out." He laughed again, like he enjoyed upsetting Ethan.

I planted my elbow on my knee and put my head in my hand, staring at the floor and trying to decide if I really believed Sasha.

Sasha said, "Are you still there?"

"Yeah." It was all I could manage.

He said, "Call me if you find the orchid." It was more a demand than a request.

"Yeah, and I'll call if I find an alien spacecraft or Bigfoot." And just to annoy him, I added, "What happens when Willow gets out?"

"I'm through with her."

"Interesting."

"What?"

"Well, I would have expected you to just kick her to the curb when her bad habits got out of control, but you put her in rehab. Doesn't sound like you're done."

He hung up. How many men did that make who'd hung up on me this week? I was losing my appeal.

CHAPTER 33

I flopped back on the bed and tried to make sense of it all. Someone had searched my home looking for the orchid. I was pretty sure of that.

And the search had taken place right after Sasha came to the Sunset for the first time. But why had someone done a financial check on us? The answer came quickly: to see if we'd had a big fat bonus going into our account and to see if we'd paid off some debts. And what else?

I closed my eyes. I wanted to stay in bed for about a year. Just stay there and not think.

Clay came in an hour later and woke me. "C'mon, sleepy-head, let's get going." He pulled a carry-all from the bottom of his closet. Either our scene that morning didn't matter to him or he was trying to patch things over. "I thought you'd be excited to go back to the island again."

"Maybe not as excited as you, not quivering with anticipation."

"You should be. This is the beginning of great things." He dropped the bag on the bed beside me and headed back to his closet. "If this goes the way I think it will, the sale of Dancing Lady will set us up for a new life."

It was the old life, the one I'd been born with, I was worrying about. I dragged myself upright and sat on the edge of the bed, arms dangling down between my legs in the most unladylike pose possible as I waited for the world to stop whirling around and watched Clay pack. "Ethan lied to me," I said

Clay didn't look up from the freshly laundered pale blue shirt he was folding. "About what?" His voice was neutral, underlined by a trace of, "Oh, here we go again." He tucked the shirt gently into the bag, patting it down and smoothing out the edges.

"Obviously your idea of a night away is far different than mine. I threw a change of underwear and a bathing suit inside my bag." I didn't add that it was mainly to hide an item I was supposed to have returned to Tully. It was one of the few things I'd lied to Clay about. Actually, it wasn't a lie. I just hadn't done what I'd promised to do.

"Ethan knew about the orchid before Ben died. Sasha told him."

He carefully folded another shirt, concentrating and not looking up as he said, "And you believe Sasha?"

"Ah, the big question."

His hands stilled and he glanced over at me. "Does it matter when Ethan found out about the plant?"

"Maybe."

His eyes went back to consider his neatly folded shirts. "Do you think two shirts are enough?"

I wanted to scream—and would have except then my head would have exploded. "It makes it possible that Ethan killed Ben."

I had his attention now. "That's crazy. Why would Ethan do that? The man has everything. What could he have possibly gained from killing his brother?"

"How about a black orchid?"

"People don't kill their brother for a flower."

"Not people like you, or people like me. Look at Martin Faust, risking jail and his reputation for a few plants. Some of these people go beyond crazy, smuggling plant material through customs, spending tens of thousands of dollars on foraging trips into the wilds of foreign countries and risking their lives." I yawned again, stretching away sleep. "There's an international trade in endangered species of wild animals and plants. Where do you think all that material goes to? Collectors."

I could see on his face that he wanted to argue. Instead, he went back to packing his immaculately arranged bag. In truth, I didn't believe it myself. It was just that everything seemed wrong and suspect these days.

On the way to the dock, while we were stopped at a red light, Clay looked straight ahead and said, "Are you sure you want to come?"

I studied him, a sudden realization dawning. He didn't want me there, was afraid I was going to mess up his deal of a lifetime. I didn't bother answering.

"Why don't you stay home and rest? You can drop me off and come back for me tomorrow night." The light turned green. "A day's rest will make a difference to the way you see things."

I felt like hell, and normally I would have been only too happy to beg off. But the thought of being separated from Clay right now gave me a bad case of the worries, scared for him and dreading being by myself. There was no way I was ever going to spend another night alone in that half-deserted subdivision. "It might be my only chance to see this fine place. Besides, I can rest there better than I can in Jac. I'll tag along."

"You can't fool me. You'd rather we weren't going." Clay

slowed and put on the blinker for a left turn through the gates of the marina. "What's got you so bothered about this trip?"

I waved to a kid with a skateboard under his arm standing just inside the gate and waiting for us to pass. "Oh, I guess I'm just a herd animal. I don't like to be cut off from the rest of the pack, like to be right there in the middle of things where no one can get at me."

"Ah, in other words, the Sunset." He pulled into a parking space and waited while the window slid silently up. "One day I expect you to put a bed in your office and move right in, never leave the place again." He grinned at me and cut the engine.

"There's a lot to be said for that idea: no rent, food at my command and company always available."

"Is that how you want to live your life?" His gaze was intent, his eyes fixed on mine as if his very life depended on my answer.

I shook my head and put my hand on his. "No, that's not what I want. I want a life with you and a family of our own. It's embarrassing, but now I want all those things I used to make fun of."

He smiled into my eyes and said, "Yeah, me too." He squeezed my hand. "So, no more jumping at shadows today, okay?"

I pulled my hand away. "You've got it wrong. It's not shadows that have got me jumpy. It's a murderer."

I heard his sharp intake of breath.

We sat in silence for a minute, and then Clay said, "Okay, let's look at this logically." He pulled my left hand towards him, rubbing it gently between his fingers as he spoke. "Ethan came to the Sunset because his brother had died and the police told him Tito had your card. Okay?"

I nodded.

"Everything else flowed naturally from that. Ethan gathered together some collectors who wanted Ben's black orchid for the ball. Right?"

Again I nodded.

"But maybe none of those people were part of what happened to Ben."

I turned to him and started to object, but he raised his hand and cut me off. "Yes, they all want the orchid, but there is no reason to think any of them are involved beyond that. It's only Ethan's suspect list. Maybe the person who killed Ben is someone we've never heard of and what happened at the nursery had nothing to do with orchids."

"Oh, shit, I hadn't thought of that." It was an astounding idea. "The first day Ethan came to the Sunset, he said he thought it was about drugs."

"Now do you see why you need to turn this over to the police and let them sort it out?"

"Yes," I said. "Yes, I need to talk to Styles."

"And do you really think you are the only person that these plant collectors are calling? The news from the Orchid Ball spread like wildfire. Orchid collectors will be checking out every possible source for Ben's black flower. Ethan told me the CEO of a bank phoned from New York and offered a bundle for the orchid."

I pulled my hand away from him, feeling stupid. "But why are they calling me?"

"They're calling you because you gave them your card." He sounded totally exasperated. "They thought you were promoting something besides a restaurant. Now that you've made it clear you haven't got the plant, they'll leave you alone." He opened his door. "Now, let's go have some fun and forget about everything else for a day."

I didn't point out to him that his scenario didn't cover the return of my sandal. There was no use in starting that argument again. I'd never convince him someone had really sent it to me, and bringing it up now would only convince him I was either lying or crazy—possibly both.

I got out of the car and smiled across the roof at him. The sun was shining and a slight breeze was blowing across the water to cool us off. I hadn't done anything just for fun since my trip to Miami, so a day on the water was just what I needed to clear my head and heart of a lot of things. "Okay, a day off from worries. I'll call Styles tomorrow and let him figure it out." I threw my boat bag onto my shoulder and followed Clay down the dock to the berth where the boat from Dancing Lady waited.

CHAPTER 34

Liz had sent her launch—at least, that's what she'd told Clay she was sending. It turned out to be an eighteen-foot white runabout with a Bimini top. The man driving it was named Silvio Rozelli. He had beef-jerky skin, a long gray braid down his back, and a green-and-red mermaid tattoo swimming up his forearm. You'll find a guy like him, pumping gas, delivering boats and emptying trash bins, in every marina in Florida. Always ready to take off at a minute's notice as crew on a boat for parts unknown, men like Silvio will never be far from the water. Boaters depend on guys like him.

We motored slowly away from the dock, easing out into the channel and barely gaining speed when we were clear of the marina. Silvio was a careful boater, respectful of the fact that inland waters are a no-wake zone, so it was a slow trip out to the open waters of the gulf. I didn't mind. I studied the few houses on the gulf side, playing the when-I-win-the-lottery game of choosing a house, until the long point of land turned into a state park. Now Australian pines grew along the shore, and here and there, boaters had pulled up to enjoy a picnic in their shade, living the dream.

After we hit the gulf, Silvio opened up the engine, but it was still a thirty-minute ride down the coast from the end of the state park. Dancing Lady Island was just about as remote as you could get on the Florida coast.

Clay felt my eyes on him and turned to smile at me. He rose and made his way back to me. "Are you all right?"

"Better than I've been for weeks. Even my cold is better, but that may be from the ton of junk I've ingested."

"Good. Whatever is making you feel better, I'm grateful." He bent down and kissed me. "This is going to be a new beginning for us."

I nodded and smiled up at him.

"Mr. and Mrs. Normal, that's going to be us." He brushed back the hair whipping around my face. "We're putting the bad times behind us." A boyish grin. "We've had a few of those, haven't we? But we got through them."

I nodded up at him again and then watched him go back to stand beside Silvio. What spun through my mind was, just because we'd always survived that didn't mean we always would. Anxiety and panic couldn't be dismissed as easily as Clay believed.

I huddled down on the turquoise cushions along the back, arms hugged to my chest and my hair beating my face, and let the rushing air clear my stuffed head. My view of events had taken on a novel twist. Clay's suggesting there might be people involved that we'd never heard of sent my brain whirling through possibilities. He was right. I'd fixated on Ethan's guest list. If there was someone else involved that I'd missed, was there any hint of who it might be? I went over every second from the time I left Miami, and then I started going over the list of people I'd already considered, searching for someone, or something, I'd missed.

Maybe Tito had told someone about me before he died. Scary thought, but a dead end. The big "aha" moment came when I listed all the people who had made me an offer to purchase the black orchid. Only one name was missing. Only one person hadn't called or come into the bar, thinking that I had the plant . . . Liz. And why was that? Because she already had it.

We were within minutes of Dancing Lady. I looked at Clay. He'd freak out if I told him what I was thinking. There was no going back.

The house looked like the prow of an ocean liner, sailing above the mangroves and palms, the sun glinting off the banks of black solar panels across the roof. It demanded attention from those passing by while offering perfect privacy.

A sixty-eight-foot Predator yacht named *Dancing Lady II* sat at anchor a hundred feet off the dock. A quarter-million-dollar yacht. You had to be seriously rich to have one of those waiting at your pleasure. I wondered why it was here and not in a marina.

The weathered gray dock had a large white sign on the end. In bold black letters on a white board, it said, DANCING LADY ISLAND, and below the name were the words NO TRESPASSING. A woman in her early twenties, with bright blue hair and a ring in the center of her bottom lip, stood with her arms folded on top of the sign. She was barefoot and dressed in shorts and a halter. At her feet lay a canvas boat bag. She stood up straight and waved furiously.

Silvio waved back. "My daughter, Cassandra. She works here with me," he said, pride and joy on his face and in his voice. He cut the engine and eased along the dock while Clay threw the bumpers over the side and tossed the girl a line.

She walked along the dock and pulled us in close to the tires lining the edge. Clay, holding the line for the stern, jumped onto the dock and tied it off.

Silvio left the engine idling and slung our gear onto the dock while Cassandra dumped her bag onto the back seat and jumped aboard, a woman who had spent her life getting on and off boats. "Hello," she said to me, and then she went to stand beside her father. They both looked at me expectantly, waiting for me to stand up and join Clay on the dock.

"Aren't you staying?" I asked Silvio.

"I'm taking Cassandra over to Boca Grande for a party and then I'll be back."

"How will we get back to Jac?"

Silvio started to make a joke, but then something in my face registered and he checked himself. "Don't worry. I'll be back in an hour or so." He put out a hand, almost touching me, and then drew it back. "You won't want to leave before that, will you?"

I shook my head, but I was thinking a lot can happen in an hour. An excuse to go back to Jac trembled on my lips. Or maybe I could ride over to Boca with them. I wanted to be anywhere but trapped on this island. I looked up at Clay. He held out his hand.

For better or for worse, I was sticking with Clay. I stepped up onto the seat and then onto the dock. Clay picked up our bags while I watched with trepidation as Silvio and his daughter motored away. And then Liz was there, hugging us and leading us up a boardwalk into the mangroves. About five feet into the mangroves, a steel gate was built across the walkway. When it was closed and locked, the tangled branches on either side formed a living fence, impossible to pass through, protecting the house from intruders. The top of the gate was finished in decorative spikes. It would be as hard to get out as it would be to get in.

But for now the gate was unlocked, the key still in the mechanism. We continued along the walkway, scaring tiny lizards off the planks ahead of us. We stepped out of the tunnel of vegetation at the base of the building. An unholy racket broke out. A giant wire cage was built half under the stilt house. Inside the cage a red parrot, perched on a bare branch, screeched at us.

"Buddy is our guard bird," Liz said. "No one gets in here without Buddy warning us." She took a nut still in the shell from the pocket of her baggy shorts. "They just have to drive down the lane at the ranch or pull up to the dock and he tells us they're coming." She pursed her lips and made kissing sounds. "Keep your fingers away from him or you'll lose them."

"Seriously?" Clay said.

"Yup. Macaws and parrots have more pressure per square inch in their beaks than alligators do. Watch." Holding an almond by one end, Liz stuck it through the wire. Buddy snapped at it. Grasping it with his talon, he cracked the almond shell like it was nothing more than a peanut, dropping bits of the casing and gobbling up the nut. Then he stretched his wings wide and began bobbing his head.

Liz made more kissing sounds at Buddy. "Sweet boy."

She plucked a feather out of the wire and handed it to me. Red. I turned the feather over to expose the underside, blue with a thin line of green. "Get real." I turned it back and forth, blue to red.

She grinned at me. "Amazing, isn't it."

Buddy grabbed the wire with his beak and turned upside down before he swooped back to his perch.

"Take a bow, Buddy." Liz bowed low. "Take a bow." Buddy bowed, ran forward on his perch and bowed again. We clapped. A mad string of bows followed on Buddy's part.

"Show-off," Liz said.

Finished with Buddy's entertainment, Liz darted for the broad steps leading up to a deck at the front of the house. Caught off guard by her sudden exit, we ran to catch up as she jogged up the stairs.

CHAPTER 35

In a way, the mansion's architecture was rooted in Florida history. Like a Seminole chickee, it had a steeply pitched roof and was constructed on cantilevered stilts to allow storm surges to sweep under it without damaging the structure above. From the dogtrot house of the early Florida settlers, the design sported a gallery that ran around the building, providing outdoor living space and natural cooling.

All similarities to those modest structures ended there. A house with attitude, it was built in the shape of a pentagon, with one of the points facing towards the north and Jacaranda. The roof rose higher as it went from the south end to the north end, where the floor-to-ceiling windows were eighteen feet high.

The roof was uneven, with the west slope rising several feet above the east side, allowing for a chain of windows the full length of the house. Wide, whitewashed plank flooring and a white handrail atop glass panels wrapped around the house.

Standing on the huge deck at the top of the stairs, you could see nearly three hundred and sixty degrees, see sailboats on the horizon eleven miles away. Black wicker lounges with white cushions, lined up along a sisal area rug, looked out over the Gulf of Mexico. It was a beautiful day and the gulf was busy with boaters on holiday, but Liz was in no mood to relax and watch the world go by. "This way," she said, already on the move.

Off the deck was the living room. There were windows on three sides of the room, making it almost like being outside. Three large couches surrounded a fieldstone fireplace. The white couches had an abundance of blue and white cushions. Oversize blue-and-white Chinese vases, so big you could hide a small child in them, stood on either side of the fireplace. All the tables in the room were made of gray driftwood and glass. On the plank ceiling above us, a giant palm-frond fan turned slowly.

Clay dropped his bag and turned in a circle, taking it in. "Beautiful. I need to come back with a photographer and take pictures."

Liz waved his words away. "Don't worry about that today. I just want to give you an overview so we can start sketching out a marketing plan."

"How many acres are there on the island?" Clay asked.

"Ten. It's completely self-contained for fresh water and sewage, and totally private."

Not good. Alone made you vulnerable—a target—like food fish cut off from the school by a shark.

Liz pointed at the fireplace. "The stone goes all the way down to the concrete pad below and has two more outlets there; three fireplaces in all."

I looked up at the mammoth structure and asked, "Is Ethan coming by?"

Beside me, Liz's body jerked away from me. "Good god, no."

"Oh," I said, still staring at the fireplace.

She grabbed me. Her nails dug into my arm. "Why did you ask that?"

I turned my face to her. Her angular features were locked

in anger. I noticed that the roots of her caramel-colored hair were growing in gray. "I thought maybe there would be a repeat of the party." I looked down to the arm grasping mine; ropy muscles stood out along the powerful forearm of an expert tennis player.

"Ethan isn't coming." She let go of me and stepped away. "Once was enough." She planted her fists on her hips and added, "You told him the island is for sale, didn't you?"

"I didn't realize it's a secret."

She frowned. "He showed up here three days ago in a company helicopter with his chief of security to look the place over." She gave a snort of disgust. "Chief of security? Digger Jackson is just a no-account bully from back home who's learned some fancy tricks. He and Ethan were always thick as thieves and rotten as hell. They came here with no warning, hoping to surprise me." Her annoyance with me was gone now, and she grinned like a naughty girl enjoying herself. "They looked this place over real good, every corner. Ethan said he might be interested in buying Dancing Lady."

I watched her closely and asked, "But you don't think they were island shopping, do you?"

Again she snorted. "They were looking for Ben's orchid." Liz pointed at Clay. "Which reminds me, if he actually offers on the island, you don't get a commission." She was on the move again and talking over her shoulder. "He viewed the place before you became the agent, Clay."

Clay, following at Liz's heels, frowned back over his shoulder at me.

"Sorry," I mouthed, but somehow I didn't think that was going to cut it if I'd screwed up Clay's commission.

She showed us around the rest of the house, rattling off facts and figures at warp speed. "There are five suites off this central hall." Liz stopped and pointed up to the ceiling of the hall. "The windows above the hall can be opened by a remote control." She pulled a remote out of a holder on the wall and demonstrated. A window silently opened above us. "Opening a window creates a giant chimney that sucks air in from the outside and sweeps it out here." She tossed the remote back in its holder and trotted off down the corridor.

Waving at each open guest door we passed, Liz said, "Of course, the house comes fully furnished."

I peeked into each room as we went along and then had to speed-walk to catch up.

She stopped at one of the entrances. "This is your suite."

In gray and sea green, with a bathroom in white marble and black granite, the suite contained every luxury a houseguest could desire. "I could get used to this," I said, turning around in circles.

Liz was already on her way out the door, a tiny dynamo on a mission. We dropped out bags on the floor and followed.

"My bedroom is at the end of the hall."

Both bedrooms in our rental home could be put in Liz's with plenty of floor space left over for dancing. Her suite contained an office, a bedroom, a dressing room and a bathroom. It ran the full width of the south end of the house. The house tour was calming my anxiety—until we got to her bathroom. A cheap plastic curtain partitioned off part of the shower—which was weird, because the walls and floors were made of travertine marble. A faint glow came from behind the plastic. I took a hesitant step towards it, curious.

Liz's voice was sharp and insistent. "Come on, Sherri." She turned and walked away.

I didn't follow.

"Hurry up," Liz ordered, waiting for me at the bathroom door with her hand on the knob. When I stepped over the sill she closed the door firmly behind me.

Glass doors along the south wall of the bedroom had been pushed back and stacked so that twelve feet of the room stood open to the outside. A brown pelican sat on the balcony railing. Liz crossed the carpet to the balcony, saying, "Wait until you see this." With a wave of Liz's hand, the pelican flew away.

Clay followed her halfway out the door and then, seeing me lagging behind, turned back to me and said, "Coming?"

"Yes." I glanced back towards the bathroom once before I followed.

Clay and I joined Liz at the rail. Below was a raised pool and patio deck. The bottom of the blue pool was covered in a mosaic mermaid.

Liz said, "I swim every morning." This was the first time on the tour that she'd been inclined to linger. It didn't last long. On either end of the deck, stairs curled down to the pool. Liz headed for the flight of steps on the left, saying, "You've got to see the physical plant, Clay. We have two cisterns for the water we save from the roof, and our own purification system."

Clay and I followed along like puppies. On the broad lawn beyond the pool, she tapped her foot on the turf and said, "The septic bed is here, under the grass."

She pointed to the far left side of the green space. "That part, the bit screened off, is the physical plant that keeps this monster of a house functioning."

They walked across the lush grass, me still trailing behind as they talked of sewage and generators and other exciting stuff.

Beyond the lawn, nature had been left to her own devices. A six-foot-wide brick path had been cleared through the jungle. Through the shadowy tunnel of undergrowth we came out on a tennis court. Liz explained that on the other side of the tennis court, the path led through a tangle of palmetto scrub to a helipad.

Back at the house Liz showed us the cool and pleasant tiled area under the house, with its huge outdoor kitchen and sitting areas. The block walls were painted a bright lime green.

The white pillars holding up the house had been strung with brightly striped Peruvian hammocks.

"This is also the living quarters for the staff, two small apartments. We won't go in." She pointed to the hammocks. "When the bugs let him, Silvio likes to sleep outside."

"There don't seem to be any insects here," Clay said.

"I think it's because we have more wind than the mainland." She shrugged. "Whatever it is, I'm grateful we can open things up without being eaten alive."

When the tour was over, Clay and Liz talked strategy while I spread on coconut sunscreen. Just the smell makes me think of good times and holidays. Out on the airless tennis court, I set the ball thingy firing yellow orbs at me while I swatted at them like they were annoying mosquitoes. I didn't last long. After forty-five minutes I wandered off to see what else there was, leaving the court littered with missed objects.

I went for a swim in the pool and sunned and waited. I didn't even know what I was expecting, but there was a small lump of dread in the pit of my stomach that wouldn't listen to reason and go away. A couple of appalling years, filled with death, had left me feeling like prey, a sensation that no amount of explanation could erase.

I told myself nothing bad was going to happen and things were just what they seemed. But the realization that Liz was the only one who didn't try to buy the orchid from me, plus the fact that we were trapped on this island, had my nerves humming.

And then there was the fact that Silvio hadn't returned.

CHAPTER 36

Dancing Lady Island was as close to paradise as most of us could ever imagine. Sitting on the dock and waiting for the boat to return, I watched a pelican fold its wings and dive-bomb for dinner. Later, a pod of dolphins fished off the end of the pier. While I watched the dolphins, a passing cruiser came about, turning towards the small dock. I got to my feet, prepared to run if the boat wasn't what it appeared to be. But the boaters were there to enjoy the gleaming creatures arching out of the water again and again, putting on a show for us while they fed.

When the small yacht cleared out I searched the horizon over towards Boca for the runabout with the Bimini top. Why wasn't Silvio back? He'd said he was only going to be gone an hour. It was now closer to two hours.

I had to do something besides sit there and drive myself crazy. I'd seen a trampoline on the outside of the house, beside Silvio's patio. It had to be Cassandra's. I couldn't see either Silvio or Liz bouncing on it, but maybe I was underestimating Liz. A woman like that, who had survived what she had and moved at a clip that left a thirty-year-old in her wake—there was no telling what she was capable of.

I climbed up on the trampoline. There was no cross in the center to keep me oriented, and with no spotters, I warned myself to take it easy and find my balance. I bounced gently, getting my feel back and finding courage, and quickly found that what I'd once thought I was pretty great at now made me feel awkward and silly. A little higher. Still okay. With each spring into the air I felt the steel bands loosening around my gut, felt my knees relaxing and absorbing the shock of hitting the mat.

I lifted my feet out in front of me and hit the mat with my butt, a little hard and off balance, falling sideways. Encouraged, I tried again. I couldn't quite make it back to a standing position, but at least I hadn't injured myself.

I bounced higher and higher, the freedom of motion taking away the apprehension and dread I'd lived with for weeks. My whole body began to buzz with the joy of soaring high enough to look through the glass panels on the walkway.

I was there twenty or thirty minutes, maybe more—long enough to be able to hit the rubber mat and bounce back to my feet again, but not long enough to get up the courage to try a somersault in the air. Some tricks are best left on the gym floor.

I stretched out on my back on the trampoline. Cumulus clouds, in separate little fleecy puffs, dotted the sky. A wedge of ducks flew over, heading down the coast to Captiva Island. God, why hadn't I thought of this before? Somewhere along the line I'd given up exercise for booze as a stress reliever. I might have to rethink my choice.

I planted my hands on the surround bar and somersaulted off. Sloppy, falling backwards onto the edge of the equipment but landing on my feet, I'd get no points for dismount.

I'd barely regained my balance when Buddy set up an uproar. Just that fast, my angst was back. I ducked low and ran to hide behind a pillar, pressing my tense body against the unyielding surface. My heart was pounding. It didn't slow until I heard Silvio talking to the parrot.

I let out my breath and wiped the sweat from my face. "Crazy woman." I went to join Silvio and watched Buddy take his bows.

Liz leaned over the railing above us. "Silvio, Sherri, come up here, please. We need witnesses for our signatures."

"Okay," Silvio answered, tucking one more almond into Buddy's cage.

After Clay and Liz had signed the contracts and we'd added our signatures, they had drinks to celebrate while I went to our bedroom and climbed into the shower. As the water poured over me, I wondered what Liz was hiding behind the plastic curtain in her beautiful shower and tried to figure out how I could get a look behind the curtain.

When I went back outside the three of them were still on the veranda, with fresh drinks in their hands, watching boats go by and enjoying the day.

I helped myself to the nuts and asked, "Do people ever try to come onto the island?"

Silvio said, "Not when I'm here." He struck a hero's pose and patted his chest. "It's my job to keep them off."

Liz placed her empty highball glass on a silver tray. "A drink, Sherri?"

"Sure, how about a soda?"

Clay looked at me and raised an eyebrow.

I said, "But first I want to make a call, check on things at the restaurant." I held up my cell phone. "I can't get a signal."

Liz said, "Cell service is spotty out here. There's no tower. There's a SAT phone on the boat. Use that, or if you want to send an e-mail, we have marine satellite Internet, but it's slow and hit-or-miss." Liz picked up the tray. "There's also VHF and EPIRB on the *Dancing Lady II*, so we're not totally cut off." A small smile teased Liz's lips. "As long as you can get down to the boats."

I said, "Even if I can get to the boats, I don't know how those systems operate."

Silvio set his glass on the table and got to his feet. "Come on, I'll show you how it works."

Following Silvio down the stairs, I asked, "Why don't you have a SAT phone in the house?"

"Lousy reception in a concrete building, better on the boat. Besides, Liz calls having phone service 'being at everyone's beck and call.'"

Liz and not Ms. Aiken; I was betting a little more than strictly business was going on here.

Silvio stopped and fed Buddy another nut.

"The guard bird does all right."

"He deserves it." He made clicking sounds at the parrot. "He's the early warning system when people get too curious."

"Ah, you mean when boaters drop in."

"Exactly."

Too curious was an odd way of putting it. I wanted to ask, "Curious about what?" Instead I said, "But don't the mangroves and the gate keep them out?"

"It's a nuisance to keep the gate locked during the day. Every once in a while an unwanted sightseer decides to venture past the dock. Buddy lets us know."

"So, at night you're behind locked gates with no telephone service, cut off from the world?"

"Pretty much."

I shuddered.

He gave me a questioning look and said, "You okay?"

"Sure, fine." I tried to smile at him. "I'm not used to being so remote."

He stepped onto the boat and held out his hand to me.

I took his hand and stepped aboard.

Silvio turned on the communication system and the large microwave antenna automatically turned to track satellites. We got a signal right away. I got through to the restaurant and started asking if the wine delivery had arrived.

Gwen clearly thought I had lost my mind. "It arrived before you left," she pointed out.

"Yes, that's right. How are reservations?"

"Fine." She drew the word out cautiously, and then Gwen said, "What the hell is going on?"

"I missed you. I'll see you tomorrow." I handed the phone to Silvio. "I've never used one before. Show me again how to make a call if I needed to. I want to be sure I know how it works."

He nodded as though he thought I was perfectly sane. When we'd gone through it again, he jumped up on the dock and waited for me. A boat pulled in close to stare at the flying fortress above us. Silvio pointed at it and said, "It's something that happens over and over. *Dancing Lady* is a marker for passing boaters, something to show the guests."

Silvio waved a greeting but waited on the dock until they'd pulled away.

When we'd passed through the gate he locked it, pulling on the steel bars to test that it was firmly in place before he removed the key and stuffed it in his pocket.

There was no leaving the compound now. So much for knowing how to use the communication system. I could no longer get to it.

Clay wasn't usually much of a drinker, but when Silvio and I rejoined him and Liz on the deck, he downed two scotches in a row, on top of what he drank while I was in the shower. It was an unheard of number for him. Working on a fresh one and becoming very mellow, Clay regaled us with stories of his sailing trip to Cuba. "The captain was a Nazi, and the only other crew member was a drunk. It was the trip from hell."

Silvio started talking about where he'd sailed, from Key West to the Caribbean and south as far as Venezuela. His trips had been just as adventurous as Clay's, making me even more determined to stay home. I hate traveling—another thing Clay and I disagreed on.

"And now it's time to think about dinner." Liz drained the last of her scotch and got to her feet, overbalancing and giggling. "Whoopsie." She was in no better shape than Clay.

"I'll come with you," I said, gathering up the glasses.

I followed as she weaved her way inside. It looked like our hostess was zipped. But then, she might be as sober as I was. I hadn't actually seen how much she'd had to drink.

"This is something of a farewell dinner," Liz said and opened the refrigerator. "Let's make it good."

"A farewell dinner?"

She stood looking into the depths of the fridge like she couldn't remember what she was there for. "Things are changing. We'll be leaving the island." She closed the door and stood there staring at the blank steel surface, lost in her own world.

I went over and stood beside her. She looked at me vaguely

and then wandered over to sit at the granite bar. I opened the French door of the refrigerator and started taking out salad greens. There was a large piece of something wrapped in butcher's paper that Silvio had brought in a cooler back from Boca. I unwrapped it and set the sirloin in a bowl to marinate and then searched around until I found potatoes and got them ready for baking.

Liz planted her elbow on the counter and propped her head up with her fist. "You're my kind of guest: one that cooks," she lisped. If she wasn't drunk, it was a damn good imitation. "I think all guests should come prepared to cook."

"I like to cook, but at the restaurant Miguel never lets me and I'm never home to make a meal." I pulled the cord on the lettuce spinner. "We eat at the Sunset most days."

Liz watched me silently. At last she said, "I think I'll have myself another little drink." Her cheeks were a lovely alcoholic rose, but I still wasn't convinced she was as inebriated as she pretended to be. Some people's faces grew flushed after one drink.

She poured the scotch over ice as I said, "I'm surprised you haven't got more staff."

Her head tilted sideways and she studied me. "Haven't you figured it out yet?"

"What?"

"I've let them all go. I invested in some risky hedge funds, and now I'm just about bankrupt." She looked confused. "What the hell are hedge funds anyway?"

"I've no idea."

There was only hurt in her eyes. "Me either, but I'm trimming my assets like I'd prune a sick plant, cutting out deadwood and rot." She gave a broad wave of her hand to indicate tossing away something unnecessary and unreliable, but the movement nearly toppled her off the seat. "I'll do anything necessary to survive this, but survive I will."

And that was precisely what worried me.

She considered me as she said, "I'm surprised Clay didn't tell you. I thought you two were the type who told each other everything."

"So did I." The truth was, Clay knew Liz's need for money would feed my paranoia. Even now, I was considering just what Liz had done for money. "So, that's why you're selling the island."

"Dancing Lady sucks money, so she has to go, and the yacht is already sold. Silvio and Cassandra are delivering it to the new owner over in Miami next week. I'll drive over and bring them back. Want to come along for the ride?"

"Sorry, can't make it." It would be a day or two yet before I was ready for that trip. "It must be hard to give this up."

She tilted her head to the side, considering. "Kurt's family owned this island for fifty years."

I crushed some garlic and dumped it into a bowl. "You mean when I was a kid, playing out here, that's who it belonged to?"

"Yup. I always dreamed of building a house here. Unfortunately I picked the worst time to do it. I got caught in the economy swirling down the toilet, like everyone else. When one thing went wrong, a whole lot followed."

I squeezed a lemon into the oil and garlic for the salad dressing, but I was focused on Liz. "It must be hard to give up on your dream."

"At least I got to have my dream; most people don't. I can't cry if the dream didn't last. They seldom do."

I whisked the dressing and studied her. "Finding the black orchid is important to you, might be the thing that saves you."

She grimaced. "Saving me would take millions, not thousands."

The amount took my breath away.

Clay grilled the steaks for the long, boozy dinner on the deck high above the water. I no longer wondered if Liz was inebriated. They all were. Except for me. I was cold sober . . . and waiting. Don't ask me what I was waiting for because I didn't know. I just knew I wanted to be ready when it came.

I was alone with three intoxicated people on a locked-down island, with evil circling. At least, I thought we were alone. I hadn't checked out the helipad or the mechanical sheds. Who knew what was waiting out there? Even though it didn't make sense, I couldn't stop my imagination from coming up with scenarios like that.

I collected the plates on either side of me. "What will you do when you sell your island, Liz?"

Liz filled her water glass until it spilled over the brim. "Ben left me his nursery." She set the water jug down but made no move to mop up the spill. "The fire destroyed the buildings and all Ben's mother's orchids are gone, but at least the land is there. I'm going to start over doing what I love, breeding plants." She raised her glass. Water slopped over the lip onto her hand. Without taking a drink, she set the glass back on the table with a thud, spilling more water.

Liz leaned forward, planting her elbows on the table and her chin on her hands. "I've been thinking about why he did that, why he left me the nursery. I think he knew about Susan, knew that she stabbed Kurt. She must have told Ben, and this was his way of thanking me."

Maybe it was true. Liz had got rich by making deals and taking chances. If she knew she would inherit the nursery, she might have killed Ben to get it. And Liz was the one who had just come back from Peru, the world center for the collection of wild orchids. Had she smuggled the orchid into the country and sold it to Ben? Or was Ben just representing her? Either way, I wasn't ruling Liz out for involvement in Ben's death.

It didn't make sense that Liz would destroy everything at the nursery she stood to inherit, but maybe the blaze had gotten out of control, with unexpected consequences. The fire was probably meant to wipe out evidence, not the whole plant center.

I carried the plates to the kitchen and was loading the dishwasher when Clay headed down the corridor to our suite. I followed him.

As I closed the bedroom door, Clay lifted his head from his overnighter. "What's the matter?"

"Let's get out of here," I whispered. "Tell Liz I'm sick."

"Are you?"

"No."

He pulled a big envelope out of his bag. "You're being irrational." He went to the nightstand and picked up a leather portfolio. "Go if you want to, but I'm staying." He left the room.

I wasn't going anywhere without Clay.

In the living room, I listened as Clay and Liz schemed on ways to maximize the profit of selling the island. First they discussed breaking the island up into lots and selling them off, something that seemed an easier sell than getting rid of the whole island. They even discussed developing Dancing Lady into a resort. Given enough time and scotch, they'd probably have drawn up plans to turn it into a pirate-themed island park for boaters. I wasn't sure if any of their ideas were practical or if they were just having fun. What struck me was that Silvio was right in the thick of it, and in the end he was the one who rejected an idea or said if it was possible. Liz, the independent woman, seemed to have a partner.

At one point, Liz turned to Silvio and said, "What do you think, Silvio?"

He replied, "It isn't any crazier than Ethan showing up here and searching for Ben's orchid." They both roared with laughter.

Clay's eyes met mine over their heads. His forehead wrinkled in concern. He was just sober enough to get what was happening between Silvio and Liz.

I rose to my feet and left them. Out on the deck the night was as soft as satin upon my skin. Beyond the mangroves the running lights of Liz's yacht were on, outlining it and keeping it safe from boats traveling at night, but making it look like a great big target for thieves. The lights must have been on a timer, because Silvio hadn't left us to turn them on. Silvio had said SAT communications were best on the yacht. That's where I wanted to be. Spending the night on the yacht seemed like a better idea than being in the house.

I stood there and told myself that my fear had gotten out of hand. Everything was just as it seemed. This was just a beautiful island. But there were too many things getting in my way. The biggest of these was finding that parcel on my desk. But there was something else, something that had happened on the night of the ball and was just out of sight. As I leaned on the rail, my mind turned over rocks of memory. It was something I'd seen, something that had frightened me. I felt a jolt of excitement as it crystallized. What came back to me was the memory of arriving at Selby Gardens. An earlier image, seen online and vaguely remembered, floated across my brain to merge with what I'd seen through the limo window.

I needed a computer. I went back inside.

"May I use your computer, Liz?"

"Sure," she said with a wave of her hand. "It's in my office."

And the office could only be accessed through her bedroom with the attached bath, the room that held Liz's little secret.

CHAPTER 37

The master bedroom was dark. I walked through to the gallery, with only the hall light behind me to guide my steps. The generator hummed in the distance. It was the engine that kept Dancing Lady going; without that thrum of machinery the house would shut down. Even as I thought that, the generator went silent. I held my breath, but the light in the hall stayed on.

I turned on a floor lamp. All the furniture surfaces were mirrored, which made the light bounce around the room. The most formal room of the mansion, with blue damask on the walls and a matching duvet, it was like stepping into a picture in a magazine.

The office was through French doors off the left side of the bedroom. I booted up the computer, then went to the hall door and peeked out to make sure no one was coming to check up on me. The hall was empty. I was alone.

Time to see what was in that shower. In the bathroom a faint glow still came from behind the white curtain. I drew the curtain back to reveal a giant orchid, almost two feet across. It was covered in black flowers.

Having my wildest fears confirmed didn't make me feel better. I took a deep breath and let it out slowly. Okay, so Liz had the orchid. Did that mean she'd killed Ben? Silvio would be the one who'd actually done the killing. Still, there were things that needed to be explained. If Liz already had the orchid, who had been in my house looking for it?

I closed the curtain. There was still one more thing I wanted to check. I searched the Internet for the picture of Angie that had appeared with the story of her murder. The article sprang up quickly. "Jumping Jesus." In shock, I pushed back from the desk. Then I pulled myself forward again to stare at the picture. The little worm that had been burrowing into my brain since the night of the ball had found its way home.

"So, now we know," I whispered to the screen. Here was the proof. I brought up Liz's e-mail program, typed in Styles's address and attached the link for the article. Then I started writing out the whole story, from the beginning of my trip back from Miami to finding the black orchid in the shower stall. Styles could sort through it, verify everything and put an end to my nightmare in the swamp. I had just hit Send when Buddy screamed in the night.

My head jerked up. I listened with an intensity that froze me in place. Then I heard a curse and more squawking and clattering in the wire cage before the earsplitting racket was sharply cut off. Somewhere, a door banged as if in a breeze. But it was a still night. They were coming. No, they had arrived.

"Silvio," Liz's voice called into the night. "Silvio, where are you?" She was somewhere on the veranda at the front of the house. "Silvio, what's wrong?" There was fear in her voice now. It jolted me to my feet.

My first inclination was to race down the hall to the living room, but I didn't know what was happening there. Besides, it wasn't safe inside where it was all lit up. Outside then. I slipped around the back corner of the house and ran down the gallery for our bedroom.

Liz called again, in a voice less certain and demanding, "Silvio?" She was begging now.

And then I heard a gasp of astonishment I thought came from Liz. I started to call out to her but bit back her name.

I moved slowly towards the window of our room. Clay had left the door to the bathroom open and the light on. In the dim glow, the room appeared empty. I slipped inside. I dug in my duffle and brought out the Beretta.

Rubber soles squeaked on the bare hardwood floor of the hall. I slipped out through the open French doors. On the veranda, I pressed my body up against the wall and held my breath, waiting.

From inside came the sound of heavy footfalls on the floorboards. Not Clay. Clay moved like a ghost, never heard and seldom seen. Silvio? Not likely. This was a bigger and heavier man than Silvio, so someone new, a man who shouldn't be here.

I could follow his movements by the squeak of his shoes on the wood flooring. I heard the click of a lamp being switched on, and then light fanned out onto the veranda. I pulled my toe from the shaft of lamplight and listened to him move about the bedroom. He wasn't trying for stealth but moved with a confident indifference, sure that he was in charge. The closet door rattled in its track as it was pulled aside. Was he looking for me? Time to move, before he checked the veranda. I ran along the covered terrace towards the front of the house, wanting to reach Clay.

Behind me a stranger's voice yelled, "Hey!"

Scissor-kicking like I once had for the high jump, I went over the rail and down, dropping the six feet onto the trampoline, landing on my ass and bouncing half over the edge before scuttling off. Under the house now, I ran north, towards the living room.

Feet pounded on the gallery above me. A voice yelled a warning. I kept running until I came to Silvio's twisted body. Stumbling to a halt, I stared down at him. Someone charged down the flight of steps in front of me. The shadowy figure came around the end of the stairs, and then I heard a gun. Chips flew off of the pillar beside me. I zigged sideways behind the pillar. I raised my Beretta in both hands. He wasn't trying to take cover, coming on without any expectation that I would return his fire. I squeezed the trigger. The sound was deafening, the scream of the guy even worse.

I darted left to the west side of the house and ran full-out down the underside of the gallery.

Without reasoning it out, I headed south towards the helipad, away from the direction of the dock and Buddy's cage, where he stood guard and warned us before his alarm call had been brutally cut off. There was likely a man there to guard the exit. At least, that was my guess.

Past the pool and out to the lawn, zigging and zagging across the grass like a crazed rabbit, sprinting frantically and leaving Clay behind. The noise from the gun aimed at me was more a popping sound than the terrifically loud blast the Beretta made. Clods of dirt flew up around me.

I had no plan, no idea what I was doing. Escape was my only thought. At the edge of the lawn some innate survival system kicked in, telling me to think before I went too far. I burrowed into the shadows of the underbrush and looked back at the house. In the light from Liz's bedroom windows I saw a man, built like a linebacker, run along the upper deck and start down the steps towards me, coming after me.

I had to hide, but where? By the water tanks? I hadn't gone there with Liz and Clay so I didn't know if they offered concealment. Besides, the linebacker would see me if I broke cover and headed across the grass in that direction. The mechanical sheds were out. But I had to find a hole to hide in.

I decided I needed to be in the thick underbrush beyond the tennis court. I moved towards the brick path. A gun exploded.

I ran. Adrenalin sent me crashing along the path and past the tennis court without thought to what was ahead of me. I was nearly to the helipad, driven by panic, before I jumped left, into the arms of the sea grapes. Digging deep into the underbrush, panting and winded, I settled down on my haunches with the gun raised. I steadied it with my left hand, just the way I'd been taught.

"I am not going to die," I promised myself over and over while I waited for the man to appear.

He didn't come. Cautious and aware that I had the advantage now, he was taking his time. But still, he was moving and I wasn't. Silence and stillness were on my side. I wiggled farther into the undergrowth. Twigs snapped against me. A branch stuck into my back. Scrunched up to make a smaller target, I watched the path for movement.

Suddenly a pulsing sound filled the night. A terrifying sound, it grew louder and more insistent. A strange wind blew. The leaves around me whipped about and sand flew up into my eyes. It grew lighter in the undergrowth. It was like a spotlight shining on me from the sky.

I looked up to see a mechanical bug hovering over me. Could it see me?

It moved off a bit and then swung around to settle down on the huge white cross of the helipad. The helicopter was bringing reinforcements.

I let the branch settle back in front of me.

When the helicopter was still, the door slid open and Ethan Bricklin jumped out. He wasn't more than a dozen feet from me and I could see him clearly in the helicopter lights. In his hand was a gun.

I aimed for Ethan's chest. My finger tightened on the trigger. "Not yet," I whispered. The sound of my own voice startled me and I hardly managed to keep from squeezing the trigger. It would give away my position, and killing Ethan might not be enough. How many men had Ethan brought with him in the helicopter?

A twig snapped under the weight of a man off to my right. They were on both sides of me now. My Beretta stayed locked on Ethan's chest, but if the other man appeared first, he was a dead man.

CHAPTER 38

Ethan was clear in the light from the helicopter for only a few seconds before he bent over at the waist and ran for the protection of the scrub. I thought I'd lost him and was about to turn my gun on the person coming from my right when I saw a sliver of Ethan's body at the entrance to the tunnel. He paused, checking to see if the way was clear before he inched forward.

I'd only get one shot. I wanted him closer.

Ethan wasn't about to do anything rash. Cautious and silent, he sidestepped his way into the tunnel, hugging the edge of the sea grapes. Big, but a country boy, Ethan knew how to move without a sound when he was stalking prey. The linebacker didn't. The man coming from the direction of the house wasn't used to operating outdoors, hadn't been trained to hunt with Tully and stay quiet the way I had.

Ethan heard the linebacker and stopped moving. The crunch of leaves under a footstep and then a flash of light exploded from Ethan's gun. The smell of gunpowder filled the air.

A scream rose in the night. The bullet, ripping through cartilage and bone and tearing into muscle, hadn't yet destroyed life. The linebacker stumbled into view and fired as he fell. A splinter of wood dug into my cheek and I jerked sideways.

Any noise I might have made was covered by the sound of the

man dying in front of me. With legs pedaling but going nowhere, he struggled for life five feet from me.

Ethan inched forward, his gun held in front of him. He turned on a flashlight and pointed it down at the man on the brick path. "Shit," Ethan said.

On the ground but trying to get up, the man whispered hoarsely, "Help me. For god's sake, help me."

Ethan moved quickly. Surging forward, he stepped over the man and disappeared into the night. I had the Beretta on Ethan the whole time, but I didn't pull the trigger. Now I had missed my chance. I bit back a curse.

He was gone. Or was he? Had he gone for help, or was he playing possum? I went over the possibilities. If Ethan had been in contact with the man chasing me, maybe Ethan knew I was nearby and was being clever, waiting in the dark for me to make a move. Was it possible for the strange men on the island to be in cell contact if there was no tower? I didn't know.

I didn't lower the gun. I kept it fixed on the spot where Ethan had disappeared.

My hands began shaking from tension and the weight of the weapon. Would I be able to hold them still enough to hit anything if Ethan returned? I eased my hands back towards my chest to relieve the trembling.

If Ethan had gone to get help for the man he'd shot, more people might be headed my way. Now was my only chance to get away.

I started to rise and then sank back down. Tully's voice echoed in my head. "Don't break cover." One bad night he'd kept us alive with wisdom earned the hard way in Vietnam.

"Don't break cover" was my mantra now. Frozen in place, I

watched the shooter, lying there in front of me, as he died. It wasn't an easy death. Slowly the guy's legs stopped moving, and then his body stopped twitching. And then nothing.

Still I waited. There was no sound to help me decide if Ethan was waiting in the dark for me.

CHAPTER 39

Blood ran down my face. I licked a trickle from the corner of my mouth, a metallic taste on my tongue, and then lifted my left shoulder and dried the blood on my cheek with my shirt, afraid to lower the gun long enough to wipe it properly. Time crept by. My cramped muscles began shaking.

Two things became clear to me. First, I couldn't stay hidden. They'd search until they found me, I was sure of that. The second thing I was positive about was Ethan wasn't going to let me leave Dancing Lady alive. Ethan didn't let witnesses live.

I had to come up with a plan, a way of saving myself. But what?

I could only hide as long as it was dark. Maybe not even that long. They had flashlights, and if they got lucky shining them into the jungle of vegetation, they'd discover my hiding place. Moving was risky. And if I did break cover, which way should I run? The pilot was still with the helicopter. Would he be armed? At the very least, he'd warn the others . . . tell them where I was. Could I kidnap him? Force him at gunpoint to take me away? I'd have to surprise him to make that plan work. It was too much of a long shot. So I couldn't go left. To my right, down the path, Ethan waited.

Behind me, towards the gulf waters, was a dense wall of vegetation, followed by fifty feet of mangroves. If I could push through all of that, it would be easy enough to swim around the island to the dock and the boat that had brought us to Dancing Lady Island. Would they have left a man at the dock? Even if they hadn't, they'd come after me as soon as they heard the engine start, and Silvio's little boat was unlikely to be powerful enough to outrun them. I hadn't heard a boat. But how else could they have got here? Maybe I just hadn't been paying attention, assuming any sound of an engine was just someone cruising by.

It didn't matter. Silvio wouldn't leave the keys in the boat any more than I'd leave the keys in my truck for someone to steal.

I searched for other options. What if I hid in the water until a boat came by and then swam out to it? How could I make them see me in the dark? If I was close enough to call out to them, I risked being run down. Besides, there would be no boat traffic until morning, hours away.

There was still the yacht and its communication equipment.

I checked behind me and to the side, trying to wiggle farther back. If I could get out to the water and swim around the far side of the island to the west, I might be able to get to the yacht and use its radio to bring help. It would take an hour for help to come by boat from Jacaranda.

I'd only managed to wiggle about five feet back into the underbrush. I knew there was no way to get through the mangroves. Even as a child small enough to fit through tiny spaces, no matter how many times I tried, there was no way out through mangroves. And then it hit me. I wasn't going to be able to call for help. And no one was coming to rescue us.

I settled back on my heels and thought. Improbable ideas tumbled through my mind. In the end it came down to two things, help myself or wait to die. The second thing I decided came as a revelation to me. I wasn't leaving without Clay. Come what may, we were going together or we weren't going at all.

Questions piled up. How many men were there? And, the question I most wanted answered, was Clay still alive? Behind me, deep in the mangrove roots, something stirred. Surprised, I gave a frightened peep of terror and then froze, expecting to see Ethan creeping back at the sound.

When nothing happened, I took a deep breath and forced myself to move. Inch by inch, I crept out of the sea grapes until I stood by the dead man. His gun lay inches from his hand. I picked it up, studying it. It was much heavier than the Beretta, but it had a silencer, and that was an advantage. I checked that his gun still had ammunition and then dropped my Beretta into the pocket of my cargo pants.

Sticking to the shadows on the right side of the dark path, I worked my way back towards the house, my heart beating so fast and hard I thought it surely would do me an injury.

CHAPTER 40

At the tennis court I hesitated for a long time. Moving out into the open was risky. Would they have left someone here in case I came back? It seemed likely, but they were two men short: the one I had shot and the one Ethan had killed.

I knelt down and waited, trying to decide what to do. At last I crept around the fenced court. Nothing happened. No one was on guard here.

I crept along the path towards the house. At the edge of the lawn I knelt down again and tried to gather my strength and courage for the dash across the grass. Twenty-five feet across that open area was the only way to get to the house.

I was still hesitating when a shape separated from a deep shadow. I raised the gun, bracing it with both hands, and waited. A flashlight flicked on and the shape became a man. Someone I didn't know. The light swept from right to left around the perimeter of the lawn, searching. The light reached me, blinding me as I squeezed the trigger. The jolt of the gun knocked me sideways.

With a surprised "umph" the man crumpled into a lump on the grass, on top of his flashlight. I scrambled to my feet and waited for someone to appear from the house. Even with the silencer, the gun sounded loud. Surely it would bring someone.

Nothing moved and no one came running. The outline of

the body glowed strangely from the illumination beneath it. Staying low and moving swiftly, I ran straight across the thick turf. Past the body on the ground, without stopping to see if he was alive or dead, but praying he wasn't going to rise up and kill me, I ran.

At the foot of the south stairs I stopped. Remembering the squeak of runners on the decking, I slipped off my runners so they couldn't give me away.

My eyes strained to see in the dark. Crouched in the shadows, I listened, but there was nothing except the night sounds of nature, just cicadas and tree frogs. Slowly, slowly, pausing on every step, I crept up the stairs, past the pool and up the second set of steps, expecting a head to appear over the railing at any moment. I was ready to take a shot.

Near the top of the stairs I paused, listening intently, before I lifted my head above deck level. No one stood guard. Where were they? Maybe Ethan was the only one left. No, I was sure he'd brought more than three men.

Moving quickly across the deck to the door of Liz's room, I plastered my body against the wall. Inside or outside? A quick look. That long hall was brightly lit, making it a shooting gallery for anyone at the other end. Darkness offered cover, so outside it was.

I made my way along the gallery, stopping at each glass door, checking inside and then running silently past. When I got to the living room, I realized I'd made a mistake. I should have come upstairs at this end instead of at the south. Here, I had to pass the floor-to-ceiling windows before I could go inside.

I flattened myself against the wall, waiting for a plan to form.

"Ben knew it was you who broke in last January," I heard Liz say. "He called me and asked me to take his orchid." I peeked around the window frame as Liz moved into view. Blood trickled from a cut on her forehead and her body wavered like beach grass in the wind, but her voice was still defiant. "After that break-in, Ben didn't feel it was safe to keep the black at the nursery. He figured he'd come home one day and find your men had come back." She pointed to the black orchid, now sitting on a drift-wood table. "It was out on the yacht when you and Digger came. You searched the whole damn house and didn't think to look there." She laughed, a harsh and bitter sound.

"Shut up," Ethan ordered.

Her laughter was gone as quickly as it came. "Why'd you have to kill Ben?" Her voice wasn't defiant anymore.

"An accident. Stay where you are," Ethan said.

Liz hadn't moved, so he was speaking to someone I couldn't see. I hoped it was Clay.

But Liz wasn't finished. She raised her arm and pointed at Ethan. "The last conversation I had with your mother was about you. She said you were a 'greedy little bastard,' just like your father." She waved her finger. "You burned the nursery to hide the fact that you took your mother's orchids."

"Where's Sherri?" Ethan asked.

I heard Clay's voice say, "I told you. We had a blowup and she went back to Jacaranda."

Clay was alive; it would all be fine now.

"Then who shot Devlin?" Ethan asked.

"I don't know," Clay said.

Ethan moved into view and raised his gun to Liz's head. "One more time, where's Sherri?"

The gun in my hands lifted. It was fixed on the middle of

Ethan's back. My finger tightened on the trigger. An arm snaked around my neck and lifted me off my feet. Someone swung me away from the windows like I was no more than a sack of potatoes as the gun bucked in my hands. My toes dangled above the deck, and my bullet dug harmlessly into the soffit.

"Put it down," the man holding me said. Something hard and metal prodded my lower spine. "Now." The barrel of a gun dug deeper into my back.

His fingers bit into my right arm, pulling it down and cutting off the circulation. "Put it down." He pushed me forward at the waist. The big gun fell from my hand and onto the deck, and then he jerked me upright.

"Okay, over there." He gave me a little shove away from him. "Move."

Stepping delicately sideways so as not to surprise him in any way, I kept my eyes fixed on him.

He was a giant, older, sixties maybe, but still formidable. He picked the gun with the silencer up off the deck and motioned with his head. "Inside."

I did as I was told, my mouth dry with fear.

Ethan was grinning with pleasure when we came through the door. "At last, the final member of our party."

My eyes found Clay. His face was filled with yearning and regret.

I started towards him, but the man behind me grabbed my hair and pulled me back against him. "Stay."

On the couch a man in his thirties was stretched out, a white towel soaked in blood wrapped around his thigh. He glared at me with hate in his eyes.

I almost apologized, but then I remembered that Silvio was dead and I soon would be.

The big man stepped around me and said, "This is all going wrong, boss. Let's kill them and get out of here."

Ethan's eyes never left my face. "Not yet, Digger. We'll clean this up and then we'll go." His gun was pointed at my chest. "You were the wild card, the one I couldn't figure out. I knew you were there at the gas bar the minute I met you. I picked that pink flip-flop up by the water after we came up the canal. As soon as I met you, I knew it was yours and you'd been there, but I couldn't figure out who you were buying for."

He paused, perhaps waiting for me to respond, and then said, "I thought you might be working with Tito. He was Nina's snitch."

"It's over, Ethan," I said.

He laughed. He wasn't frightened at all.

"You just shot one of your own men."

"I shot him because I thought he was one of you." Ethan made it sound like the most rational thing in the world.

"You screwed up big-time." I was babbling like an idiot to keep him from shooting me. "There was that picture."

His brows furrowed. "What picture?"

"The one of your Cadillac with Angie sitting in it. You shouldn't have let Angie have her picture taken with the car. Did you know the newspapers used that picture when they reported Angie's death?"

"What difference does it make?"

"It proves you were there and that you knew Angie."

Confusion on his face.

"The girl at the gas bar, the same girl murdered over in Homestead, Angie Martinez. The newspaper article has a picture that shows Angie with your Caddy."

He wasn't indifferent now.

"That photo proves you were out near the nursery before Ben died. Her family will remember when it was taken."

I had his full attention.

"So what?"

"Why would you go see Ben except for the black orchid?" I was trembling with anger and exhaustion. "You went back and killed Ben, and then you killed Tito because he saw it happen."

He shrugged. "Tito's dead. They can't prove anything."

"No? Shall we call the cops and see if that's true?"

His gun rose to point squarely at my chest. "They'll never hear about it because you'll be dead."

"The cops already know. I told them everything."

Behind me, the man named Digger released me and stepped away.

"I sent an e-mail just before your guys arrived." A silly kind of joy filled me until I remembered one brutal truth. No way was Ethan going to let me walk away from this. I was going to die. My legs could barely hold me up.

If I was frightened, Ethan looked like he'd swallowed something nasty. He was doing the calculations and trying to decide if technology was somehow going to mess him up. He didn't see Digger edging towards the hall with his gun covering Ethan. Digger knew it was over.

Ethan was concentrating on me, working out his story. "I'll tell them I went over to talk to Ben a week before the fire. I stopped at the gas bar and a girl asked to have a picture taken with the car. No big deal."

"Horseshit!" Liz roared. "You never went near him before the night of the fire. He would have told me. It could only have been the day Ben died. And you never drove that thing unless you felt you were sticking it to Ben. Do you honestly think he cared that you had it?" Her chin went up and she cackled in disgust and triumph. "He called it your pink pacifier." Liz was out of control. Perhaps she didn't realize he was going to kill us, or maybe she just didn't care. She surged towards him, shoulders back and up on her toes like a boxer, bouncing in outrage. "You were no good back when you were a kid and you still aren't." She jabbed a finger at him. "Your mother knew just what you were."

"Don't," Clay said and pulled her away. Stepping in front of Liz with his hands raised, Clay said, "Get away now, Ethan, while you still can. It's over."

"Boss," the injured man said, pushing himself off the couch and trying to stand, "Digger's going. We've got to get out of here too."

Ethan turned as Digger ducked into a bedroom and disappeared.

Clay said, "Can't you see you've lost, Ethan?"

Ethan said, "And so have you." His gun exploded. A red flower of blood marred Clay's crisp blue shirt with the cuffs turned neatly back.

My hand scrambled to my pocket and the Beretta.

The sound of the helicopter filled the room. Ethan pivoted. Gun raised, he stared down the hall in the direction of the helipad.

That's when I shot Ethan in the back. The bullet hit him high in the left shoulder, but it didn't take him down. He gave a startled grunt and staggered forward. And then he slowly turned on me.

I stepped backwards with the Beretta held out in front of me.

He looked down at the small exit wound on the front of his

shirt. Confusion flooded his face and he said, "I thought you'd be easy."

"You thought wrong," I said and shot him again.

Ethan's eyes opened wide and he stumbled backwards. Then he sat down hard on the floor and fell back against a chair, still staring at me.

I took a deep breath and tightened my finger on the trigger, ready to shoot him a third time. The front of his shirt turned red. He didn't move.

I ran to Clay.

Clay whispered, "Sorry, Sherri . . . mistake." Blood pulsed from his open lips. His eyes fluttered closed. His body went limp.

I lifted him in my arms. Frightening animal sounds of grief; I didn't realize they came from me.

CHAPTER 41

I have no memory of the next few hours. It was Liz who called in the police, leaving me in the house while she went down to the boat.

She told me that she tried to take Clay's body away from me when she returned, but I wouldn't release him. She said that when the sound of the first emergency helicopter filled the house, I struggled to carry Clay out of the house. By then my mind had gone somewhere else. It took a long time for it to come back.

It came back to a mess. The man I'd shot clarified much of my story in exchange for a lighter sentence. Digger Jackson and the pilot were found. Digger told the police that Ethan had killed all those people not only for a black orchid, but also for his mother's orchid collection, which he stole before burning down his brother's nursery. The cops had a hard time believing the story. How could anyone understand? Greed and obsession make no sense to normal people.

One day when we were in the bar and talking about progress, Ethan had said, "Once things start rolling there's no going back." That's pretty much what had happened when he went out to Osceola Nursery. Events just spun out of control.

I've had lots of time to count the ways I could have changed things. But even if I'd told the cops the little I knew as soon as I was out of the swamp, I doubt it would have made a difference to the outcome. Ethan always thought I had the orchid. He would never have believed that my being there was just an accident.

All and all, it feels most times like there was no one right thing, no act that would have left me without regrets. But there's one thing I could have changed. Deep in the night, I admit to myself that Clay would be alive if I hadn't stayed for that final martini.

It was the Sunset and its strange family of misfits, people who had accidently washed up on the same beach, who helped me heal.

Life became as simple as someone saying, "The sun's going down. Looks like it's going to be a good one. Let's take a drink outside and watch it."

Seeing the dying sun explode across the sky, and trusting it would come back in the morning, helped me believe that life would get better.

The End

Award-winning mystery author PHYLLIS SMALLMAN's writing has appeared in *Spinetingler* and *Omnimystery* magazines. Her Sherri Travis mystery series was chosen as a summer read by *Good Morning America*, and the first book in her new series, *Long Gone Man*, won the 2014 Independent Publisher Book Award gold medal for best mystery e-book. Before turning to a life of crime, Smallman was a potter. She divides her time between a beach in Florida and an island in the Salish Sea. Visit her website at phyllissmallman.com.